Velvet

MARY HOOPER

BLOOMSBURY

LONDON   BERLIN   NEW YORK   SYDNEY

Bloomsbury Publishing, London, Berlin, New York and Sydney

First published in Great Britain in September 2011 by Bloomsbury Publishing Plc
49–51 Bedford Square, London, WC1B 3DP

'There are more things in heaven and earth' quote on p156:
Hamlet by William Shakespeare, Act 1 Scene 5

A CIP catalogue record for this book is available from the British Library

ISBN 978 0 7475 9921 0

Mixed Sources
Product group from well-managed
forests and other controlled sources
www.fsc.org Cert no. SGS-COC-2061
FSC © 1996 Forest Stewardship Council

Typeset by Hewer Text UK Ltd, Edinburgh
Printed in Great Britain by Clays Ltd, St Ives plc, Bungay, Suffolk

1 3 5 7 9 10 8 6 4 2

www.bloomsbury.com
www.maryhooper.co.uk

Contents

Chapter One

In Which Velvet Faints, and Gains a
New Position in the Laundry

Velvet had fainted too many times, according to Mrs Sloane, and was liable to be dismissed from Ruffold's Steam Laundry.

'It's the rules,' said Mrs Sloane, the laundry supervisor, following Velvet out to the yard and waving a bottle of smelling salts under her nose. 'Anyone who can't discipline themselves not to swoon has no place here. You've already gone down twice today.'

Leaning against the wall to try and gain some relief from her aching back, Velvet turned to face her. 'But it's stifling inside today, ma'am,' she said as politely as she could, 'and I've been working right beside a boiler.' Saturday was the worst possible day to be standing next to any of the boilers – everyone knew that. All the giant water heaters in the laundry were turned off on Sundays, so at the beginning of the week conditions in the laundry weren't too bad. As the week went on, however, the heat in the vast room became worse and worse; condensation ran in rivers down the walls, whilst sweat beaded the girls' faces, dripped into their eyes and trickled between their shoulder blades. Every breath they took was a gasp of exhaustion.

Mrs Sloane pursed her lips and looked at Velvet over the wire-rimmed glasses which were almost permanently steamed up. 'Rules is rules,' she said. 'You know that. If anyone makes a habit of fainting then they're deemed incapable of carrying out a proper day's work.' She nodded towards the raggle-taggle group of girls standing just outside the yard by the curved iron sign that said, *RUFFOLD'S STEAM LAUNDRY*. 'Look at all those girls – they're waiting for a job here and *they're* willing to work for a shilling less a week.'

Velvet glanced over at the girls. Tiny, thin, shoeless and mostly with neither jacket nor mantle on this first really cold day of the winter of 1900, none looked older than nine. 'But they wouldn't be able to work nearly as quickly or as skilfully as me,' she said to the supervisor, who was known to be softer than she looked. 'They're as scrawny as day-old rabbits. They could never manage to carry a pile of bed sheets on their own.'

Mrs Sloane pushed her glasses back up her nose and frowned. Velvet was right, of course. It took at least six months to train a girl and Velvet – apart from her fainting – was a fast and diligent worker, able to switch between the washers, mangles, box pressers and flat irons as required.

'Please, Mrs Sloane.' Velvet filled her lungs with cold air and closed her eyes briefly, thinking of what could happen if she lost her job. 'If I could just work a little further away from the boilers.'

'Girls can't pick and choose where they work! You knew that rule before you started here.'

Velvet shivered. Her dark hair had congealed into a mass of damp frizz which stuck to her cheeks, and her eyes itched with tiredness. Her skin had been hot, her blouse and smock wet with sweat when she'd fainted, but now she felt clammy and cold. 'Could I, perhaps, go into packing and folding?'

'There's no vacancies there. Besides, I keep those jobs for my older ladies.'

'Then please, Mrs Sloane. I'll try really hard not to faint again.' Velvet hung her head. 'It's my time of the month, you see – that and being on my feet so long. I shall be fine on Monday!'

Mrs Sloane rolled her eyes. 'You girls!'

God knew she wasn't a hard woman, but there were schedules to maintain, bosses to keep happy and customers to placate, and every day a mountain of sheets, pillowcases, towels and tablecloths arriving from every boarding house and hospital in the area. At Ruffold's everything was soaked, washed, boiled and blued, rinsed three times ('We rinse them Thrice to make them Nice' was their motto), put through a box mangle, dried, pressed and finally folded into cardboard boxes ready to go back from whence it came. If too many girls fainted, the schedules would go awry.

'One girl going down too often can lead to the others playing copycat,' Mrs Sloane admonished. 'It can spread faster than scarlet fever. Why, I remember once when the girls went down in fainting fits one after the other right across the room. Fell like skittles, they did!'

'I'll work an hour next week without pay,' Velvet said desperately. She straightened up, trying to look bright and alert. If she lost this job it would be near impossible to get another, and without a regular wage she couldn't pay for her room, buy food, coal or anything else. And then what would happen? She always kept a silver shilling hidden in her shoe for an emergency, but that was all that stood between her and the workhouse. The workhouse . . . that fearful institution where the destitute were made to live and work under harsh, prison-like conditions. 'You've always been most fair to me.' As she spoke, Velvet's eyes suddenly filled with tears. 'Please, Mrs Sloane . . .'

Mrs Sloane hesitated, looked at the unhappy girl again and sighed. She knew Velvet had no family to support her, and besides she was a quick and intelligent girl who could read and write well

– certainly better than the others, most of whom had only had a year or two's intermittent education at a ragged school.

After thinking for a moment, Mrs Sloane decided on the course of action which was to seal Velvet's fate.

'Well, I'll probably live to regret it, but there's a vacancy in Personal Laundry, if you think you're up to it,' she said. As Velvet gasped and said she could do it – *of course* she could do it – and would be most grateful for the opportunity, Mrs Sloane continued, 'It needs the utmost care and attention to detail, mind; a meticulous awareness of a fashionable lady's adornment and decoration.' She took off her glasses, polished them on her apron and looked at what Velvet was wearing under her regulation white smock: a dark skirt made of hard-wearing gabardine and a plain, high-necked blouse. Mrs Sloane looked doubtful. 'Usually, a more mature lady fills this sort of position, someone who's worked as a haberdasher or seamstress.'

'I'd be suitable, I'm sure! What would I have to do?' Velvet asked, thinking that whatever Mrs Sloane said, she would certainly say she was capable of it.

'It means taking responsibility for our most valued clients' personal garments,' said Mrs Sloane. She paused for these portentous words to take root and Velvet nodded at her, wide-eyed. 'It means you would work at the top table and take charge of a laundry box containing a particular customer's laundry. You would remove any delicate buttons, lace or precious embroidery, deal with stains, then wash each garment by hand and see to its drying. Once dry, you'd replace whatever fine detailing you'd removed, then press everything into shape, reform any frills, ruffles or pleats, and return the garments to their box ready to be delivered to the customer.'

Velvet nodded eagerly. 'I can do all that!'

'I need hardly add that the good name of our laundry rests on this particular exceptional service that we provide for our wealthiest clients,' Mrs Sloane went on, although she was not being perfectly truthful here, for the reputation of Ruffold's had actually been based more on the fact that they used washing water hot enough to kill bedbugs.

'I know how to look after fancy things, ma'am,' Velvet said. 'My ma was a laundress – and before that, a governess,' she added proudly. 'When I was small I used to watch her. I learned how to do buttonholes and make repairs, too.' This, at least, was true. Necessity demanded that all working-class girls knew how to repair, mend and make do with whatever materials they could lay their hands on.

'It's exacting, finicky work,' said Mrs Sloane. 'Our private customers tend to be *very* fussy.'

'Then I'll be just as fussy,' Velvet said eagerly. 'I'll take care of their precious garments, Mrs Sloane – I'll look after them like they're babies!'

'It must be understood, mind, that any less than perfect results, any little mishaps that might befall these most treasured garments, will result in your instant dismissal.'

'Of course, ma'am,' Velvet agreed hurriedly. 'I wouldn't expect otherwise.'

'Very well,' said Mrs Sloane. 'That's all settled, then.'

'Thank you, ma'am.' Velvet bobbed a grateful curtsey. Her aching back, her swollen ankles, the cramps in her stomach and her sore, chapped hands – she could bear all these just as long as she kept her job.

'Missus! Oh, missus!' one of the little girls waiting in the yard called over to Mrs Sloane as they turned to go in. 'Begging your pardon, but is there any casual work today?'

'No, none at all, I'm afraid,' said the supervisor.

'If you please, missus! Me ma says I'm not to come home with me pockets empty!'

'Then I'm sorry for it,' said Mrs Sloane, 'but there's still no work. If I do have any, you'll be the first to know.'

The girl looked across at Mrs Sloane and Velvet, then turned away without another word. She lifted one bare foot and held it in her hand for a moment to try and rub some life into her blue-tinged toes, then exchanged it for her other foot.

'Ask again on Monday,' Mrs Sloane called over to

her, relenting slightly, 'but I can't promise, mind.' She said to Velvet that she hoped there would be no more fainting from her that day, and that she should report to the laundry's upper table the following Monday at seven thirty in the morning.

Returning to the vast space that was the laundry, the wall of heat and noise hit Velvet so that she recoiled instinctively. The steam billowing from the huge washers, the hissing jets of the gas irons, the scorching heat of the ironing machines and the damp reek of sweat pervading from the massed lines of one hundred girls hard at work always made her feel she wanted to run and hide in a corner. The laundry was a heaving, vile nightmare of a place – as hot as hell and twice as nasty, as the girls were fond of saying. There were large circulating fans above the boilers in the centre of the room, but these did little to move the air around, and the windows were never opened because of the risk of smuts coming in and spoiling the newly washed linens. It was no wonder, Velvet thought, that most girls could only manage two years, or at most three, in the steam laundry before succumbing to a life of marriage and babies with the first boy who asked them. If they couldn't find anyone to wed, then quite often their health – affected by both the relentless work and the humid, unhealthy atmosphere – would break down completely and they would 'fall into a consumption', as they said. They were then left with no option but to take up some badly paying home employment, such as stitching shirts or sewing on buttons for a few pennies a day.

Mrs Sloane returned to the top of the room where, standing on an upturned crate, she watched proceedings with – steamed-up glasses notwithstanding – the eye of an eagle. If more than a few words were exchanged between workmates, if someone took longer than half an hour for dinner, if a white towel touched the floor, or if some procedure was not carried out correctly, she always knew.

Velvet went back to her ironing table, meeting the eyes of her friend Lizzie and giving her a quick smile.

'Velvet Groves! I thought you'd gone for good!' Lizzie whispered. The room was dense with noise – a hissing and roaring from the big steam washer, a whooshing as the paddles turned in the wooden washing barrels, and dull thuds from the pressing machines – so that Lizzie had to speak right into Velvet's ear in order to be heard. 'I thought she'd shown you the door.'

'No! Actually, I have a new position.'

Lizzie gaped at her. 'Never! Doing what?'

'I'll tell you on the way home,' said Velvet, for Mrs Sloane was still on her crate and Velvet was anxious not to do anything which might cause her to change her mind about the job.

A little girl learner appeared at Velvet's shoulder

bent double under a basket of wet, freshly washed sheets, and Velvet heaved them on to the enamel table and began folding them ready to go into the box mangle. The sharp smells of washing soda and carbolic soap stung her nose and the sweat was already beading on her forehead again, but now that it seemed her fortunes had turned, she could stand it. She scraped her hair off her face and wound it into a knot at the base of her neck. With luck, she thought, these might be the last linen sheets she would ever have to fold in her life. A better sort of laundry life awaited.

'And I said my ma was a laundress and made out that I knew all about the sewing-on of trimmings and such,' Velvet said to an amazed and envious Lizzie on their walk home. 'Mrs Sloane said I could start next week.'

'And *was* your ma a laundress?' Lizzie asked, for the girls had not known each other for very long. It was only a month ago that one of Lizzie's numerous aunts had managed to get her a regular job at Ruffold's.

Velvet shrugged. 'I suppose so, if that's the same thing as a washerwoman.'

She made a quick sidewards glance at Lizzie to see if her face registered disapproval, but Lizzie merely nodded. Velvet's father had always been bitterly ashamed of the fact that his wife washed the dirty clothes of strangers for a living, though it was clear enough to Velvet that if her ma hadn't done so, they would have starved. Besides, occasionally the families who she had washed for would pass on their old clothes and, though these were often patched, faded or the wrong size (sometimes all three), they were more than welcome, for they could never afford to buy new. Her father had hated them wearing other people's cast-offs, of course – but then, she thought, he hated most things. He had once ripped a waistcoat from Ma's back, saying that she should have more self respect than to wear discarded leftovers, but Ma had retaliated for a change, saying that sometimes you had to wear what fortune had provided or go naked. Ma hadn't often spoken back to him, for to do so meant risking a slapped face. Or worse.

'When did you say your ma passed away?' Lizzie asked gently.

'When I was about eight.'

'And can you remember much about her?'

Velvet smiled. 'I remember little bits.' Sometimes she would spend hours trying to recollect more; wondering what she'd been like as a girl, going over old times and guessing what might have caused her to marry the miserable old grouch who was Velvet's father. 'If I'd known my ma was going to die I would have kept those past times a bit safer,' she said. 'I'd have gone over and over them so that I could remember every single day.'

Lizzie gave her a sympathetic smile and the two girls linked arms as they crossed busy Hammersmith Broadway to take the road towards Chiswick. 'And what about your pa? You told me once he did children's parties,' she said when they were safely on the other side.

'That's right.' Velvet gave a wry laugh. 'He was Mr Magic.'

'Mr Magic!' Lizzie said, and then the tone of her voice changed to one of concern. 'But how long have you been an orphan?'

Velvet swallowed and hesitated, trying to sound as natural as possible. 'My father died last year.'

'That must have been very hard.'

Velvet didn't reply to this, for in all honesty she couldn't pretend that – apart from her guilt, of course – she'd felt anything but relief after his death. She'd been his housekeeper since her mother had died, and had found it a hard and thankless job.

'If you don't mind speaking of it, how did he die?' asked Lizzie.

Velvet took in a deep breath. 'He drowned.'

'Oh, how awful!' Lizzie gasped. 'What happened?'

There was another long pause, then Velvet said, 'We had a room in a worker's cottage next to the canal in Duckworth. It was night-time and . . . and

12

he was chasing me. It was raining hard and he slipped and fell down between two boats.'

She didn't say any more. She couldn't possibly tell her friend that she'd heard the splash of him going into the water, heard him shout for help – and just let him go under.

Chapter Two

In Which It Is Discovered That Velvet Did Not Begin Life as Velvet

That night, after her father had fallen in the canal, Velvet did not go back to the room they shared – at least, not to live in it. There seemed little point in doing so. She'd known nothing but misery in the place. Indeed, not only could a legion of rats be heard scuttling under the floorboards at night, but eight weeks' rent was owed on it. Even without her father in it, it would never be home.

After Velvet heard the splash she kept on running along the canal until she was exhausted, then took a convoluted route back to their room, where she retrieved her best shawl, her Sunday hat and an old lace petticoat which had once belonged to her mother. After spending a night curled up like a dog in someone's garden shed, she ventured into a baker's to buy bread with a portion of her emergency shilling and saw a large, bright advertisement for Ruffold's Steam Laundry. Thinking, rightly, that a company which boasted of employing over one hundred girls must have a high turnover of staff, she made her way to Brook Green in west London, where the laundry was. After waiting in line for three days, she was taken on at half pay as a learner, with the hope of being elevated to the position of fully fledged laundress after six months. Velvet wasn't to know this, but it was a case of her filling a dead girl's shoes, for her arrival at the gates of Ruffold's coincided with the deaths of several young laundry workers who had fallen ill with consumption and then died, for none of them was able to afford the medication, fresh air and healthy diet necessary for its cure.

Finding a new room wasn't difficult once she had a job, but she couldn't afford to be too fussy. The room Velvet secured in the big house in Chiswick was little more than a store cupboard, but at least it was cheap. It had a bed, a chair, a small window and – most importantly – a door which could be closed against the world.

During the time she spent waiting outside Ruffold's, Velvet slept on park benches and in doorways under layers of old newspaper, blessing the fact that it was summer. In one of these papers she'd read that, following the landlord reporting him missing, the body of her father, Fred Marley, *also known as Mr Magic*, had been found in the Duckworth Canal. It gave notice of a funeral service but she was too frightened of being implicated in his death to attend, nor was she such a hypocrite that she could have gone along and pretended sorrow at the demise of the man she'd come to dislike so much. Even the thought of his funeral service irked her, for she knew he had put away enough money for a proper gentry funeral with a glass carriage, black horses and mutes, as if he were a man of some standing; a man held in respect. No, she decided there and then, what was over was over. She would try to forget her past and resolved to build a new life for herself.

Exhausted by the working week and a little over-wrought, wondering what might be expected of her in her new role, Velvet slept until noon on Sunday. She'd intended to go out to one of the morning markets and buy some meat – a pork chop or meat pie at a bargain price just before the stalls closed – but woke too late for that. She had just enough time to go to the local public baths where, after paying tuppence, she washed herself with three inches of tepid water in a tin bath. She then went back to her room, tidied it and swept the floor, darned her stockings, washed her work clothes, read a story in an old copy of *The Young Ladies' Journal*, and ate some bread and cheese before the light faded (she didn't want to go to the expense of light-ing a candle) and it was time to go to bed again. She was exhausted, yes, but grateful to be so, for it meant she was in work whilst so many in London were not.

Most mornings she was woken by the church clock on Turnham Green striking five, but that particular Monday, despite all the extra sleep she'd had, she didn't wake until six o'clock. By this time, the house's other lodgers were up and about and she had to wait ten minutes to get into the privy in the yard. Then, having forgotten to fill her water jug the previous evening, she had to join a small queue in the kitchen to fetch washing water, so she wasn't ready by the time Lizzie arrived and called up to her window.

Velvet put her head out, said that she'd be just a moment and asked Lizzie if she wouldn't mind waiting. She was glad it wasn't raining so that she didn't feel obliged to invite Lizzie in; she was too ashamed of the room for that. It wasn't that it was dirty (she was always going over the floor with a dustpan and brush), but because it was such a small and poor room. Bare of any furniture except the single iron bed and chair, it had dusty floorboards, faded paper, peeling paintwork and patches of damp under the uncurtained windows. The many small black beetles scurrying about between the floor planks were another potential embarrassment, and altogether she felt it was not a room to which you could invite someone without making apologies and giving explanations. Perhaps later on she would ask Lizzie to come in, Velvet thought, when they knew each other better. She'd been to Lizzie's house several times and realised it must appear somewhat unfriendly not to return the gesture, but hoped that when her friend eventually saw the room she would understand. Lizzie's family, she knew, were not wealthy by any means, but although she had three younger sisters to be fed and clothed, her father was in employment as an omnibus driver. Consequently their house was a proper one with curtains and carpets, furniture, pictures of the royal family on the walls and a full larder. It was a home rather than a cold and anonymous box to sleep in.

The walk to work from Chiswick took nearly an hour and although the horse buses went in that direction, neither girl could afford the fare; it was only clerks and office workers who could spend *that* sort of money every day. Lizzie and Velvet were glad to be able to walk together, therefore, and usually spent the time chatting about young men they knew (or hoped to know), the current story being serialised in the paper, the misdemeanours of younger members of the royal family, or whether it was quite the done thing for young ladies to wear bloomers on bicycles. They spoke to each other a lot more in the mornings; in the evenings they were sometimes too tired to do more than put one foot in front of the other.

On this Monday morning, as well as all the normal topics of conversation, they spoke about Velvet's new role in the laundry, whether the work was going to be difficult, and exactly what type of customers use the service.

'My sister said you might get members of the royal family,' Lizzie reported.

'Surely Buckingham Palace would have its own laundry,' gasped Velvet.

'Oh, perhaps. But then my ma wondered if well-known actresses would use it. Ellen Terry, maybe. Think of that!'

Discussing the relative beauty of various actresses and music-hall singers, the two girls stood waiting to cross the high road, which at that time of day was thronged with hansom cabs, private carriages, farmers' carts, horse riders and omnibuses. As they waited for a gap in the traffic, they kept a lookout for a motor car, for one had been seen chugging around Turnham Green a few weeks previously and this had caused great excitement, especially so since it had been a lady driving it.

Nearing Hammersmith Broadway, they could see the grisly remains of turkeys squashed on the road here and there, for not two hours previously a whole flock of these had passed by on their way to the poultry market at Leadenhall, and many had been run down and trampled on by horses. The more complete carcasses disappeared almost immediately, of course, and several families enjoyed an unexpected turkey dinner as a result, but the odd mangled leg, wing or clutch of feathers remained compacted on the cobbles. It was as the girls were negotiating their way past a whole heap of turkey innards, their faces registering disgust, that they heard a piercing whistle and a sudden cry of 'Kitty!' over the noise of the traffic.

Outwardly, neither seemed to react to this, but a careful onlooker might have seen Velvet's shoulders hunch in a nervous way. 'Quickly!' she said to Lizzie. 'Let's cross now before we get run down.'

As she hurried her friend along, there came another cry of 'Kitty! Hey, Kitty!'

Lizzie, intrigued, looked round at the young man on the far pavement, who waved and then gestured towards Velvet. 'Oh!' Lizzie said. 'There's a nice young man waving at you. Do look!'

Reluctantly, Velvet turned. She realised she could no longer ignore this particular young man.

Seeing a break in the traffic the man ran across to them, a broad smile on his face.

'Kitty!' he said to Velvet. 'By all that's wonderful, I've been looking for you everywhere.'

Lizzie's mouth opened, round as a coin, and her eyes travelled backwards and forwards between the two of them. She and Velvet had often spoken about the possibility of having sweethearts, but Velvet had never said that she actually had one. And why was he calling her Kitty?

Velvet looked at the young man with resignation. Charlie! The tow-haired boy at the end of her old road who had stood up for her in fights, chosen her as his Valentine and once given her a bunch of flowers he'd picked from someone else's garden. He was part of her childhood and part of her past . . .

She considered pretending she didn't know him, of saying he must be mistaken, or affecting a faint, but none of these options seemed credible. If only she'd woken up on time, she thought, they would have been at Ruffold's by now and he would never have found her.

Charlie, dressed in new boots, breeches and a tweed jacket a size too large for him, pulled off his cap, causing his tawny hair to stand on end. He looked so droll, so anxious, that Velvet couldn't help but smile at him.

'Hello, Charlie,' she said with a little sigh.

He seized both her hands and kissed them each in turn, then, noticing Velvet's face and seeming to realise what he was doing, dropped them and gave a small bow instead. 'I do beg your pardon, Kitty,' he said. 'I was just so pleased to see you.'

Lizzie gave a small squeak of surprise. '*Kitty?*' she asked. 'Why is he calling you Kitty, Velvet?'

Now it was Charlie who looked from one to the other. '*Velvet?*'

Velvet sighed again. 'Well,' she said to Lizzie, 'my real name is Kitty, but . . . but after my father died,

21

I decided I didn't want to be Kitty any longer.' The name Kitty, she thought – and had always thought – was a sweet little puss of a name; the name of someone feeble who might easily be trodden underfoot and taken advantage of. The other reason was simple: if anyone wanted to find a girl named Kitty Marley to ask her questions in connection with a certain drowning, then they would find it difficult if Kitty Marley was now Velvet Groves.

'You changed your name?' Lizzie asked.

Velvet nodded. She and Lizzie had had a conversation about her name only the previous week, she remembered uncomfortably, and Lizzie had said rather wistfully that she wished *she* had been christened with such a rich- and luxurious-sounding name instead of Lizzie, a name that she thought was surely best suited to a between-stairs maid.

'Ah,' Charlie said. 'I see. So your name's Velvet now?'

Velvet nodded.

'I think Kitty's a nice name,' Lizzie said, slightly disgruntled. 'Why ever would you want to change it?'

'I needed to make a new start.'

'But why did you just disappear from my life?' Charlie asked. He twisted his cap round and round in his hands. 'You fair broke my heart, Kitty. You didn't even say goodbye!'

'*Velvet!*'

'Oh, all right, *Velvet*, then,' Charlie said, 'but I don't see why.'

Velvet looked at him stonily.

'Anyway,' he went on, 'after we heard about your father drowning, I came looking for you, you see. Ma said you shouldn't be on your own and I was to bring you to live in our house for a while, until you got on your feet.'

'Well, thank your ma kindly for me,' Velvet said, remembering the comfortable warmth that had emanated from both Charlie's mother and Charlie's house, 'but I needed to get away and begin again. You know what my father was like . . .' She bit her lip, longing to declare how much she'd hated her father, loathed the wretched room they rented and despised the life they'd lived. She did not dare, however, for fear that she would start weeping.

Charlie took her hand in his and looked searchingly into her eyes. 'But Ki— . . . Velvet,' he said, lowering his voice, 'I always thought we'd be wed one day. I remember asking you to marry me when we were about seven.'

Velvet, embarrassed and rather shocked, gave a nervous giggle. 'Exactly! We were seven years old. That was just the silly sort of thing that children say to each other.'

'It might have been just silliness as far as you were concerned,' Charlie said, 'but I meant it. You know I've always . . .'

Fearing that a declaration of love was forth-coming, Velvet tightened her shawl around her shoulders and took Lizzie's arm with some haste. 'Sorry, Charlie. We have to go. We're going to be late for work unless we leave right now.' She couldn't resist adding, 'I'm taking up a new position this morning, too.'

Charlie tried to catch hold of her arm. 'Don't go! Not yet!'

Velvet bobbed a little curtsey. 'Goodbye, Charlie.'

'At least let me know where you are. Tell me where you work!'

Velvet set off and pulled Lizzie's arm to come along. Despite knowing that they'd be fined if they were late for work, Lizzie was hanging back, fasci-nated to see a romantic encounter being played out at first hand.

'I'll get in touch soon, Charlie!' Velvet called above the traffic.

'But where are you living? Where do you work?'

Lizzie, feeling desperately sorry for Charlie, suddenly turned and called, 'Ruffold's Steam Laundry!' and saw him nod and smile.

Velvet turned on her friend. 'Oh, how could you!'

The two girls didn't speak to each other all the rest of the way to work. On parting with set, frown-ing faces, however, they agreed that they might possibly see each other at dinner time.

At Ruffold's the girls' working day began at half

past seven, although the men who stoked and primed the great boilers which heated the water were there long before that. On arriving, Velvet hung up her shawl, put on her smock and cap, and went to the top end of the huge laundry room to the long, white enamel-topped table. Around this were seated the personal launderers: six young women on high stools, all with a laundry box in front of them, bent over some form of domestic needlework. Velvet bade them good morning and received murmured replies.

A moment afterwards Mrs Sloane came along to remind her of her duties. She was to work as she'd been instructed the previous Saturday: to take a box and be solely responsible for its contents, only taking another when the first had been completed, checked with Mrs Sloane and deemed by her to be satisfactory in every way. Using this method, each girl only had one customer's personal laundry at any one time and there was very little likelihood of a garment going astray or being put into the wrong box. Mrs Sloane checked the cleanliness of Velvet's hands, nails and smock, bade her be seated at an empty stool and put a box in front of her. Velvet lifted the lid, and her new career began.

It took her the whole of her first morning to do the contents of the first box – five petticoats in white cotton broderie anglaise. Two required their lace trimmings to be repaired and all needed to be washed, starched and flounced to an icy perfection.

At dinner time, sitting in the corridor (the girls were never, of course, allowed to eat near the customers' laundry), she and Lizzie made up after their little falling out.

'I just felt so sorry for him,' Lizzie said by way of apology. 'He seemed so nice and was very much in earnest.' She quickly came to the main thing she was bothered about. 'Anyway, you never told me you had an admirer!'

'I don't think of him as that,' Velvet said firmly. 'Charlie was just a childhood sweetheart, a neighbour's son I used to play with as a child. I know he's a very nice boy, but . . .'

'Did you have a lovers' tiff and run away?'

Velvet shook her head. 'Nothing as exciting as that.' She sighed. 'Really, have you never had the feeling that you want to change everything about your life; become someone else?'

Lizzie shook her head. 'All I want – all I've ever wanted – is to meet a nice young man with a trade, marry him and live somewhere near to my ma and my sisters.'

'But you know last year, when the century changed from the nineteenth to the twentieth?'

Lizzie nodded.

'Didn't that make you feel just a little bit giddy

and excited, as if anything could happen? As if you might become anyone you wanted?'

Lizzie looked at her in astonishment. 'I don't know what you mean,' she said. 'The likes of us . . . well, we work in the laundry or somewhere like it, and then we fall in love and, if we're lucky, get married wearing a nice dress of white sprigged muslin.'

'Lizzie! There must be more to life than that.'

'Yes. After that, we have babies!' said Lizzie happily. 'Who could want more?'

'Me,' said Velvet.

Lizzie shook her head sadly, as much as to say that Velvet was going to be sadly disappointed.

Chapter Three

In Which Velvet Receives a
Special Invitation

During her first week, Velvet's laundry boxes were very commonplace: a cache of white collars to be laundered, starched and shined with an agate for a gentleman in the legal profession, four ecru linen jackets for a clergyman posted to work in the tropics, a child's christening robe to be washed and to have its lace bodice repaired, two cotton blouses for a woman who needed all the buttons taken forward because the garment had shrunk in a previous laundering. Velvet also took a laundry box which contained two beautiful peach satin sheets and a matching counterpane. These caused her no end of time and trouble as they needed (following Mrs Sloane's explicit instructions) to be ironed damp with a cool iron under a cloth. Velvet did her best with them, but they would keep sliding away from her and falling off the table in cascades of silkiness. This made the other girls smile, for they knew the sheets from their previous visits to the laundry and had purposefully left them for her.

By the following Saturday she had discovered some important things. The first was that if you got to know how a particular customer liked his or her laundry done, and managed it well enough for them to mention their satisfaction to Mrs Sloane, then that customer was said to be yours, and you laid claim to all their subsequent boxes of laundry. If someone else then took your customer's box, it was considered rude in the extreme. On her second day, Velvet did this by mistake, taking a laundry box full of under-shifts and lace-trimmed bloomers and going so far as to put them in suds before hearing an outraged cry of '*My* lady, if you don't mind!' and having them snatched out of the tub. Maisie, the girl whose box it was, later apologised to Velvet, saying she realised now that Velvet could not have known which ladies and gentlemen were already taken. 'We like to keep close to our special customers, you see,' Maisie explained, 'because sometimes – near Christmas – we find a little extra something tucked in amongst the laundry.'

The other thing she discovered was that the girls on Personal Laundry were hoping that the skills they learned there would be a means to an end, for previously some girls had bettered themselves by taking up jobs in a gentleman's or lady's household as laundresses or personal maids. Indeed, one Ruffold's girl, by carefully applying blue-bag, bleach and soap to the white shirts sent daily by a single man, had made herself indispensable to him. 'She went to work as his housekeeper and ended up as his wife,' Maisie told Velvet in awe.

Wondering if she, too, might find herself a rich patron, Velvet took to looking on the sides of the boxes to check the names of customers, hoping to find someone titled or wealthy-sounding. In this way she found a Madame Natasha Savoya and, after asking around to make sure she wasn't already 'owned', was told by Maisie that Madame was a new customer whom no one knew much about. 'I had one of her boxes last week,' Maisie said. 'Rather you than me with all *her* flummery.'

Velvet, intrigued, opened the newly arrived laundry box and gasped at the delicious assortment of pastel silks and satins it contained: a strawberry pink blouse, a silk bed jacket with embroidered yoke, a shawl as fine as a spider's web, a creamy blue nightdress, a long pleated linen skirt and a cashmere morning gown appliquéd with moss roses.

'Look at these!' she cried, pulling everything out. 'What lovely things.'

'Lovely they may be,' Maisie said, looking over her shoulder, 'but they'll prove the very devil to launder.'

Nevertheless, Velvet set to. In all, the box took

near two days to get through and she needed to learn several new skills, for the hem of the night-dress was unravelling and it was missing some pearl buttons, one of the appliquéd roses was coming adrift from its backing, and there were various other small and careful repairs required, as well as all the garments' washing, drying and pressing. Taking advice from Mrs Sloane and the other girls along the way, Velvet completed everything carefully and, on finishing, sprinkled the garments with lavender and layered them in tissue paper before putting them back in the box.

Some days later, a message arrived saying that the distinguished customer was very pleased with what had been achieved, so Velvet laid claim to Madame Natasha Savoya's personal laundry from then on. She wasn't sure how to pronounce this name, nor even what nationality she was, though Lizzie said she must be Russian, for someone in the royal family had a Russian cousin named Natasha.

As the days and weeks passed, Velvet felt she grew to know Madame pretty well. She knew which colours were her favourites (lilacs, blues and greys), could guess if she'd had a quiet week at home or been to a party, and whether or not her outings had been of a formal nature. She even knew when Madame attended a funeral, for a black grosgrain gown with underskirts of black netting came in to be sponged and pressed. Madame's garments were often fragile or difficult but Velvet, stroking a length of soft green cashmere or touching her cheek to a silvery gossamer shawl, found great satisfaction in lavishing care on them. They made a pleasant change from the shapeless smocks, drab linens and cheap wool garments which had been her everyday wear for years.

December arrived with the promise of the new year. Some people said that the new century hadn't really begun last year, but would properly start on 1st January 1901. Velvet liked this idea. Last year her life had changed direction; next year it might change again. It was another chance for something tremendous and exciting to happen.

It grew much colder, so that initially everyone at Ruffold's was happy to be working inside in the warm, but it took no more than half an hour or so in the close, steamy atmosphere for them to be gasping for fresh air again.

All the girls were to be given Christmas Day and Boxing Day off work and, having nowhere else to go, Velvet had been invited to have dinner at Lizzie's house. She was happy to be going, although spent some time anxiously wondering if she would be expected to bring presents for Lizzie's mother and three sisters as well as for Lizzie herself, for – their two days off being unpaid holiday – she would be very short of money that week. After much deliberation, therefore, she decided to buy a box of sugared plums that all the family could share.

Some of the girls on Personal Laundry had received Christmas boxes from their ladies and gentlemen; four sixpences were discovered in a silk bag, a silver crown in amongst the creases of a shirt. One fortunate laundress received the almost unbelievable sum of ten shillings and, because many of the girls had never seen a ten-shilling note before, it was passed around and remarked on by all. A few gifts arrived, too: a silk scarf, a box of shiny bonbons from the proprietor of a small Christmas-cracker factory and a Bible. Money was what the girls hoped for, however, and money was mostly what they got, although some customers didn't deem it necessary to give anything at all.

Velvet didn't receive anything until Christmas Eve, when she opened a newly arrived box from Madame Savoya and discovered a white sealed envelope with *Velvet* written on it in blue ink. Thrilled, she put it on the middle of the table, where it sat until dinner time, the focus of much speculation amongst the others.

'It's got to be a banknote!' Maisie said as dinner time came and Velvet held it aloft.

'It couldn't be another ten shillings, surely!' said the girl who had received that amount, whilst someone else warned Velvet that it could be just a Bible tract or a Christmas card, so she shouldn't get her hopes up.

Velvet pulled the seal from the back of the envelope, then looked in and shook her head, disappointed. 'It's not money,' she said, pulling something out.

'Just a card!' someone cried, and there was a collective groan of disappointment.

'No, something else,' Velvet said. 'It's . . . two tickets!'

In honour of the Season, one of London's Leading Clairvoyants,
Madame Natasha Savoya,
will be hosting an Evening of Mediumship
on 26th December 1900 at 7 o'clock
in Prince's Hall, London, W.

Discover what the New Century has in store for you.

'Oh!' Velvet gasped. 'My lady, she's one of those . . . *mediums*!'

'They talk to dead people!' someone said.

'Or they say they do,' someone else returned.

'Prince's Hall,' Maisie said. 'That's shocking posh. Will you go?'

'Certainly,' said Velvet, just a little dismayed that the envelope hadn't contained money. She felt a rush of apprehension. 'But *mediumship*. What sort of thing do you think will happen?'

'It will be table-rapping and so on,' said one of the others. 'My aunt went to a séance and the table leaped into the air.'

'People will materialise out of smoke,' said another girl.

'Ethereal spirits will lay their ghostly hands on you,' said Maisie in an eerie voice, and someone gave a terrified shriek which, the girls being rather over-excited because of the festive season, made everyone collapse in giggles.

A shiver ran down Velvet's back. Her mother and father were both dead and though she wouldn't mind hearing from her lovely ma, she had not the slightest wish to have contact with her father. Suppose he turned up and railed at her for not saving his life? Suppose other people heard and she was accused of his murder? She was pleased and excited to be given Madame's invitation, but a little nervous about what might come from it . . .

Velvet and Lizzie left work as usual that evening, and by then Lizzie had been told about the tickets and offered the spare one. She accepted immediately.

'I've always wanted to go to one of those!' she said as they walked across the laundry yard. 'My aunt went once and my dead uncle came through and spoke to her about all sorts of things: how he wanted the garden planted and what she should name her new dog. He said that she had a new friend whom she shouldn't trust.' Lizzie frowned. 'She had an admirer at the time, you see, and because of what my uncle said, she finished with him.'

'Really?' Velvet said. She had next to no knowledge of psychic mediums and no way of determining how accurate or truthful they were. When she thought of them at all she presumed they were just another form of magic – and she associated magic with her father and therefore some deviousness. Perhaps spiritualism was different, though, because it was said that even Queen Victoria and the royal family practised table-turning, and certainly the papers were full of the aristocracy attending the sessions of this or that famous London medium.

Outside Ruffold's, a figure was standing, a small box in his hand. Velvet recognised Charlie and sighed a little.

'Kitty!'

'Velvet,' she coolly corrected him. She'd imagined that Charlie would have turned up at Ruffold's before now, and had been just the tiniest bit put out that he hadn't. He couldn't have missed her that much, then, despite his declaration of love.

'Yes, I meant Velvet. I came to wish you happy Christmas and to give you this.' He pushed a small box into her hands. It was wrapped in plain white paper and had her name – her new name – written in sturdy block capitals on the top.

'Thank you, Charlie. How kind.' He grinned and proffered his cheek, so she couldn't do much else but brush it with her own. 'And a merry Christmas to you,' she said.

A small group of Ruffold's girls passed them. All turned to look at Charlie, sizing him up, arching their eyebrows and casting enquiring looks as to whether he was there for Velvet or Lizzie. Velvet waited until they'd gone by, then thanked Charlie again and turned to leave.

'Please don't go yet!' he said, putting a hand on her arm. 'I want to tell you something. That day you saw me, I was going for an interview.'

Velvet paused. 'Yes?'

'I'm a police cadet now,' he said proudly. 'I should make a proper policeman in three years' time, and I want to train as a detective after that.'

Velvet smiled, though she shivered a little inside, for in her mind the word *policeman* was inevitably connected with the word *crime*, and the one that she held herself responsible for. 'That's wonderful, Charlie. I'm very pleased for you.'

'My father says being a policeman is the most rewarding job a man can have,' Lizzie put in.

Charlie smiled at her warmly, then turned back to Velvet and took her hand. 'When I'm fully qualified, I'll come and find you and ask you to marry me.'

'Thank you, Charlie,' Velvet said. 'But I think you'll find that my answer is just the same as it's always been.' She spoke kindly, however, because every girl liked having a follower and he had bought her a Christmas present. Being Charlie's wife, though, whether he was a policeman or not, was most definitely not how she saw her future.

Velvet managed not to open Charlie's present until Christmas morning. When she did, she was disappointed, which was extremely wicked and ungrateful of her, she knew, but she couldn't help thinking that Charlie's mother must have chosen the gift within – a pink and green flower corsage for an outer coat, made of felt and not at all fashionable. She'd been hoping that the box might contain a pretty hair decoration with which to keep back her curls, or even a little silver necklace to enhance the Sunday best dress that she intended to wear to Lizzie's house that day. But she admonished herself. What was she thinking of? If it had been a costly piece of jewellery, then she would have had to return it. A girl couldn't accept a gift like that from a male friend unless they were engaged, and it wouldn't do to give Charlie ideas. He was a sweet boy and she liked him very much, but he wouldn't make a husband for her. He was part of the past which she intended to leave behind.

At Lizzie's house she was delighted to find that the family kept a good Christmas – the sort she'd never experienced before. In the doorway hung a kissing ball of ivy and mistletoe, and in the hall the Christmas tree was liberally decorated with candles, gold tinsel and ivy ribbons. She felt shy at first, but was welcomed so warmly into the family that before long she was joining in everything – even the raucous singing games around the piano – as if she'd known them all for years.

Mr Cameron, Lizzie's pa, was a source of amazement to Velvet. Whereas *her* father had always seemed to be teetering on the edge of a display of bad temper, Lizzie's was a happy-go-lucky chap who whipped off his jacket and waistcoat to show his daughters how to dance the hornpipe, and made paper hats for their pet dogs. When they sat down at the table and Lizzie's ma discovered that she'd forgotten to put the stuffing into the breast of the roast goose, Velvet went cold, fearing a terrible row, but Mr Cameron roared with laughter and called his wife a flibbertigibbet, then kissed her and said he wouldn't have her any other way.

After the goose came a flaming plum pudding containing small silver charms: a boot, a coin, a top hat, a dog, a lucky horseshoe and a ring. Velvet got the tiny horseshoe (she thought that Lizzie's kindly mother had likely arranged it that way) and everyone made much of the fact that this was the best token to have and that the coming year was bound to be very lucky for her. After the meal there were charades with forfeits if you didn't guess the answer in a certain number of minutes, then blind man's buff and – as the afternoon grew more boisterous – a game with a Ouija board which Lizzie's sisters played most enthusiastically, getting in touch with all sorts of 'spirits' but failing to get anything sensible out of them. *HSTRETYZZ*, one said in reply to a question about his name. *WERPRSIT*, said another when asked where he came from. At teatime everyone had a barley sugar stick from the Christmas tree, a slice of iced fruit cake and a bonbon. When Velvet pulled her cracker with Lizzie's mother, she was delighted to discover within it a tiny pair of nail scissors, a paper hat and a joke (*My dog has no nose. How does it smell? Dreadful*) which sent everyone into near hysterics.

Complimenting Mrs Cameron on the wonderful fruitfulness of the cake, Velvet, looking around the table and feeling very happy, wondered if her ma and pa had ever had such good times together. She decided they had not for, as far back as she could remember, her father had been an impossible man to please. Why, only last Christmas she'd made an effort to create a little cheer, buying a joint of ham for their Christmas dinner and studding it with cloves, but her father had sniffed it, said that he hated cloves and thrown the whole thing to the floor. He'd taken exception to the way she'd decorated the room, too, and tossed the evergreens outside, saying they were a pagan tradition which he would not tolerate (although he certainly could not be called a religious man).

'Lizzie tells me that your mother and father are no longer with us, my dear,' Mrs Cameron said as they sat, much later, toasting chunks of bread before the fire. 'I'm sorry to hear it.'

'Thank you,' Velvet murmured.

'And you have no brothers or sisters?'

'None that survived their childhood,' Velvet replied.

'And had your father a trade?' asked Mr Cameron, who was immensely proud of his position as an omnibus driver.

Velvet nodded. 'I suppose you might call it so,' she said. 'He was a children's entertainer and called himself Mr Magic. He performed conjuring tricks at private parties.'

'Oh!' everyone exclaimed. 'What fun.'

'Did he play tricks on you?' Lizzie said.

'Were you always finding rabbits in his pocket?' Mrs Cameron asked, making them all laugh. 'What a merry time you must have had.'

Velvet looked around her, wondering how much to say and, because the faces turned towards her were kindly, shook her head. 'No, it wasn't really a merry time.'

'Might one ask why?' ventured Mrs Cameron.

Velvet took a deep breath. There was so much she could say. She thought of the big things – his wickedness to her mother, his cruelty to animals, the way he'd lose his money gambling and then rail at her if there was no hot dinner, his enormous capacity for self-pity, and the smaller things – the way he'd ask for a sugary sweetmeat from a party saying it was 'for my daughter' and then eat it in front of her, the way he'd make her run behind his hired transport carrying his cases. So many things, a hundred unhappinesses, but which to choose? And how could she air them now and spoil everyone's day?

'He was like . . . two different people,' she said eventually. 'He was jolly Mr Magic to the children at the parties, but when he came out of their houses he changed and his jolliness disappeared. He became someone else and I was always frightened of him.'

'Never!' said Mrs Cameron. 'He sounds beastly. I'd like to find him and give him a piece of my mind!'

'Now, now, dear,' Mr Cameron put in. 'The man's passed away, remember.'

'Even so . . .' Mrs Cameron dabbed at the corners of her eyes with a lace handkerchief. 'But were you well nourished, my love?' she asked Velvet. 'Who kept house after your dear mother died?'

'I did,' Velvet said, 'though sometimes I didn't have much to housekeep.' She smiled wryly. 'Father was a gambler, you see, and I don't know what was worse: when he won at the races and got roaring drunk, or when he lost and got dismal drunk. Either way, it was never pleasant.' She looked around at their kindly faces. 'I know one shouldn't speak badly about one's father, but I fear he wasn't a good or decent man. My mother had a miserable life with him, and I believe he drove her to an early grave.'

'I've known men like that,' said Mr Cameron. 'Nice as pie when they're out and about, but the very devil to live beside.'

'But I mustn't speak ill of the dead,' Velvet said. 'He's gone now and there's an end to it. You've all been so nice to me and I don't want to spoil the festivities.'

'Nor have you, my dear!' said Mr Cameron. 'You needed to get that off your chest.'

'And as you haven't had a fortunate past, we'll drink to your happy future. The future of the girl who got the lucky silver horseshoe!' toasted Mrs Cameron, raising her glass of plum wine in Velvet's direction.

The family joined in, then settled down even closer to the fire for what Mrs Cameron assured Velvet was the way they always concluded Christmas Day – the head of the family reading from *A Christmas Carol*.

Chapter Four

In Which Velvet and Lizzie Attend
an Evening of Mediumship

The excursion to Prince's Hall for an evening of mediumship had been planned, timed and talked about in detail. The most urgent matter was what to wear, of course, for neither Velvet nor Lizzie had ever been to what Mrs Cameron assured them would be a 'proper do, with society and all'. Deliberations about their costume did not occupy them for very long, however, because each girl had only two outfits: one for work and one for Sunday. Their hats were to be given new trimmings, however, and here Velvet put to use the felt corsage she'd been given by Charlie, breaking up the flowers and sewing them individually around the brim of her hat. Regarding their outerwear – and feeling that the woolly shawls the girls usually wrapped themselves in would not do for such an event – Mrs Cameron lent Lizzie her best black mantle, and

Velvet borrowed a similar one from Mrs Cameron's sister, who lived next door. Velvet also washed her hair and dried it wrapped around rags, so that, away from the heat and damp of the laundry, it was transformed into shiny dark ringlets instead of a cloud of frizz.

The travel arrangements were quite straight-forward: the girls were to catch the number fifty-one omnibus which would drop them almost outside Prince's Hall. To save them from being pestered by young men or street sellers afterwards, Mr Cameron would meet them and escort them home.

Prince's Hall turned out to be a small, intimate theatre with gold-painted chairs arranged in semi-circles before the stage. The girls were seated halfway down the hall, which suited Velvet. She was very much looking forward to seeing Madame, but she would have felt exposed if she'd been any nearer to the front. She really didn't want to be called upon and told that someone from the spirit world wished to speak to her in case that someone was her father. She hadn't actually killed him, she repeatedly reassured herself. Surely she couldn't be accused of murder . . .

'Look!' Lizzie said, pointing to a chair and table before them on the otherwise bare stage. 'Those things will go up in the air – my sister said that always happens. It goes dark and then there are rapping sounds and things fly everywhere.'

'Not with Madame Savoya!' the large woman beside Velvet said in a somewhat admonishing tone. 'Madame does not do party tricks.'

'Then, if you'll excuse me for asking,' Velvet said politely, 'what does she do?'

'We've never been to such an evening before,' explained Lizzie.

'Why, Madame Savoya communes with the spirits,' replied the woman. 'She asks them questions and they answer. Madame has the most wonderful rapport with those on the Other Side.' She lifted a finger and waggled it at them. 'She doesn't need to sound trumpets and make furniture fly in the air!'

Velvet and Lizzie thanked her, nudging each other in excitement, then began a game of counting the number of fur coats they could see in the front four rows. They had just reached seventeen when the gaslights were dimmed, a voice called for complete silence and the audience immediately became hushed. Velvet, who'd earlier been scared that she might giggle nervously at an inappropriate moment, now felt herself much too overawed to do so.

After perhaps three minutes, a curtain parted at the centre back of the stage and a young man in an evening suit came out, holding the drape open for a small, darkly beautiful young woman with elaborately coiffed hair, dressed in – Velvet gripped Lizzie's arm in excitement – the grey silk, pin-tucked blouse that she personally had laundered not four days before! She instantly recognised it because it fastened all down the front with mother-of-pearl buttons, and one of these had broken in half before it came to Ruffold's and had had to be replaced with an identical one from Mrs Sloane's button tin.

'I laundered that!' she whispered in Lizzie's ear. 'That very blouse she's wearing.' But Lizzie was too rapt watching the stage to answer.

Madame Savoya walked towards the chair. Her skirt (soft cashmere in dove grey) was pulled back at each side into an elaborate bustle which fell to the floor in gentle drapes and revealed the toes of shiny silver shoes. As she sat down, the young man standing to one side of her bade everyone welcome on her behalf, introducing himself as her assistant and saying his name was George. 'Gorgeous George,' Lizzie breathed in Velvet's ear, for he was very handsome indeed.

'What you are about to witness will amaze and confound you,' he told the enthralled audience. 'Madame Savoya's grandmother was a Russian princess, one of the Romanovs, and the women of her family have always had the Sight.'

Madame Savoya smiled faintly and nodded as George continued. 'On her sixteenth birthday, she had a vision in which her grandmother appeared and told her that she was going to become a medium of enormous talent. She said that Madame would gain immense influence and respect in the world, but must never allow her talents to corrupt her. Her grandmother told her she must always give half of everything she would earn to charities, institutions and those poor creatures less fortunate than herself.'

A murmur of appreciation ran through the hall.

'Madame has, of course, always abided by this rule, and is now the leading medium in London – perhaps in all of England. Tonight, in Prince's Hall, she is going to give you a demonstration of her powers. We hope to be blessed with help from the spirits this evening, although one can never guarantee visitations from the world beyond.'

The audience's eager faces dropped just a little at this, as did Velvet's and Lizzie's. 'I hope they *do* come,' Lizzie whispered. 'Fancy us doing ourselves up like this and not hearing any messages.'

'Madame Savoya is a ray of light into the spirit world, a rainbow which links their existence to ours,' the young man elaborated. 'Madame is an open book wherein the spirits can write.'

Madame smiled and inclined her head gracefully.

'The large number of you here tonight means an equally large number of spirits is waiting patiently on the Other Side, for they know that we're hoping to hear from them. Channelling messages from this dense throng will be extremely tiring for Madame and she will not, at this time, be able to deal with those newly passed spirits, who are usually somewhat bewildered and demand a lot of patience and attention. Madame asks, therefore, if you have someone who has recently passed, to contact her so that she may conduct a private sitting and dedicate more of her time and consideration to you.'

George finished his introduction and bowed, then Madame rose and came forward to address the audience. She was not foreign, Velvet realised straight away. Her voice was low, cultured, and she was younger than she first appeared, perhaps only twenty-two or twenty-three. Her face was pale, her lips full and her eyes dark and expressive under thin, arching brows. She had glossy black hair, pulled back and piled into curls on top of her head, leaving a few wisps about her face. She looked both beautiful and serene.

'I see some tense faces amongst you,' she said. 'But I must tell you that tonight there will be no dire prophecies or tales of woe. Tonight is a light-hearted diversion to show what help our guiding spirits can provide. Perhaps it will give you the courage to have a longer and more personal sitting with me.'

'She is *such* an inspiration!' the large woman beside Velvet was heard to murmur.

'Underneath each of your chairs is a pencil, a slip of paper and an envelope,' Madame went on. 'If you would care to, please write down a question, place it in the envelope and tuck in the flap to ensure that it cannot be seen by me. It is not I who will answer your questions, ladies and gentlemen, but the spirits.'

There was a pause and then the scraping of chairs as the audience located their pieces of paper. After that came some whispered consultations, followed by the soft scratching of pencils.

Velvet and Lizzie exchanged glances. What to write? Nothing that might mean her father being called back, Velvet thought. After a moment or two she wrote, *For how much longer will I be working at Ruffold's?* Lizzie, who had spent near three years at a dame school and so had quite a passable hand, wrote, *Will I marry a rich man?*

The questions were collected by the young gentleman assistant who, Lizzie and Velvet were sure, smiled and crinkled his eyes at them as he took their envelopes. 'Not that I'm surprised at him being saucy with us,' whispered Lizzie, 'because everyone else here is so very old.'

The envelopes were dropped into a top hat and taken to Madame. 'You will have seen that your questions cannot be viewed through the envelopes,' she said, 'and they will be in your full view the entire time I'm on stage. I have absolutely no way of knowing what you've asked before I open your envelope.'

'Madame and the spirits will try to answer as

many questions as possible,' said the young man. 'But we ask for your support and understanding if she becomes exhausted by the demands upon her.'

The audience was still and silent as Madame dipped into the top hat and pulled out an envelope. She closed her eyes for a moment, held the envelope to her heart and spoke out brightly. 'Ah, a lady here wishes to know if she will receive a proposal of marriage in the near future.'

There was a murmur of interest from the audience and Madame asked if the lady who had asked the question would please rise. A woman stood up, not in the first flush of youth but very elegantly dressed in a black-and-white silk costume with a small feathered hat. When she smilingly confessed that the question had been hers, Velvet noticed that she had prominent front teeth which made her lisp slightly.

Madame was quiet for a moment, then said, 'You will be happy to know that the answer from my spirits is a very positive one. They tell me that the gentleman in question is on the verge of proposing . . .' this produced another murmur from the (mostly female) audience '. . . and that you will marry before next Christmas.'

'How marvellous!' said the lady.

'They have even given me sight of the outfit you'll be wearing when you receive the gentleman's proposal,' Madame said, and she smiled. 'It'll be an azure satin gown.'

'I shall go and buy such a garment tomorrow!' the questioner said, clearly delighted.

'But you must try and look surprised when the gentleman asks you,' George the assistant said, and everyone laughed.

'May I confirm your question?' Madame asked. The woman assenting, Madame pulled out the flap of the envelope she held, removed the slip of paper and read out, *'Will I marry soon?'*

An excited buzz ran around the hall. 'How did she know it said that?' Lizzie asked, truly amazed, but this time it was Velvet who was too transfixed to reply.

Madame took another envelope and held it to her heart for a moment, as before. 'A question from someone who signs himself, *A gentleman from Scotland,'* she said. Then followed a long pause during which Madame held her head on one side, as if listening. She eventually continued, 'The spirits tell me that you will live a long and happy life, sir. What's more, you and your wife will be blessed with one more child.'

The 'gentleman from Scotland' who stood up to own this question looked sheepish, but gave Madame permission to open the envelope and read out his question: *'I fear I will die young. Can the spirits tell me otherwise?'*

Madame held the next envelope aloft. The question inside was from someone who wanted confirmation that her father was in the spirit world, for she said he'd gone abroad and hadn't been seen for many years. A stocky woman stood up to claim the question, and Madame told her that he was indeed on the Other Side, but that she shouldn't grieve, as he was happy with another woman in spirit. 'His wife or his sister?' Madame asked.

'That would be his sister,' the stocky woman agreed. 'She passed just last year.'

'Indeed it is,' Madame confirmed.

'Has my father no messages for me?' the woman asked.

Madame Savoya listened, then smiled. 'He says he always was a man of few words. Is that correct?'

The woman laughed, saying, 'Yes, he was.'

'Do come and see me privately if you wish to communicate with him more fully,' said Madame.

The questions and answers resumed, following the same format. Occasionally Madame would put aside an envelope, saying that the question within was too intimate and that the questioner might care to consult her privately. Laughter was provoked when, holding an envelope, Madame said, 'Well, there's someone here whose maid must have dressed them completely in the dark, for they're asking me what colour gown they're wearing. Would the lady who wrote this please own her question.'

A woman wearing a fashionable dress in dark green velvet rose to her feet, smiling and a little embarrassed.

Madame addressed her very kindly. 'I'd say that you're wearing moss green, madam.'

Madame continued as before, occasionally putting her hand to her forehead and looking somewhat strained. As it neared ten o'clock, there was still a number of envelopes left in the top hat but the young man said that they could only take two more.

Madame pulled out the next sealed envelope and held it close. 'Here's someone who asks about her future,' she said. 'A nearby spirit tells me that it's from a young lady, who's enterprising and bright, who's not content to let the grass grow under her feet.'

Velvet nudged Lizzie and held her breath. This could be her question!

'I see the young lady in a hot and steamy environment . . . could it be a place similar to the hothouses at Kew?' Madame paused a moment, holding the envelope between her palms, as if praying. 'No, I believe it to be a laundry, or something very like.' She looked around the hall. 'Will the young lady own her question, please?'

Velvet, her legs shaking at the thought of being conspicuous in such company, got to her feet. Several fur-coated ladies looked at her and exchanged glances of surprise, for it was highly unusual for a working-class girl – not only that, but someone who apparently worked in a laundry – to attend such a gathering.

Madame smiled at her kindly, however, and Velvet no longer felt small and insignificant but – as she told Lizzie later – as if she were standing in a pool of sunlight. 'My dear girl,' Madame said sweetly, 'don't be nervous. The spirits say there are great things in store for you. You won't continue long in your present position, but will rise up in the world.'

Overawed, Velvet could do no more than say, 'Oh! Thank you very much, Madame.' She would have liked to ask many other things – when she might meet her future husband, what he would be like, how she would know he was the one and how soon all this might come about – but she did not dare. She merely stammered that she was grateful for the information and sat down.

Following the last question, which sadly was not Lizzie's, Madame left the stage leaning heavily on the young man's arm. He returned to apologise on her behalf because she hadn't been able to answer everyone's questions and repeated that those who needed specific advice, or wanted messages from their relatives on the Other Side, should attend a private session. He spoke so elegantly, seemed so solicitous of the feelings of others and had such chis-elled cheekbones that Velvet and Lizzie both returned home to dream of him.

Chapter Five

In Which a Terrible Disaster Leads to
a Very Surprising Outcome

Velvet's life continued as before – if it was going to be her lucky year there was no indication of it. Every day was the same: rise, wash and dress by the light of a candle, breakfast swiftly on anything left over from supper the night before, meet Lizzie outside the house for the brisk, icy cold walk to work and spend the next near-twelve hours in stupefying heat before walking home again, ashen-faced with tiredness, and falling into bed. Velvet found that it was a little cooler working at the Personal Laundry end of the room, but this was negated by the intense concentration required for the exacting, detailed work she had to do so that she felt just as weary. Every day bar Sunday was the same, and the routine was only briefly interrupted at the start of February when everyone was given a day off work to mark the funeral of Queen Victoria.

The queen had been in deep mourning and more or less permanent seclusion on the Isle of Wight since the death of her husband Prince Albert forty years before. Mindful of all this gloom and anxious to start a new, forward-thinking regime, her son, the new King Edward VII, put a three-month limit on the mourning of her by her subjects. Within this time, however, a great deal of black garments descended on the laundry to be freshened, sponged and pressed.

Velvet thought a lot about Madame Savoya whilst pressing black bombazine skirts, black-beaded bodices and the tight little black jackets which were so much in fashion. In fact, she had a recurring dream in which Madame adopted her and brought her up as her own child. She knew this was quite ridiculous because Madame was probably not more than five or six years older than her – and anyway, she herself was over sixteen now and surely too old to be adopted. Nevertheless, the dream was often repeated and proved strangely comforting. Waking, shivering, in her miserable room in the middle of the night, Velvet would imagine that she was safe and comfortable, a daughter in Madame's house, only momentarily feeling chilled because her feather-filled quilt had slipped from the bed. Soon she would wake to a warm house, find hot water for washing and her clothes laid out for her by her maid, then go downstairs to breakfast on kedgeree.

Sometimes the make-believe would work and she would easily fall asleep once more, but mostly it did not and she would lie awake until the church clock struck five and then rise to the same poor room, her washcloth frozen hard and the water in her jug having formed itself into a block of solid ice.

Madame's success as a medium gathered momentum. Velvet sometimes saw a mention of her in a newspaper, and once overheard a woman in the street talking of some remarkable happening: 'And Madame Savoya said she saw him actually standing there before her. Standing there – and him five years dead!' Madame's laundry boxes continued also, and although Velvet laid claim to several other regular customers, it was Madame's clothes that she cherished. No other customer wore such wonderful materials in so many different fashions and styles, no other gowns had such lavish embroidery or bore such an extravagance of smocking, lace, tucking, ruffles and beads.

It was a silk ruffle which led to a dreadful happening, however, for when Velvet was slowly and carefully twirling the frilled edge of one of Madame's precious blouses, disaster struck. Something – afterwards she wracked her brains to think what it might have been – took her attention away from the job and she left the ruffle iron in position a moment longer than she should have done. A moment was all it needed: the tip of the iron became caught up and, in the blink of an eye, a flounce of purest silk melted into a shrivelled grey lump.

'No!' Velvet stared at the lump in horror, tears starting in her eyes. 'Madame's beautiful blouse!' She touched the frizzled material with her fingertips. It bore a Parisian label and she didn't dare to think what it must have cost.

Hearing her cry out, the other girls turned to look and gasped or urged her to go and plunge the blouse into cold water. Mrs Sloane jumped down from her box and was on the spot almost immediately, snatching the blouse from Velvet's hands and carrying it to the light to inspect the damage. Whilst Mrs Sloane was studying it, Velvet felt there was a chance that it might not be as bad as she'd thought, but as soon as the supervisor turned from the window she shook her head.

'It's beyond any help,' she said. 'Completely ruined. You careless girl! What were you thinking of?'

Velvet burst into tears, knowing that this would mean instant dismissal. It wasn't just that, though – it was knowing that she'd let Madame down, and destroyed something that she held dear. Why, she'd rather have burned her own arm than spoiled one of Madame's beautiful garments!

'You were chattering, I suppose,' said Mrs Sloane. 'Chattering and giggling like you all do. Oh, I knew that something like this would happen sooner or later.'

Velvet was crying too hard to even begin to say that she hadn't been talking. Besides, she knew it was useless to protest, for a girl had been dismissed only the previous week for making a tiny burn mark in a sheet, even though she'd pleaded that it was a rust stain which was already there.

Mrs Sloane looked at Velvet's heaving shoulders, then pursed her lips and steeled herself. Velvet was a favourite of hers, but rules were rules and she'd already given the girl one chance. 'You can stay until the end of the week,' she said.

Velvet sniffed back tears and looked at Mrs Sloane bleakly. It was Thursday, so she had two more days earning money before she had to join the massed ranks of London's unemployed. 'What if you took payment for the blouse out of my earnings?' she asked. 'Couldn't you do that, Mrs Sloane, please?'

'And how long do you think *that* would take?' Mrs Sloane snorted, then lowered her voice. 'I'm already going against rules letting you stay on an extra two days. Dismissal is supposed to be instant.'

Velvet said no more, but wept on and off for the rest of the afternoon. Mr Ruffold himself was informed of the unlucky incident and went to see Madame Savoya personally to apologise and to try and make good, in financial terms at least, what had occurred.

That night Velvet went home anxious and very miserable, imagining Madame's horror and disappointment at the damage done to her blouse, and spending a sleepless night wondering how on earth she was going to manage without a job. Saturday was to be her last day at Ruffold's. She would collect her wages that afternoon, pay her rent for the following week and then have just a few coins between her and the dreaded workhouse.

When the girls made their way into the corridor for their dinner break that Saturday, Velvet sat huddled, worry gnawing at her, unable to eat – unable, even, to respond to Lizzie's sympathetic suggestions as to what she might do next. How could she earn money? Where could she go? She had no particular experience except at washing and ironing, but she couldn't possibly take in laundry at home because she had no access to hot water and certainly nowhere to hang lines of drying sheets.

Sunk in despair, it took her a while to become aware that one of the little girl learners was tapping her on the shoulder. 'Mrs Sloane wants to see you,' she said, 'and you're to come as quick as you can.'

'Is Mr Ruffold there?' Velvet asked, for she was fearful that the boss might take some of her wages as partial compensation for the accident.

The girl shrugged. 'Dunno, miss. She just told me you must come and see her straight away.'

Velvet went towards the supervisor's office and, hearing voices from within, almost fled. To do that would have meant running away from her wages, however, so she took a breath and knocked at the door.

'Come in,' Mrs Sloane called.

Velvet entered and was both alarmed and comforted by the sight of Madame Savoya, smiling and beautiful in a dress and jacket of lavender wool. Beside her stood George, the young man who had assisted at her evening performance, looking tall, slim and elegant in dark-green livery.

Velvet gave a low curtsey.

'Now, Velvet, what do you think?' Mrs Sloane said in her most genteel voice. 'Madame has come here specially to ask us to keep you on.'

Velvet gasped and was about to bob another curtsey to Madame when she saw, to her great consternation, that this lady was shaking her head.

'I beg your pardon, but I haven't come here for that, Mrs Sloane.'

Mrs Sloane looked confused. 'Oh, allow me to beg *your* pardon,' she blustered. 'I presumed that your appearance here could only mean one thing, and this seemed to be confirmed when you said you wished to talk to me about Velvet and asked if she could attend us.'

Velvet kept her eyes on the floor, hardly knowing where to look.

'No, I wished to talk to Velvet for quite a different reason,' Madame said.

'I'm most terribly sorry about your lovely blouse!'
Velvet blurted out. 'I loved having your clothes to
look after – they're so beautiful. I wasn't really
being neglectful of my duties. I don't know how the
ruffle iron got caught but –'

Madame lifted a hand encased in a lilac suede
glove. 'No more need be said about that.' There was
a pause, then she added, 'I came to offer you a position in my household.'

'A . . . position?' Velvet stuttered.

'As a laundress?' Mrs Sloane asked.

'As a . . . well, I'm not sure of the name for what I
need,' Madame said thoughtfully. 'I understand
your mother taught you several skills, Velvet?'

Velvet bobbed a curtsey. 'I can read and write
well, Madame, and I can embroider and smock, and
also draw a little. I can even speak a few words of
French.'

Madame Savoya smiled at this.

'You see, before my mother was a laundress, she
worked for a big family as a governess. She taught
me everything she knew,' Velvet finished.

'May God rest her soul!' put in Mrs Sloane piously.

'She has passed over, I understand,' Madame said.
'You are quite alone in the world?'

'I am, Madame.'

She nodded thoughtfully. 'You've cared for my
clothes so beautifully here, I'm sure you can do the
same thing at my home.'

'I would be . . . like a lady's maid?' Velvet asked.

Madame smiled. 'Partly that, although we already have a housekeeper and a daily maid. You would, perhaps, do a little light sewing and work of that ilk, but mostly you would be my companion and assistant, opening the door to my clients, accompanying me to the shops, laying out my clothes, walking my pet dog, answering the telephone – duties of that nature.'

Velvet gasped anew at each of these duties – the last especially, for she had only ever seen a telephone once, in Mr Ruffold's office, and certainly had never answered one.

'What do you think, Velvet?' asked Madame. She glanced up at George. 'What else can we tell her, George? I'm not too hard a task-mistress, am I?'

'You are the kindest and very best, Madame,' George said. He smiled at Velvet and she noticed that his eyes were almost a match for the dark green of his uniform. 'Won't you come and join us at Darkling Villa?'

Velvet, beaming with pleasure and amazement, already felt herself to be half in love with both Madame and George. 'Oh, yes, please.'

Chapter Six

In Which Velvet Begins Living in Her New Home

Darkling Villa was just off Hanover Crescent in Regent's Park, an expensive area in north London, and Velvet was delighted to find herself even further away from the place where she'd spent her childhood. Madame had given her the fare for a hackney carriage from Chiswick and she very much enjoyed the ride through the streets, taking with her all her possessions (which did not amount to much more than the few clothes she wasn't wearing, the old lace petticoat which had once been her mother's, her washing things and a spare pair of shoes) in a large brown paper bag. The area was very well-to-do and when the driver stopped outside Darkling Villa, a beautiful Regency house with bay windows and columns either side of the door, he'd looked at the house and then back at Velvet in disbelief. 'Are you sure you're for *this* house, miss?' he asked.

'Yes, I am, thank you,' Velvet said, and she paid him and climbed out of the cab, trying not to look amazed and incredulous. When she'd bade good-bye to Lizzie the evening before, she'd not thought for a moment that somewhere as genteel as this would be her new home. She looked up at the house – and up again – thinking that it was probably one of the most beautiful she'd ever seen. Her father had sometimes presided over children's parties in wealthy homes, but none had been as lovely as this, with its pale-grey shutters, marble columns and elegant bay trees in great wooden tubs outside the door.

Madame had told her to come to the front door (rather than the back entrance for tradesmen, or the side door which led to her private quarters), and it was George who answered when she knocked. George's duties, she was to discover, were those of a chief valet or manservant in a house where no gentleman resided. He made sure the house was safely locked up at night, escorted Madame to functions, drove her in her own gig to various engagements and, when necessary, dealt with any gentlemen of the press (Madame's revelations from the Other Side sometimes made headline news, he told Velvet). He also took notes at Madame's private sessions and generally provided a charming, reassuring presence for the many wealthy, middle-aged ladies who were Madame's principal clients.

'Shall I call you Mr George?' Velvet asked, feeling herself blushing.

'*George* will do,' he said, and he took her bag from her and ushered her inside.

She thanked him with a bobbed curtsey and, hoping she would soon be able to speak to him without going red, straightened up and looked around her. She saw a sweeping staircase coming down to a magnificent hall tiled in black-and-white marble, in its centre a long, polished display table containing a large vase of exotic blooms and greenery. To one side were two curved wooden coat stands empty of any garments.

'Do come through to the kitchen,' George said, opening a panelled door on to stairs leading down. 'Madame is sleeping, so you may not see her until later this afternoon. We were at Egyptian Hall last night and the poor lady was overwhelmed with messages – they fair exhausted her.'

'Messages from . . . from dead people?' Velvet asked as they reached the bottom of the stairs.

George nodded. 'Only we don't call them dead,' he said. 'We say they're in spirit, or on the Other Side.'

'I see,' Velvet said. She wanted very much to learn and understand. She wanted to prove invaluable to Madame so that she'd never regret taking her on and she wanted to show George that she wasn't just a simple laundress, a nobody, but a girl who was teachable, capable and clever. And then (she was a romantic, so could not help wishing this), when he'd discovered all that, she wanted him to also discover that she'd wound her way around his heart and he couldn't live without her.

'This is Mrs Lawson, our housekeeper,' George said as they reached the kitchen. A wiry, middle-aged woman nodded at Velvet. 'Mrs Lawson, this is Velvet.'

'Velvet, is it?' said Mrs Lawson, looking up from the dough she was pounding. 'Were your sisters Wool and Linen?'

Velvet smiled, although she had heard the joke – or one very like it – before.

'Mrs Lawson looks after us, cooks our food and keeps the house in order,' said George.

'All on your own?' Velvet asked politely. 'Such a big house!'

'I manage well enough,' replied Mrs Lawson, still pummelling dough. 'Sissy, my daughter, comes in as a daily maid and always attends when Madame has one of her evening soirées.'

'Mrs Lawson is a marvellous cook,' George said. 'Her puddings are things of wonder.'

'And what about my puddings, Mr George?' A girl came out of the scullery and stood looking at George, hands on hips. By her challenging tone and impudent manner, her meaning was clear, but George (to give him his due, Velvet thought) did

68

not continue the banter but pretended to take the question at face value.

'Your lemon meringue is excellent, Sissy.'

The girl laughed.

'Sissy, this is Velvet,' George said. He held up his hand. 'And she's already heard the jokes about Wool and Linen, so I trust you'll spare us those.'

'I'd spare you anything!' Sissy said, and she winked at her mother, who shook her head and gave George a look as if to say, *what would **you** do with her?*'

Velvet was not surprised to find a rival at Darkling Villa, for it was obvious to her that a young man as good-looking as George would attract the eye of any girl, young, old, rich or poor. Not all of them would be as forward as Sissy, of course, but this, Velvet thought, could work to the other girl's disadvantage. Surely she was much too vulgar for anyone as refined and gentlemanly as George?

Velvet was taken by him on a tour of the rest of the house. There were three servants' bedrooms at the top, and Velvet was very pleased to have a room of her own and not to have to share with Mrs Lawson. On the next floor down, a suite of rooms were occupied solely by Madame, consisting of a bedroom, dressing room, small sitting room and a proper bathroom with running hot water. 'Madame is very keen on the latest gadgets,' George said, and went on to say that plans were being drawn up to have electric lights fitted throughout the house. 'Light at the flick of a switch,' he said. 'Imagine that!' On the first floor was an elegant private dining and drawing room, and on the ground floor two large rooms which were used almost exclusively for hosting evenings of mediumship.

These 'Dark Circles', as George referred to them, were usually held in the room facing the street. In this spacious front room the only furniture was a piano and a very large round table with twelve matching chairs placed at regular intervals around it. George explained that Madame either presided at this table or, if the number of visitors was too great, the table could be folded down and the room used to accommodate up to thirty people seated in rows down the room.

'Does Madame use a Ouija board?' Velvet enquired.

'No, she certainly does not!' George said, and Velvet wondered at first if she'd offended him. 'Ouija boards have long been discredited by serious mediums. We consider them no more than playthings.'

Velvet nodded. 'I did wonder,' she said. 'At Christmas we played on one at my friend's house, but I believe her naughty sister was directing things, and spirits came to the board who weren't even dead.' She hesitated. 'That is, weren't even on the Other Side.'

'That's why proper mediums don't use such objects,' George said. 'A Ouija board is all too easy to manipulate.'

Whilst they were in this front room, George paused by a curious arrangement consisting of a thick damask curtain hung across an alcove with a sumptuously cushioned easy chair inside. 'That's Madame's cabinet,' George said. Upon Velvet looking puzzled, he added, 'But I forgot that you haven't attended a closed séance.'

'I've been to Prince's Hall,' Velvet said.

'Those sessions are rather different. This . . .' he indicated the curtain arrangement '. . . is Madame's cabinet and, if she and her guests aren't seated around the table, she'll come in here in order to commune with the spirits.'

'Commune with the spirits,' Velvet repeated, and looked at George wonderingly. He was speaking of strange and remarkable things as if they were everyday happenings. 'Really? How does that happen?'

'When everyone is assembled, Madame goes into the cabinet, enters a trance state and summons the spirits,' George said. 'When the curtain is opened, the spirits speak to the audience through Madame. Sometimes objects belonging to the person in spirit are apported.'

'What's that?'

'It's where an object connected with the person on the Other Side materialises; a certain cigar that a man used to smoke, perhaps, or a child's toy, even a musical instrument.'

'Surely not!'

George nodded, amused, and Velvet wondered if she sounded silly and unsophisticated. She'd make an effort to be a bit more worldly, she vowed.

'But why does Madame have to be in the dark?' she asked.

'Because spirits are shy creatures, insubstantial beings who come and go as they wish. They seem to find it easier to appear before Madame in the darkness.' He hesitated, then continued, 'Occasionally, it's said, spirits may actually appear to other people – people in the audience.'

In spite of her vow just a moment before, Velvet could not but stare at him in amazement. 'They *appear*? And everyone can see them? Are they ghosts? Where do they come from?'

'No one knows exactly,' George said. 'What happens is that during the séance some sort of substance – they call it ectoplasm – comes from the medium's body and forms itself into the shape of the spirit's last manifestation on earth.'

Velvet looked at him, shocked and rather alarmed. 'Does it? I've never heard of such a thing.'

'It's a talent that, at the moment, only a few mediums possess.'

'And does Madame . . . ?'

'Not currently, although she believes her skills will shortly be developed enough for her to do this. She's already adept at so many other things.'

'Oh,' Velvet breathed, quite awestruck. She

looked inside the cabinet, patted a pillow on the chair and half expected to see something rise up from it. 'May I ask how long you've been working with Madame?'

'Several years,' George said. 'I'll tell you my story sometime.' He looked at Velvet, raised his eyebrows and smiled.

Velvet felt her stomach turn right over and she asked quickly, 'Do *you* ever receive messages?'

He shook his head. 'I've no one close to me in the spirit world. An uncle once came through, but I hardly remembered who he was in life and he had nothing in particular to say to me anyway.'

'My mother and father are both d— in spirit.'

'Then you may get a message,' said George. 'Although during an evening session Madame has so many messages for her paying clients that, unless a message for you or I were very compelling, she wouldn't have time to receive it.'

'I see,' Velvet said, and didn't add that she didn't really want one . . . that she would be terrified if she got any messages from her father. She asked instead, 'How do people hear of Madame? Does she advertise?'

'Only when we first arrived in London,' George said. 'After that, it was word of mouth – ladies are informed of her talents by their friends and they in turn tell others. We get all the swells, you know.'

'And does everyone receive messages?'

'Most of them,' George said. 'It's what they come for. But if for some reason their relative doesn't come through and they have a special question for them – perhaps a daughter wants to ask her father if she should marry a certain man, for instance – then Madame will see them privately.'

Velvet nodded. It seemed a good system.

'As long as they can afford it, of course,' George added. 'We're at the top end of the market and Madame's time is very valuable.'

Madame Savoya's First Private Sitting with 'Mrs Lilac'

'*D*o be seated, Mrs Lilac,' Madame Savoya said. 'I believe you've already met my assistant, George?'

Mrs Lilac nodded. A lady in her late sixties, she wore a long dark coat and veiled hat. Under the coat, the glimmer of several rows of pearls could be seen and there was a large gold-and-diamond brooch in the shape of a flower pinned on her lapel. Mrs Lilac seemed somewhat nervous and Madame took pains to put her at ease.

'George will attend us today and be present at any subsequent sessions. This will enable him to take a record of everything conveyed by the spirits,' she said. She added gently, 'You do understand that for the purposes of confidentiality – both yours and mine – your name will not be recorded in these notes?' Upon her client nodding, she continued, 'I identify all my clients according to the colour of their aura. Yours, dear madam, is pale mauve, a rather pretty lilac, signifying that you will soon be able to come out of mourning.'

Mrs Lilac managed to smile.

'George attends us with his notepad because I find that my clients are sometimes so overwhelmed by what they hear from the spirits that they arrive home to find they've forgotten much of what has been said.' Mrs Lilac nodded and Madame went on, 'One more thing: could I ask you to always use my private entrance at the side of the building? You'll find that the stairs lead straight up here to my private apartments.'

'Yes, of course,' said Mrs Lilac. She looked around her apprehensively, although everything seemed perfectly pleasant and ordinary. No ghosts lurked behind statues, there were no eerie noises and no shadowy shapes forming in the alcoves.

'I believe your mother was in touch with you at one of my evening gatherings?' When Mrs Lilac nodded tremulously once again, Madame added, 'You must forgive me if I can't remember the details. So many spirits, so many people . . .'

'Yes, my mother came through,' Mrs Lilac said. 'She told me that I mustn't come out of mourning clothes for a wedding I was invited to, but I should attend in unrelieved black crêpe. She also said that she had not forgiven me for . . . for . . .' Here Mrs Lilac stopped and bit her lip.

Madame took Mrs Lilac's hand. 'No need to elaborate. The spirits will let me know anything I need to.'

George smiled. 'Excuse me for saying so, Mrs Lilac,

but Madame's reputation is second to none. You can place yourself in her hands unreservedly; you may trust her implicitly.'

Mrs Lilac seemed to gain strength.

'Your mother was of a good age,' Madame said. 'Over ninety?'

'Ninety-three,' Mrs Lilac said, 'and she'd lived with me since she was seventy.'

Madame nodded. 'What a dutiful daughter you've been.'

Mrs Lilac didn't reply to this, but looked nervously at George, who patted her arm and gave her a reassuring smile.

'It is time,' Madame said. She gazed upwards and closed her eyes.

The three figures sat immobile for some moments, whilst Madame's breathing grew stronger and more laboured and the Honiton lace fichu at the bodice of her gown rose and fell.

After two or three minutes, Madame said in a deep female voice quite unlike her own, 'I am here! I have come.'

'Mother?' Mrs Lilac cried, her hand to her mouth. 'Mother dearest . . .'

'Really, Esther,' said the deep voice. 'I hope you haven't called me back for some trivial matter.'

'No, I . . . I merely wanted reassurance that you're quite content,' Mrs Lilac said, trembling all over.

There came a snort from Madame – or the one who was occupying her body.

'I trust and pray,' Mrs Lilac began nervously, 'that you've quite forgiven me for placing you in Runnymede.' There came no reply from her mother so she went on in a rush, 'I just didn't feel I could cope any longer, you see. I tried and tried, but I could hardly lift you, and you weren't eating and then when you began waking and walking around the house at all hours of the night, I was at my wits' end.'

'To think you couldn't cope with one old lady. Pish!'

'I decided that you'd be better off in Runnymede with proper care and a nurse on call every moment of the day and night.'

'You wanted to be rid of me, you mean.'

'Mother, no!'

'Most daughters would consider it a privilege to care for their dear mamas; a repayment of the care that their mother had lavished on them as children.'

'But I couldn't manage on my own at home,' Mrs Lilac said, wringing her hands. 'Even with Wilson helping me, I couldn't manage. Oh, do you forgive me, Mother? May I have your blessing?'

'I may forgive you,' came the answer, somewhat petulantly. 'I haven't decided yet. Next time you come, we'll speak of it again.'

'But are you content there?' Mrs Lilac asked, peering at the space around Madame Savoya as if her mother might be standing behind her. 'What's it like? Have you met Father?'

'Questions, questions!' came the querulous voice. 'I

see you're wearing my diamond flower and my pearls.'

'I thought you'd be pleased.'

'Tricking yourself out in my things when I'm hardly cold in my coffin! Anyway, pearls are unlucky – pearls symbolise tears.'

'Shall I wear your emeralds next time, then?'

'You should take care if you do!'

'Why's that?'

'Jewels set up a strong magnetism which may call you to the Other Side before your time.'

'Oh dear!' Mrs Lilac said, clutching at her necklace.

'Besides, such fripperies mean nothing at all. It is the light from one's soul that's important.'

'I'll try and remember that, Mother,' Mrs Lilac said humbly.

Madame sighed, and her head suddenly fell on to her chest as if she couldn't hold it up any longer.

'Mother!' Mrs Lilac cried. 'Don't go yet, please.'

However, the voice did not come again and Madame seemed to fall into a deep sleep, so after a few moments, George put his notepad to one side, led Mrs Lilac out of Madame's sitting room and accompanied her down the private stairway. She was dabbing at her eyes, quite overwhelmed.

'Is that really true about the magnetism?' she asked George.

George inclined his head. 'I believe it is. I've heard such things before.'

'Really, fancy Mother being so unconcerned about her jewellery as to refer to it as fripperies. They were all she ever loved before – one heard nothing from her but talk of her emeralds and sapphires, and how she had a ruby which was twice as large as one owned by the queen. She lived for her jewels.'

'On the Other Side, you see, there are no possessions and no wealth,' George explained. 'People undergo a sea change.'

'I suppose they must do,' said Mrs Lilac. 'Oh, but it was wonderful to speak to Mother! Will Madame sit for me again?'

'I'm certain she will,' George said, 'although I'm sure you appreciate that these private sessions are very tiring for Madame. She won't be able to do any other work for several days now.'

'I understand, and I bless the dear woman's heart!' Mrs Lilac hesitated and then dropped her voice slightly, although there was no one else around to overhear. 'I am, by the way, willing to pay a considerable amount of money for the privilege of speaking to Mother again.'

George nodded.

'I need assurance that I'm forgiven by her . . . that she's happy on the Other Side.'

'Of course,' George said. 'I'm sure Madame will be pleased to help you in any way she can.'

Chapter Seven

In Which Velvet Shops with Madame, and Is in Attendance at a Dark Circle

'What do you think, Velvet?' Madame Savoya asked, holding the dove-grey gown in front of herself. 'Isn't it quite the nicest day dress you've ever seen?'

'It is, Madame!' Velvet said with enthusiasm. Such beautiful material, she thought: the front tucked and folded with two rows of pearly-grey buttons and the cuffs prinked around with smocking. They were in Marshall and Snelgrove, one of the well-appointed new stores which sold dresses ready-made to take away, and Madame had been trying on outfits all morning. 'It'll look lovely with your white fur collar and muff. And perhaps, in the warmer weather, you could wear some lace around the neck instead.'

'Perfect!' Madame said, smiling at Velvet. 'I knew I could trust your judgement. You have quite the best dress sense of any young woman I know. How

I bless the day you picked up my box of laundry.'

Velvet blushed, pleased. She had been working for Madame for only two weeks but (owing, she thought, to Madame's convivial manner, her generosity and her charm) it felt much longer.

She had, it seemed, come upon the good luck presaged by finding the silver horseshoe in her Christmas pudding. Why, not only had she a charming little room of her own and the most interesting job in the world, but she and Madame got on so well that, though she would never have dared voice such an opinion, they seemed more like friends than employer and maid. As for the bliss of being under the same roof as George, taking meals and working alongside him – well, what girl could ask for more? They had already become good friends and this, she thought, was the very best basis for a relationship. Now *this* was established, Velvet was anxious to reach the next stage and spent a considerable amount of time imagining herself in his arms, sharing a passionate kiss in the quiet hall, perhaps, or whispering endearments as they passed on the stairs. George didn't know about any of this, of course, and Velvet was trying hard to keep it that way – at least until he had made it plain how he felt about her. Until then, she thought that one girl in the house making a giddy fool of herself was quite enough.

Madame nodded to the shop girl to confirm that

she would be buying the dress. 'Please have it delivered with the other garments and I'll try them all on at home, then return any that need alterations.'

The shop girl bobbed a curtsey. 'Yes, Madame.'

Velvet smiled at the girl as she rose. What a lovely job; working amidst taffetas, silks and precious fabrics, helping ladies to look their best. Working for Madame was the perfect job, she decided, but this must come a close second.

'And what else can I see?' Madame swept across the floor of the shop, touching fabrics, standing back to take in the overall look of something, rejecting those orange and yellow shades which did not suit her, and finally lifting from the rail a close-fitting, emerald-green dress with a small draped bustle and matching jacket. 'What do you think of this, Velvet?'

Velvet studied the outfit. 'Oh, it's very smart,' she said, 'but I don't think the colour is quite right for you, Madame. It's a little too strong. The colour would wear you, rather than you wear it.'

'Oh, how wise!' Madame said. 'You really were wasted in that laundry, Velvet.' She deliberated a moment. 'Well, in that case, as I like this outfit very much and am determined to buy it, you shall have it instead.'

Velvet could not speak for a moment, she was so overwhelmed. Then she said, 'I would not dream of . . . I mean, it would take me so long to pay you back, I really could not . . .'

'It'll be a gift, of course,' Madame said. 'If you're to be my assistant, then you must be dressed accordingly. I've already looked through some of my gowns from last season which can be altered to fit you, but I want you to have something new and very fashionable, too.'

Velvet fought down the urge to fling her arms around Madame. Never before had someone been so generous and acted so kindly towards her. Never, indeed, had she had a new gown of her very own, one which hadn't been worn by at least two people before. She gave Madame a little curtsey. 'I am very grateful, Madame,' she said, 'and will endeavour to be the best maid – or assistant,' she corrected (as Madame seemed to be about to object to the first word), 'that anyone could want.'

'I'm perfectly sure that you will,' Madame replied.

After ordering the green gown in Velvet's size, they carried on shopping, going next to Harrods in Knightsbridge, as Madame had a wish to ride on the marvellous moving staircase which had lately been installed. They managed this very well, certainly having no need of the tot of brandy which the Harrods assistant was offering to those ladies rendered faint by the experience.

It had been quite the most splendid day of her life, Velvet decided later. And didn't her new name fit her new life so well? Kitty would never have experienced such things. Kitty would never have had an emerald-green gown bought for her, or ridden on a moving staircase, or become someone's assistant. Kitty would still be living in a squalid room at the beck and call of the cold-hearted and bitter man who had been her father . . . But perhaps if Kitty had been a better daughter, then that father would still be alive, she thought suddenly, and felt horror and guilt creeping over her, almost overwhelming the pleasure of the day.

Another few days passed, during which there was Madame's little dog, Emile, to exercise, Madame's extensive wardrobe to take care of, her hair to arrange, her silk stockings and personal laundry to attend to, her breakfast and lunch to take up, her bedroom to tidy and her appointment book to keep. Velvet might have been daunted by any of these things, but George was always on hand to offer advice and guidance.

George had been with Madame for a good while. 'She rescued me from the gutter,' he told Velvet starkly. 'I would have starved if it hadn't been for her.'

'What were you doing back then?' Velvet asked.

'I had a raree-show,' George replied.

Velvet smiled back sympathetically, knowing that at one time nearly every street entertainer in London had had a raree-show: a set of pictures concealed inside a box mounted on a stick. For a small sum, a ha'penny or two, the customer was allowed to look through a peephole in the box to see a prospect of Venice, a succession of pictures of scantily clad women or a panorama of scenes from foreign lands.

'Did you not make a fair living from it?'

'I did at first,' George replied, 'but then the box was rained upon a few times, the pictures became shabby and torn, and it seemed that every other beggar in town had a peep show. Eventually I got down to my last penny and then I lost that, too.' He shrugged. 'I was at my very lowest and hadn't eaten for several days when Madame came across me. I had literally fainted in the gutter.'

Velvet's heart began beating fast as she imagined the scene: George, stretched out on the cobbles, pale, thin and near death, his dark hair awry, beseechingly looking up at his rescuer with sea-green eyes. Oh, if only she, Velvet, had been the one who had found and saved him!

'I regained consciousness to find her kneeling down beside me saying all manner of solicitous things. I was delirious and thought I was in heaven and she was an angel! She summoned a cab and took me to her house, then called her own doctor and spent two days feeding me nourishing soups. At death's door, I was, and she pulled me back into the land of the living.'

Velvet looked at him. Whether he'd been at

death's door or not, he would still have been most awfully good-looking, she thought. Finding herself blushing again, she hastily looked away.

There was very little that was gloomy and portentous about the atmosphere of Darkling Villa and although Velvet was not privy to the sessions which Madame gave for the most affluent of her clients, it never gave the impression of being a frightening place where spirits walked or wraiths appeared from the Vale of Darkness. Madame did not give herself superior airs, either, but was always interested and friendly towards Velvet, constantly maintaining a kindly concern in her welfare.

Velvet didn't have long to wait to witness Madame's considerable talents at first hand, for there was to be a Dark Circle, a gathering of ten or so eminent people at Darkling Villa, all anxious to contact a relative or friend who had passed over. Mrs Lawson was to bake small savouries which her daughter would serve, there would be glasses of port wine and, after a short recital on the pianoforte by a guest pianist, everyone would be seated for a séance. During this séance, instead of the more casual arrangement with spirits which Madame often utilised, she was intending to go into a proper trance.

On the afternoon of the séance, she spoke to Velvet. 'I shall want you to be in the front room in charge of lighting. I'll ask you to turn the lamps down and up at different times. Before that you will be needed in the hall to greet our clients, hang up their mantles and hats, and show them through to the front room, where George will be waiting with the port wine.' She looked at Velvet carefully as if to judge her reaction and added, 'I'd like you to stay in the room for the séance. I trust you will be quite happy to do this. You don't feel apprehensive?'

Velvet said that she did not.

'Because those experiencing close contact with spirits for the first time can sometimes feel rather overwhelmed.'

Velvet shook her head. There was only one thing she was nervous about. 'I'm quite prepared to hear messages from other people's relatives,' she said. 'It's just that I don't wish for any of my own. From my father in particular.'

'I believe you mentioned that he quite recently passed over.'

Velvet nodded. 'Yes, but not . . . peacefully. I was a little frightened of him in life and I don't want to be in contact with him in death.'

'What was his calling?'

'He was a children's entertainer,' Velvet replied. 'Mr Magic. He presided over parties for the children of wealthy people.' She managed to smile. 'It's strange, that, because actually he didn't like children at all. He certainly hated me.'

Madame put her hand over Velvet's and squeezed it sympathetically. 'You've survived the past and are a better person for it,' she said. 'And you'll be pleased to know that I rarely get a spirit trying to contact someone who doesn't want to hear from them. They have better things to do on the Other Side than send messages to someone who is indifferent.' She patted Velvet's hand. 'And besides, I shall be very much occupied trying to channel messages for the ten very important guests I shall have around the table.' Her eyes brightened. 'Why, I have two Members of Parliament, a very famous novelist and two titled ladies amongst the group.'

'Is there anything else I can do to help?' Velvet asked.

'Well, when they come in, perhaps say a word or two to put them at their ease.'

Velvet quashed a feeling of panic. She? Speak to members of the aristocracy? 'How shall I do that?' she stammered. 'What shall I speak about?'

'Dear girl!' Madame said. 'You must learn to make small talk! Ask if the weather was clement for their journey here, if there is any likelihood of fog, or if they have come far. Move people who are on their own towards each other so that they may converse.'

Velvet nodded and relaxed a little. She thought she could probably do that. She would act like her father had acted when meeting one of his customers in the street: all smiles and compliments, pretending an enormous interest that he really didn't have. The difference would be that she *did* feel interest – and an enormous respect – for what Madame was doing. To give comfort to the bereaved must surely be one of the most satisfying and important jobs in the world. And after all hadn't her mother, who'd been educated to a reasonably high standard before marrying somewhat below her, taught her how to make conversation with her betters; how to be polite without being obsequious and to enquire kindly about someone's status without appearing vulgarly curious?

Early that evening, after a quiet afternoon embroidering a cushion for Madame with the signs of the zodiac and some practice in her best speaking voice of '*Good evening. So pleased you could come tonight. Have you travelled far?*', Velvet took her place in the hallway. There had been some excitement earlier when the telephone had rung for only the third time since Velvet's arrival, making her jump out of her skin, and George had taken a message to say that the caller was sick and unable to attend that evening. George replaced the receiver and then picked it up again and dialled '0' for the operator, so that Velvet could hear someone, far away and crackly, speaking on the line. She found this quite amazing – almost as unbelievable as the thought of speaking to spirits.

Velvet was wearing her new emerald-green costume

and her hair was pulled back from her forehead with a curved comb topped with a green ribbon bow. Really, she thought, pleased with her reflection in the hall mirror, no one would ever guess at her humble beginnings, would ever know that her mother had taken in washing and that only three years ago, when her father had been going through one of his worst gambling phases (she couldn't remember now whether it was horses, greyhounds, cards or dice), she had survived for near a week on stale bread someone had thrown into the street for the dogs.

The door knocker sounded and Velvet took a deep breath and opened it. 'Good evening, madam,' she said to the woman standing there in the purple of half mourning. 'Do come in and get warm. It looks like snow, don't you think?'

The woman, smiling, agreed that it did indeed look like snow and, Velvet having relieved her of her mantle and hung it up, wafted her towards the reception room, where George stood with the port wine. Another knock came and Velvet left the first woman to answer it, a smile ready on her lips.

The smile died away, however, because instead of a hallowed member of society, it was Charlie who stood there. Charlie, wearing his old tweed jacket and a flat cap, with mud on his boots.

He took in what she was wearing, her outfit and her ribbon, her lips shining with the tiniest touch of lipsalve, and his jaw dropped. '*Kitty?*'

It was in Velvet's mind to close the door with a firm '*No, I am not*', but she glared at him for just a little longer than she should have done, giving him enough time to stutter, 'I mean, Velvet, of course. *Velvet.*'

'What do you want?'

'I came to see you.'

'But how did you know I was here?' Velvet sighed. 'Really, Charlie Docker, are you going to follow me wherever I go?'

'Your friend Lizzie told me. She felt sorry for me, I reckon.'

Velvet looked behind her, but George was occupied speaking to the first lady. 'You should have come round the back, for a start,' she whispered. 'Anyway, I'm not allowed followers, especially tonight.'

'Why not?'

'We have an evening of mediumship. A Dark Circle,' Velvet said, unable to stop a slightly self-important note from creeping into her voice. 'Madame is sitting for a number of well-known clients.'

'What, you think she's genuine, do you?' Charlie's voice registered amusement. 'Why, these so-called mediums are two a penny now.'

Velvet turned on him crossly. 'Please go away. I can't talk now.'

'When, then?'

'Well . . .' Velvet hardened her heart. 'Really, Charlie, I don't want to be unkind but I'm trying to make something of myself now and . . .' Her voice drifted away. She could hardly talk about her hopes for a future with George when the man himself was standing so close by, and nor could she talk about such hopes to Charlie.

'Who is this?' came a sudden voice, and Velvet and Charlie both turned to look at George. In his butler's dark livery with gold trimmings he was taller, broader and infinitely smarter than Charlie.

Charlie was about to speak up for himself but Velvet answered quickly, 'No one. A carpet salesman!'

'My good man,' George said. 'This is an area where the quality resides. No one here buys carpets at the door – especially the front door.'

'But I –' Charlie began.

'Away with you!' George pointed down the road and Charlie, after a moment's glance at Velvet, retreated. The door was closed behind him. 'You have to be firm with these fellows,' George said.

Velvet nodded, swallowing hard.

Another knock came. For a moment, Velvet, horrified, thought it was Charlie back again, but it was actually a distinguished-looking man with a walrus moustache whom she presently discovered was the famous novelist and cricketer Mr Arthur Conan Doyle. He brought with him a small clique of ladies, all of whom seemed (to Velvet, at least) to be terribly interested in George, asking him about a cold he'd had the last time they'd seen him and vying to tell him of their experiences in horseless vehicles. Velvet, stung with jealousy, found some compensation in the fact that Sissy Lawson was reduced to being a dumb maidservant, albeit one who was deliberately brushing herself up against George whenever she passed him.

Madame was due to come down from her rooms at eight o'clock, and a little before this George whispered that Madame would like to say a few words to Velvet. She went upstairs, rather apprehensive that Madame might have used her psychic talents to somehow deduce that she'd had a male caller at an inopportune time, but it appeared that she merely wanted to make sure that her clients were at ease.

'I do find that if a sitter is too agitated or upset it disturbs the spirits and they don't appear,' she explained to Velvet.

Velvet assured her that all was in order downstairs and that her clients seemed perfectly happy.

'George tells me you are managing very well with the small talk,' Madame said. 'Of course, I knew you would. Has anyone been speaking of anything in particular? About those dear loved ones they hope to hear from, perhaps?'

Velvet had heard several things spoken of: it was the anniversary of someone's passing, Mr Conan

Doyle had made a trip to Dartmoor, and someone's deceased aunt had spent her last years cultivating a wonderful rose garden.

'How interesting.' Madame nodded her thanks. She was wearing a new gown, its bodice encrusted with pearl and coral beads, and looked, Velvet thought, especially lovely. 'Was there anything else?'

Velvet shook her head. 'It was mostly talk about the weather – oh, and a gentleman's dog had died and he was wondering if dogs passed to the Other Side.' Velvet waited for Madame to respond to this latter statement, for Velvet herself had been wondering the same thing, and if dogs passed over, then what about cats, rabbits, horses, cows and so on? Why, if they all went on, then the Other Side must be fair teeming with livestock.

Madame, however, did not have anything to say on this subject, she merely spoke to say that she hoped it would be a successful séance. 'My clients rely on me so much,' she sighed. 'Some of them merely exist from one séance to the next, waiting for news of their nearest and dearest, waiting to be told how to live.' She shook her head. 'They cling to me like leeches, some of them.'

'But think of the good that you do, Madame!' Velvet cried. 'No job could be more worthwhile or more admirable.'

'Ah. If you say so.' Madame smiled weakly and then seemed to rally a little. 'Would you ask George to seat our guests around the table, please, and then announce me.'

Velvet curtseyed. 'I will, Madame.'

These instructions being carried out, on Madame's command Velvet extinguished the two lamps, and the large front room, apart from the dim glow of a candle burning on the sideboard, was plunged into almost total darkness. Standing at the back of the room ready to turn on the lamps when directed, Velvet could only see those sitting around the large table in faint silhouette. She was, however, enjoying gazing upon the lowered head of George – such shiny and thick black hair! – who was sitting opposite Madame.

Madame explained to the assembled company that George was becoming sensitive to spirits in his own right and it was especially helpful to have him in the circle when there were other gentlemen present. 'Of course, we hope that many spirits will attend us this night,' she continued, 'and that those who arrive at our Dark Circle troubled will hear from their loved ones and go away with lighter hearts.'

'Amen to that!' Mr Conan Doyle intoned, and the others murmured agreement.

Rapt, Velvet held her breath, waiting. She felt strangely moved, almost tearful with the honour of being present at such an important occasion.

'I'd like everyone to put their hands on the table with their fingers spread out,' Madame said.

Everyone did so. 'And would you please make sure that your little fingers are touching those of the people on each side of you. This is to ensure unity between us, and to make certain that there is no cheating of any description.'

Madame's left little finger, Velvet noted, was touching that of a lady with a tall, feathery decoration in her hair, and her right hand touched that of Mr Conan Doyle. George, she could not help but note, was sitting next to a young lady with pink ribbons in her hair who was remarkably pretty.

When Madame finished speaking, the only sounds in the room were a man's wheezy breathing and the distant noise of traffic. Velvet held her breath, tense and expectant, as Madame's eyes closed, her breathing became more laboured and her head fell forward.

After several more moments, she lifted her head and said in a level tone, 'I have a lady here in spirit, a lady who loved roses. She is telling me that her name began with a letter at the start of the alphabet. A, B or C, perhaps. Will anyone claim her?'

There was a little gasp of excitement, then a lady responded by saying that this surely was a dear aunt of hers, for her name had been Barbara and she had grown roses in her walled garden.

There was a murmur around the table at this, which turned to startled exclamations when a pink rose suddenly appeared, flying through the air to land in the middle of the table. Velvet gasped aloud, so surprised was she. Where *had* that come from? It was winter and roses were very much out of season.

Madame laughed. 'Your aunt is being very playful!' she said, and then put her head on one side as if listening. 'Oh, Barbara says roses grow in heaven,' she reported, and the woman who was Barbara's niece gave a sob of joy.

'Barbara' then spoke of different relatives who had passed on before her, saying they were content, then she was succeeded by a gentleman spirit who knew Mr Conan Doyle had visited Dartmoor and who wondered if he intended to set his next story there.

The imposing figure of Arthur Conan Doyle shifted in his seat. 'I certainly do,' he said. Then he added, amidst some laughter, 'Can the spirits tell me if it'll be a success or not?'

Madame next spoke of an old gentleman who said that today was the very anniversary of the day he had passed over, causing a young lady present to give a little scream in surprise. He did not have much to say, but asked if a last photograph of him could be put in a frame and placed on the mantelpiece, and his granddaughter promised to do this.

Madame moved on. More messages were delivered, flowers fell from nowhere (another rose, plus some more seasonal tulips), then a whistle sounded and a bell tinkled, both unseen by human eye. Velvet was awestruck and completely overcome by Madame's abilities. She was surely the best and cleverest medium in London!

At the end of the session, with the guests departed, George took himself off to lock up the house and wind the clocks. Velvet collected up the sweetmeat dishes and took them downstairs where, Mrs Lawson having retired to bed, her daughter was polishing crystal wine glasses. Knowing that Sissy had a long walk home, Velvet offered to finish them for her.

Sissy shook her head. 'That's all right.' She smirked at Velvet. '*Quite* all right,' she repeated, making Velvet look at her curiously. 'Because when I stay late I always get walked home by Mr George, you see.'

Velvet didn't hesitate in her response. 'But of course. Mr George is far too much of a gentleman to allow any girl to walk home on her own.'

Then she went to her room and fumed.

Madame Savoya's First Private Sitting with 'Lady Blue'

'*H*ow very pleasant to see you, my lady,' said Madame Savoya. 'I'm delighted that you decided to come and see us privately.'

Lady Blue smiled. A frail-looking, painfully thin woman of well over seventy, she was still in full mourning, though her husband had been dead over a year and one might have expected to see the black enlivened by touches of purple or cream. 'I had to come to you,' she said, adjusting the spotted veil which covered her face, 'for you're the only medium who has been able to bring my husband close.'

Madame nodded. 'I believe I did form a special bond with him. Your husband was a very devout and gentle soul; his spirit seemed to reach out to me.'

'Indeed it did,' said Lady Blue. 'And I look forward to more sessions with you. It's such a comfort to know that I can speak to my dear husband any time I choose. It lessens the pain of being without him.'

'Of course, my lady,' said Madame Savoya, 'but please be aware that the spirits may not always be willing to present themselves. Also, I have many other clients to attend to, so sometimes it may be impossible for me to drop everything and sit for you.'

Lady Blue raised a lace-gloved hand. 'I am very willing to pay you handsomely for the privilege.'

Madame Savoya gave no outward indication of having heard such a detail. 'We will use the colour of your aura to distinguish you, and your real name will not be used anywhere,' she said kindly. 'We'll refer to your husband and yourself in any notes as Lord and Lady Blue.' Lady Blue nodded and Madame went on, 'As usual, my assistant will take notes for us. I believe your husband rather took to George at our original séance.'

'Yes, I think he did,' agreed Lady Blue. 'My husband and I never had children, you know, but he always took a considerable interest in our friends' sons and daughters.' She shook her head and pressed a lace handkerchief to her eyes. 'Oh, I can't believe that he's no longer with me.'

'But he is,' Madame said gently. 'There's merely a gossamer web between his world and ours.'

'Ah,' trembled Lady Blue.

George saw that Lady Blue was seated comfortably with a cushion at her back, and then sat down beside her with his notepad. Madame pressed one of Lady Blue's hands and, ascertaining that her client was quite at ease, moved back a little, closed her eyes and tilted her face heavenwards.

After three minutes or so, she opened her eyes and said, 'What do you think? I have the noble lord with me already. The dear man knew you were coming here and was only waiting for me to go into trance.'

'Bertie!' Lady Blue exclaimed, a tear forming in her eye. 'Is it really you?'

Madame's voice, when the reply came, was deeper and more solid-sounding than it had been before. 'Yes, it really is me, my dear.'

'Only some people say it's not possible to . . .'

'Ceci! You may put your trust in Madame Savoya and her assistant. Their hearts are pure; they seek only your happiness.'

Lady Blue gave a nervous little smile to George. 'Only my husband called me Ceci!' she whispered. 'Short for Cecilia, you know. Oh, I'm terribly lonely without you, Bertie.'

'Then you must seek me out here as much as you can. Make speaking to me a regular part of your life. Why don't you also pursue some new interests? The youth just here . . .'

Lady Blue's eyes went to George. 'Yes? You mean George?'

'I see well his steadfast and untainted soul. My dear, he's the sort of son we might have been blessed with.'

Lady Blue nodded sadly.

'It would be wonderful if we could enhance his life in some way; help him make his way in the world.'

'Yes, I suppose it would, dear,' came the slightly hesitant answer from Lady Blue.

'If we could assist him, I'd feel that my life hadn't been in vain.'

'Dearest!'

'Perhaps you could think about what might be done for him – some patronage, a step up.'

George looked at Lady Blue in surprise and shook his head, frowning. 'Oh, I couldn't possibly accept such a thing . . .' he said in a very low voice.

'The fellow might be reluctant,' interrupted the strong voice, 'but after all, Ceci, we have no one else to leave our money to, have we?'

'I was wondering about leaving it to the animals,' said Lady Blue. 'There are several donkey charities and –'

'Oh, my dear, surely not! Animals already have many societies and charities to care for them. It would be far, far better to put money directly into the hands of humans, perhaps even donate it to someone who'll use it for the furtherance of spiritualism.'

Lady Blue nodded. 'I see, dear, yes. How wise you are! It does so help me to speak to you and hear your thoughts.'

'Let us talk more of this anon. In the meantime, please promise me that you'll look after yourself. You mustn't go outside when the temperature is too low, nor when it looks like snow. Make sure that you have at least nine hours' sleep a night and that the house-keeper cooks nourishing breakfasts every day.'

Lady Blue nodded intently. 'Anything else?'

'You must trust in Madame Savoya, for she is one of the very few true mediums. Don't lower yourself to visit others.'

Lady Blue looked somewhat embarrassed. She hesi-tated for a moment, then said, 'But it's rumoured that Mrs Otterley can make spirits materialise – that's why I went to her. I so wanted to see you again!'

'And you were disappointed in that, I believe.'

'Yes, dearest, I was,' said Lady Blue meekly. 'Something materialised – some shape – but it didn't appear anything like you.'

'Then there's your answer.' The voice paused. 'You'll see to it that my hunter is exercised daily, won't you? Such a pity if the animal turned to fat.'

'I will, dear.' She wrung her hands. 'But what's it truly like there, Bertie? Are you in heaven?'

No reply came from his lordship, but after a moment Madame's own voice was heard to say, 'Oh, must you go?' A few seconds later she jerked upright, blinked several times and then asked, 'What happened here? Was it a good sitting?'

Lady Blue began to mop up a stream of tears. 'Oh, it was wonderful. Thank you so much, Madame Savoya.'

'And was anything of significance imparted?'

George looked at Madame but didn't speak.

'Much was said that I must think on,' Lady Blue replied, dabbing her eyes. 'I'll come again quite soon, I think.'

'Just as you wish,' said Madame.

Chapter Eight

In Which Velvet Attends an Evening of Mediumship at the House of Miss Florence Cook

More than two months had elapsed since Velvet started work at Darkling Villa, and spring had arrived. Velvet learned more about Madame Savoya's business every day, mastering exactly when to dim and raise the lights at a séance, the right words to comfort someone overcome by events and when to appear with handkerchief and smelling salts if a lady had an attack of the vapours. She was able to speak quite naturally and easily to both lady and gentleman visitors and, by their second visit, could usually recall exactly who it was on the Other Side that they wished to be in contact with. She grew to know some visitors so well, in fact, that they would greet her by name and often slip a sixpence into her hand on leaving. This did not endear her any further to Sissy Lawson, for it had been she who had collected coats and sixpences before Velvet had come to the house.

The routine for the séances, whether taking place around the table or with Madame using the cabinet, was always the same: Velvet would answer the front door, greet the visitors and, as she helped them off with their coats and hats, exchange light conversation about the weather or enquire if they'd been to Madame's before, then show them into the reception room, where George was waiting with a drink. Once everyone had arrived, Velvet would join George and mingle with the clients, chatting in order to ease the nerves of anyone who was anxious. After more drinks were served, first George, then Velvet, would visit Madame upstairs to assure her that everything was well and impart any little pieces of overheard conversation which might be of interest. Madame would want to know if any clients had mentioned that it was their birthday, for instance, or were there to mark the anniversary of someone's passing.

The strange thing, Velvet began to notice, was that nearly every tiny fragment of information she gleaned and then passed to Madame came to be mentioned during the following séance. Sometimes it led to an important three-way meeting between Madame, the audience member and the person on the Other Side; at other times a date or name might just be mentioned in passing. Mentioned it always was, however, making Velvet wonder if this could be more than just a coincidence.

She decided to ask George about it and waited until they were in the kitchen, alone, one morning. She was carefully dipping a white linen collar of Madame's into starch, whilst he was brushing his top hat.

George listened to her carefully and then put the brush down, looking shocked. 'You surely don't suspect Madame of anything underhand?'

'Of course not!' Velvet assured him hastily. 'It just seems strange that all the little things the clients tell us are brought up later at the séances.' She bit her lip, anxious that George should not be annoyed with her. 'I would never think Madame was . . . was anything like underhand. She's surely the cleverest and most wonderful person I've ever met.'

George's face cleared. 'We are both agreed, then, that Madame is a near perfect employer.'

'A near perfect *person*!'

He smiled. 'But, yes, in some ways you are quite right. Madame does use us as lookouts, and the reason for this is that the spirits – especially if they're coming back to earth for the first time – are often rather shy about making an appearance. Some don't even know how to span the bridge between our world and theirs, and if Madame can give them a little hint that someone they love is waiting for them, if they hear a familiar date or name, then they're more willing to come forward. They just need a helping hand.'

'I understand,' Velvet said eagerly. 'And I suppose it works both ways.'

'Indeed! Those left here on earth may be too shy to claim a deceased loved one in a crowded room in case they're wrong, but if a special name or date is mentioned, then it opens things up and gives them the confidence to speak.'

'I see.' Velvet smiled at him tremulously. 'You didn't mind me mentioning it, did you?'

'Of course not,' George said. He patted her shoulder lightly. 'You and I are two of a kind, eh?' Velvet hoped for a moment that he meant there was something – a romantic connection – between them, but he went on, 'We're both orphans brought in out of the storm by Madame. Me, the owner of a raree-show, and you, plucked out of a steam laundry. What a pair!' He hesitated, then asked, 'You did say you were all alone in the world?'

'I did. My mother had two sisters, but she lost touch with them long ago because my father didn't like her seeing them. He knew they disapproved of him.' Velvet sighed. 'Quite rightly, as it happened.'

George began brushing his top hat again, smoothing down the nap so that it all swirled in the same direction. 'Madame has great plans for you, you know,' he said. 'She told me that, with the right training, you might become sensitive.'

'Sensitive?' Velvet looked at him, amazed. 'She thinks I could communicate with spirits?'

'Indeed. I'm undergoing some training, too. I thought it was highly unlikely that I could do it at first, but now I know that you just have to open your mind and let the light in.'

Let the light in, Velvet repeated to herself, and tried to look as if she understood what this interesting phrase meant. She realised that there were mysteries in the world about which she, a mere domestic servant, could know absolutely nothing, but as for being psychic herself – well, she seriously doubted that she had any abilities at all. 'I really don't think I could,' she said to George.

'Are you implying that you understand these things better than Madame?' he asked teasingly.

'Of course not!'

He laughed, then finished smoothing the hat and placed it on his head at a jaunty angle.

'Are you going somewhere special?' Velvet asked.

'Ascot – the races!'

'I didn't know you were a racing man,' Velvet said and, because of what she'd been through with her father, a little warning flag was raised in her mind.

'I'm not, but Madame thinks it a good way of gaining new clients.'

Velvet frowned, very surprised. 'What do you mean?'

'I'll be candid with you,' George said. 'There's terrific rivalry between mediums, and only a limited number of rich clients to go around. When one is in the club room at Ascot . . .' he waved his top hat in the air and made an elaborate bow '. . . one can mention one's contacts and gain valuable new clients.'

'I see,' said Velvet. It all seemed a bit mercenary, but if Madame was going to help people regain contact with their lost loved ones, then they may just as well be rich as poor, she supposed. She could appreciate that living to Madame's elegant standards couldn't be cheap. Why, she was even talking of replacing her horse and carriage with a motor car!

It was a week later that Madame sent for Velvet, saying there was something she especially wanted her to do.

'On Saturday, I'd like you to attend an evening of mediumship at Florence Cook's,' she said. 'I think you'll find it of interest.' She looked down at the card she was holding and read out: *Miss Florence Cook promises the manifestation of certain diverse spirits, including her own personal spirit guide.*' There was a slightly disdainful quality to Madame's tone as she said these last few words, for although some mediums had spirit guides – Indian chiefs or Egyptian queens who advised and nurtured them – Madame scorned such entities, saying that she was the only guide that the spirits needed and that they preferred to make contact through her directly.

'An evening of mediumship,' Velvet repeated. 'What would I have to do?'

'Merely observe,' Madame said. 'Miss Cook is an extremely popular medium – rather too popular, perhaps. I understand her Dark Circles sometimes become somewhat unruly.'

'And is there anything in particular I should observe?' Velvet asked, secretly rather thrilled at the thought of an unruly séance.

'Yes, there is,' Madame said. 'Miss Cook made headline news in the papers last month by managing to manifest a spirit in its last earthly shape.'

Velvet gasped. 'Like a ghost? George told me something of this!'

'Yes, and I'd dearly love to know how this happens and how complete and clear are these bodily forms. Are they made of smoke or light, or of something more substantial? Do they leave the medium's side and glide around the room, or do they stay within her cabinet?'

'You don't wish to go and see this for yourself?'

Madame shook her head. 'I would like to, very much, but I'm afraid Miss Cook knows me by sight, and she also knows George, come to that. She'd refuse to sit if we were there. That's why I want you to go and be my eyes and ears.'

Velvet agreed, of course, and, as the venue where Miss Cook was to appear was in west London, asked if she might have a few hours off beforehand to visit Lizzie – Velvet knew that the girls at Ruffold's finished a little earlier on Saturdays.

Madame, Velvet thought later, had seemed slightly taken aback when she'd explained this.

'A friend from your past life?' she said. 'From the laundry?'

'Lizzie and I were very good friends,' Velvet said. 'I spent Christmas Day with her family and I miss her.' She really did, she realised. The two or three short letters which had passed between them were no substitute for having a real chum close by. The coarse Miss Lawson was too much of a rival to ever be her friend and George, she hoped, was something else.

'But we're your family now, are we not?'

'Indeed you are!' Velvet said. 'And I could never thank you enough for all your kindnesses. It's just that Lizzie was a particular friend of mine and I really miss talking to her.'

Madame, after saying that she hoped Velvet knew she could call upon herself or George any time she wished, agreed that she could certainly have the afternoon off.

Velvet, her hair up in curls, was wearing a new and flattering outfit (a rose-pink jacket with a matching striped skirt, worn by Madame two seasons ago) in order to look the part for her evening appointment, so her appearance was very different from the last time she'd been to Lizzie's house. When her friend answered the door, therefore, she just stared at Velvet, puzzled.

'Yes, miss? Can I help you?'

Velvet giggled. 'Lizzie, it's me!' She loosened the ribboned cap she was wearing and shook her hair free so that Lizzie could see her the better.

Lizzie stood there, hardly knowing, as she told Velvet later, whether she should kiss her or curtsey, but Velvet broke the spell by flinging her arms around her and giving her a hug. Seeing Lizzie, she realised how very much she'd missed all their chats and their ordinary everyday togetherness. Madame was wonderful, of course. Madame was the best, most generous employer in the world, but that was what she was – her employer. Velvet knew she could never be a proper friend.

'But what have you done to yourself?' Lizzie exclaimed, and she showed Velvet into the front parlour. (The parlour, Velvet noted, not the kitchen.) 'You look like a proper lady.' She giggled. 'You look like one of those customers who come into Ruffold's to complain that their sheets have been folded into the wrong creases.'

Velvet laughed. 'It's just trappings,' she said, very pleased nonetheless that there was such a big change in her. 'Just clothes and hair.'

But it wasn't just that. Velvet now slept in an airy room on a comfortable mattress with clean sheets, ate fresh food instead of two-day-old scraps and didn't work herself to the point of exhaustion in the stifling conditions of the laundry day after day. She shared the luxuries of Madame's house, too: the hot water, the expensive soaps and creams, the soft towels, flowers and elegant surroundings, and all these things combined to make a difference to her. Plus, she felt herself to be in love, and this above all else made her happy with her life.

Lizzie stood, still gazing at Velvet in wonder, then picked up a fold of her skirt and felt it. 'Glazed cotton?' she asked.

Velvet nodded. 'And the very devil to press!'

Lizzie laughed, then began to minutely examine Velvet's outfit: her dainty shoes and her crochet-trimmed kid gloves, the small drawstring velvet bag, the ruffles on the sleeves of her jacket, the ribbons on her cap. 'You look very lovely,' she said finally.

'I don't look like this every day,' Velvet felt obliged to say. 'It's because I'm going out later for Madame.'

'Where to?'

'I'm visiting another famous medium, Miss Florence Cook, to see how she works.'

'How she works?' Lizzie repeated. 'Does she employ tricks, then?'

'No, of course not!'

'Only my pa says that there was someone, a

115

medium, in the paper the other day, who was clapped in jail for extorting a great amount of money out of someone who'd been bereaved. We thought it was your lady at first.'

Velvet shook her head indignantly. 'It certainly wasn't Madame. She's very highly respected. Why, titled ladies attend her sessions.'

Lizzie shrugged. 'Titled ladies went to this medium, too, and she was having them on just the same.' Perhaps realising that her comments were a little untimely, Lizzie added, 'Still, I'm glad your Madame is on the level. Is it all right, working for her? Is it exciting?'

'Oh yes!' Velvet said. 'It's not like work. She's so generous and everything's so interesting. We have all sorts of famous people come to the house.'

Lizzie gave an exaggerated shiver. 'What, wanting to talk to dead relatives?'

'Wanting to talk to those on the Other Side,' Velvet corrected.

'Yes. There.'

'But it's all treated as quite normal and ordinary. Really! And I work alongside George, of course.'

'Oooh! That handsome fellow who was on stage with her?'

Velvet nodded. 'He's part of the household. Not that we see a great deal of each other, because he's out a lot driving Madame in her carriage or down at the mews grooming the horses or somesuch. But we mostly have our meals together, although Mrs Lawson is around then and soon puts paid to any larking. Her daughter works as a daily maid and is a terrible forward baggage! Talk about having no shame!'

'But George, now. Do you think that he has romantic intentions towards you?'

'I don't know,' Velvet said, blushing. 'Maybe. I think he likes me.'

'And if something happened between you, what d'you think your Madame might have to say about it?'

'If George and I . . . ?' Velvet considered the matter. 'I think she'd be very happy for us.'

'So you really and truly are not walking out with Charlie now?'

'Charlie?' Velvet said. 'Goodness, no! I've *never* walked out with Charlie.'

'He's been round here, you know. He asked for your address, but I didn't have it – only Madame's name.'

Velvet nodded. 'He found me.'

'He came back here to tell me he'd called on you,' Lizzie said with a giggle. 'Said you'd answered the door and pretended he was a carpet salesman.'

'I had to say that! He arrived in the middle of a special evening at Madame's.'

'Yes, and the next time he came here he –'

'He's been here three times?' Velvet interrupted in surprise.

'Four, I think.'

'Oh!'

'It's just that this house happens to be on Charlie's beat – he's moved police stations now. And he's got a proper uniform! Made to measure, he looks ever so smart in it. And . . . well, you did just say that there's nothing between you two, didn't you?'

Velvet paused a moment, then nodded. 'That's right.'

'So you wouldn't mind if . . . if he and I walked out together?'

'Not at all,' said Velvet after another little pause. It would have been churlish, surely, to say otherwise.

'Not that he's asked me yet,' said Lizzie. 'But I want to be ready for when he does.'

Miss Florence Cook's house was almost as grand as Madame's and its location, on the river at Barnes, even more salubrious, so that despite Velvet's elegant appearance she was very nervous as she went up the steps and knocked on the front door.

It was opened by a girl about her own age who greeted her politely and, after ascertaining that she did not wish to take off her jacket, led her towards an older woman, who introduced herself as Miss Cook's mother. This older lady spoke briefly to

Velvet, asking if she'd been before, making sure she was quite at ease and – just as Velvet did at Madame's – asking who she might be hoping to hear from on the Other Side.

Velvet told Mrs Cook that she didn't really have anyone close on the Other Side but was attending out of interest, seeing as it was quite the fashion, and Mrs Cook replied that her daughter was one of the leading mediums in London and so, if ever Velvet did want to contact someone, then this was absolutely the best place to come.

Champagne was served and following this, everyone there – about thirty persons in all – was seated in rows before the curtained alcove at the end of the room. The gaslights were turned off and then Florence Cook entered the room (to applause, Velvet was surprised to note) and went behind the curtain. In another moment this was pulled open and Miss Cook could be seen through a thin muslin screen, awake and smiling.

Velvet studied her appearance as well as she could, for black blinds hung at the windows and, as at Madame's, the only illumination was from a single candle. Miss Cook seemed to be in her late twenties and was most attractive, wearing a deep-purple velvet gown. She had long fair hair which was braided with flowers, wore a quantity of silver bangles on her arms and had bare feet.

She began to speak to the audience and as she did

so, a great number of spirits seemed to arrive willy-nilly and be greeted by her. Some brought strange, garbled messages for people in the audience whilst others arrived and then went away again, disappointed, when no one said they owned them. Sometimes, as indeed happened at Madame's, messages were given to certain people in the audience who seemed to have no knowledge of the person on the Other Side, but Miss Cook assured them that when they got home and pondered on these messages, their meaning would become clear. Miss Cook's spirit guide (a very learned Oriental man, apparently) was also there and, after being introduced to the audience, conveyed certain wise words through Miss Cook along the lines of 'Peace be with you' and 'Do unto others what you would have done to yourself', which Velvet did not find terribly enlightening.

There was an interval when Miss Cook left the room, the lights came up and another glass of champagne was served, then everyone took their seats again and Mrs Cook stood up to announce that during the second half of the evening, her daughter would attempt to materialise someone. This might take some time, she said, so she begged the patience of the audience. They were to remember that very few mediums could actually do such a thing and it was tantamount to witnessing a miracle if it did happen. If any ladies in the audience were of a particularly nervous disposition, then they were advised to leave the séance now, for what they were about to see might alarm them.

No one left, however, and Miss Cook reappeared and went behind the curtain. In the next room, someone began to play a piano; a mournful air which sent shivers up and down Velvet's spine. She began to grow a little apprehensive at the thought of what she might see. How real would it be? Was it a spirit, or should it rather be called a ghost or apparition?

Moments passed and the heavy curtain was pulled back to reveal Miss Cook in an armchair, her head slumped on to her chest. The whole room fell completely quiet and Velvet even forgot to breathe. All eyes were on the cabinet, where, at the bottom, a swirl of smoke had appeared.

Velvet watched it grow dense and then became aware that something was forming beneath the smoke; something with a more tangible quality, white, like thin-bunched muslin or chiffon. This, she thought, must be the ectoplasm . . . She strained forward in her seat but was unable to see more, for the one candle in the room was behind her and threw barely any light on to what was happening in the cabinet.

All around, people began gasping and calling out as the ectoplasm grew and formed itself into the rough shape of a person standing next to the medium's chair. A woman started screaming and there was a heavy thump as if someone at the back had fainted and fallen off their chair. Several other members of the audience rose to their feet and Mrs Cook had to stand up and appeal for calm.

'The manifestation comes from my daughter's body,' she warned, 'and it would cause her considerable pain – maybe even loss of life – if anyone were to lay hands upon the spirit form. Please remain in your seats!'

The spirit form had stopped developing when Miss Cook herself spoke for the first time since the interval. 'I have a woman here who has partially materialised,' she said. 'She may not be fully visible to you, but I can see her clearly. She passed over when she was about seventy years of age. She is a stout woman with her hair in a bun and she wears mourning clothes . . .'

'Is it our dead queen?' a woman at the back called, and was immediately shushed. 'Well, it could be,' she was heard to retort indignantly.

Miss Cook resumed, 'She has been dead six years or more. She ruled her household with a rod of iron and her family lived in awe of her. Does anyone claim her?'

Velvet knew, of course, that it could not be her mother, whom she had never known to be anything but sad and overworked.

'I believe the lady belongs to my family,' a man called out.

'Her name is . . .' Miss Cook paused, then continued, 'her name is the name of a flower.'

'No. My mother's name was Eleanor,' the same man said, disappointed.

'But my mother's name was Violet,' a lady's voice came from the front row. 'It sounds like her – she wasn't a shrinking violet, that's for sure!'

Miss Cook smiled. 'She's laughing about what you've just said. She's quite a different character from the way she was on earth. Is there anything you wish to ask her?'

Given such an opportunity, the woman was suddenly struck dumb.

'Should I perhaps ask her if she is with your father?' Miss Cook suggested gently.

Through the medium of Miss Cook came the answer, 'We have met, but we are not as we were, for we are in spirit.'

'Ah,' the woman said, and sat down again.

'You must make peace with the person you've been avoiding, for they mean you no harm,' said either Miss Cook or the spirit of Violet (Velvet wasn't sure who it was). 'Remember what I told you. Remember my last words to you before I came to the Other Side.'

There was more in this vein and Velvet watched and listened as closely as she could, trying to remember everything so she could report back to Madame. She tried to make sense of the spirit form, hoping to see if it was attached to Miss Cook in some way. It was too smoky in the cabinet to tell, however. Did the ectoplasm emanate from under Miss Cook's bare feet? Was that a human shape which could be seen, or just shadows? What was the strange, filmy-like material? Could it all really be true?

Madame Savoya's First Private Sitting with 'Mr Grey'

'Good morning, Mr Grey. Do be seated,' said Madame Savoya. As the client looked at her, surprised and about to speak, she added, 'I will be referring to you as Mr Grey in the interests of both your confidentiality and mine, and your real name will not be recorded in any notes.'

'Right-o!' said Mr Grey cheerily.

'Thank you for using my private entrance to this house, and please continue to do so.'

'Certainly, certainly.' Mr Grey nodded. True to his name, he had thick grey hair and a full, fluffy grey beard which went some way to softening his craggy features. 'And – if you don't mind me asking – why am I Mr Grey, and not Mr Brown or Mr Black?'

'A very good question,' Madame said. 'I name special clients of mine, those who come for private sessions, by the colour of their auras.'

'Auras, spiritualism, mediums – all these words are

new to me,' said Mr Grey, 'although I know from the newspapers that all the top people are doing it. You can see my aura, eh? And what might that be when it's at home?'

'An aura is the luminous glow which surrounds you and all living things, but which can only be seen by those of a spiritual nature, such as myself.'

'Well, I'm blowed!'

Madame looked at Mr Grey consideringly. 'But I'm afraid **your** aura does not glow with colour and light, as it should, but is a rather sad grey. Hence your name.'

Mr Grey heaved a sigh. 'That doesn't surprise me. Doesn't surprise me at all.'

'But, my dear sir, we hope to be able to change that. Perhaps, in time, we will be able to get in touch with your beloved wife. When you have made your peace with her, your aura will glow with colour once more.'

'Right-o!'

'I believe you said that it was she whom you had wronged?'

'It was indeed. I've been a wicked man in the past, you see. Most wicked. It would ease my mind greatly to know that my wife has forgiven me.'

'We have all done things we are ashamed of,' Madame reminded him gently.

'But some have done more than others,' Mr Grey responded.

George tapped on the door, came into the room and,

after bowing and shaking hands with Mr Grey, sat down on a footstool ready to take notes.

'I know you've already met George. It was at Ascot, I believe,' said Madame.

'Indeed. We are both racing men. Racing, the sport of kings!' Mr Grey said expansively. He then frowned and looked at George. 'But, if you'll pardon me for asking, young man, why doesn't someone like you, with such a job, win every time he goes racing? You surely know which horse is going to come in first?'

'I'm afraid spiritualism doesn't quite work like that,' Madame said. 'A medium is a mere vehicle through which important messages from those on the Other Side are conveyed. Who might or might not be going to win the two-fifteen on a certain day is of no concern to the spirits.'

'Besides, a good medium does not operate for profit,' George put in. 'It would be completely against everything Madame believes in.'

However, Mr Grey had moved on to more important things. 'They call it the sport of kings,' he said, 'but when I consider how I neglected my dear wife and child, and kept them in penury whilst I gambled everything I owned, it seems to me now that it is the sport of fools! Oh, I deserve to suffer for my past sins –'

'My dear sir,' Madame interrupted, 'you must look forward. And at least your interest in racing led to your marvellous win – and to your meeting George.'

Mr Grey shook his head reflectively. 'A six-horse

accumulator. So much money that it changed my life. Well, I say it changed my life, but it merely changed the way I live. There's a difference, you know.' He paused for Madame and George to nod. 'Money can't change the past, can it? Money can't erase a lifetime of cruelty. Money, in all its –'

'Mr Grey, I'm going to try and help you,' Madame said swiftly. 'To do so, I'll have to concentrate on you, my especial client, and on you alone. I intend to put all my endeavours and strength into contacting your late wife.'

Mr Grey nodded eagerly. 'I want to tell her how sorry I am, how desperately sorry for all the wicked, wicked things I did and . . .' He stopped here, convulsed by sobs.

'Mr Grey, I beg you to pull yourself together,' George said, handing him a handkerchief. 'Madame will do her very best to contact your wife, even if it means neglecting her other clients. If you wish, she will concentrate all her resources on you and your problems.'

'Yes, that's what I want,' came the muffled reply.

'It may prove extremely difficult and it may take some time because, if you're being truthful in your assessment of your past life and did indeed treat your wife badly, she may not want to return and speak to you. Madame will therefore need to use every ounce of her strength and ability to entice her back.'

'Yes. Yes!' Mr Grey said. 'I'll pay whatever it takes.' He suddenly reached forward and seized Madame's hand in his own. 'I have been a cruel man – and not only to my wife. I had a beautiful daughter who should have been looking after me in my old age, but I treated her so badly that she deserted me.'

Madame extricated her hand, massaging it gently where Mr Grey's nails had dug into her palm. 'I dare say you had a hard life, though, and found a wife and child too much to cope with.'

Mr Grey looked up at her, seemed about to agree with her sympathetic judgement, but then changed his mind. 'Oh no, I was proper wicked, I was. My wife died too young; I drained all the life out of her. And my little girl, why, she found herself a dog once, made a pet of some little puppy she found wandering the streets . . .' He broke down here, and George began to speak but was interrupted with, 'Oh, but I was a wicked beast! I told her the dog had fleas and couldn't come into the house. Do you know what happened then?'

Madame and George shook their heads.

'It froze to death on the coldest night of the year. Found it dead on the doorstep, I did, stretched out next to the boot-scraper.'

Madame shook her head, removed herself from the reach of Mr Grey and closed her eyes. 'I am now going into trance, Mr Grey.'

'If you would be so kind as to remain silent until Madame speaks again,' said George.

'And when she does speak again, will my wife be there with her?'

'I very much doubt it will happen that quickly,' said George. 'It may take several visits to the Other Side before your wife can be located. However, rest assured that Madame will achieve this in the end.'

'I know I've got to be ready to take the stick when she does find her, but I'm prepared for that,' said Mr Grey. 'I was Mr Magic, the children's entertainer, you know. You don't find many of us around, do you?'

George put his finger to his lips to silence Mr Grey, but not before he and Madame had exchanged a secret look of utter astonishment.

An hour later, Mr Grey's dead wife still had not been found and Madame confirmed that several more private sessions would be needed in the coming weeks in order to locate her. Mr Grey said that seeing as he had been most especially wicked in his past life, he quite understood and was prepared to pay whatever the price.

Chapter Nine

In Which Madame Materialises
Sir Percy Malincourt

'So, I had a raree-show, but what about *your* early days?' George asked one morning when he and Velvet were in the kitchen, polishing glasses for that evening's séance.

'You know about me,' Velvet said. 'I worked in a steam laundry. Such hard work my back felt like it would break in two. It was so hot you could scarce draw breath and my hands were always red and sore.' She stretched her arms in front of her and wriggled her fingers. 'My hands are still as rough as sandpaper.'

'Nonsense,' George said, catching hold of one and examining it carefully. 'Your hands are lovely. A *lady*'s hands. They look as if you've been doing nothing but embroidering flowers on pocket hand-kerchiefs all day.'

Velvet laughed, but George was looking at her so intently that she felt her cheeks warming. He turned her hand over so that the palm was uppermost and he traced his finger across the centre of it in a circular motion. Velvet held her breath, feeling her stomach fluttering. That such a tiny movement could have such an effect!

George gently tugged at her hand, moving his fingers up her arm so that she came towards him, closer and closer. Closer still, so that she felt his breath on her cheeks and then – at last – his lips were on hers and they were kissing and Velvet felt her head spinning with giddy wonder.

Oh, but it lasted only a moment before there was a commotion at the kitchen door and Mrs Lawson came in muttering and complaining, struggling to carry a large cardboard box containing white lilies and pink roses. 'I was at the back, calling out!' she said as Velvet and George sprang apart. 'Didn't anyone hear me?'

'Mrs Lawson! I do apologise,' said George. 'Velvet and I were intent on talking about our lives before we came here.'

'It looked like it,' Mrs Lawson said with a sniff.

'We honestly didn't hear you,' George said, getting up. 'Let me take that heavy box from you, then you sit yourself down and I'll put the kettle on the fire.'

'Hmm' was all Mrs Lawson said, but she allowed herself to be propelled towards the easy chair which stood by the window.

Velvet began to breathe again. Oh, thank goodness they had kissed at last! There had been so many
other times when George had looked at her with a
spark in his green eyes as if he were thinking certain
things, certain naughty things, and intended to carry
them out, and she'd thought *now*, now they would
kiss and fall in love properly and her fate would be
decided. Something had always interrupted the
moment, though: an excited shout from the street
that a motor car was coming past, the strident ring
of the telephone ('Quick! Answer it and save the
electricity!'), or Madame's footsteps on the stairs.
Now it had actually happened, and Velvet was
certain that he must like and admire her.

That day, however, there was to be no more time
for daydreaming, for Madame was holding a special
event for some of her wealthiest clients and was
hoping to materialise at least one spirit during the
second half of the evening.

Over the last weeks, the materialisation of spirits
had become quite the thing. It seemed that the
longer the public's interest in spiritualism continued,
the more complex the subject became. The whole
business had started off some years ago in quite a
simple way, George had told Velvet, with tapping on
tables, then chairs and tables had started moving,
then spirits had begun writing and drawing. After
this had come the appearance and movement of
objects, the playing of instruments that might or

might not be visible, and direct messages from spirits. Now nearly every medium of note was either offering materialisation to her clients or was saying they would be able to do so quite soon.

George explained to Velvet that Madame had been honing her talents and sensitivity, not wanting to hurry things until she was sure she could cope with spirits in actual bodily form. He was certain, however, that anything Miss Cook and 'those other poor imitators', as he called them, could do, Madame would be able to do also, for he was of the opinion that the spirits acclaimed and respected her above all other mediums. Madame had asked him to assist in this new enterprise and they had spent several evenings shut away, quietly working together, trying to decide which method of operating would be the most conducive to the spirits. Velvet, too, had become involved, and had been summoned to these talks to impart every last detail she could remember about the evening at Miss Cook's, whilst George and Madame listened avidly and questioned her on each point.

Greeting the guests that special evening, Velvet could pick out immediately those who were newly bereaved: the young lady, her face white and drawn, clutching a child's lacy shawl around her; the tall man with blotchy, tearful eyes; the woman in early middle age who was dressed entirely in black and remained behind her veil for the whole evening. These three seemed somewhat removed from the rest of the gathering who were, perhaps, there for the purposes of entertainment. This part of the audience consisted of two opera singers, an actor, a poet, a sprinkling of titled ladies and Lillie Langtry, the beautiful actress who had not only been the new king's long-term mistress, but (according to the newspapers) mistress to half the men in London. She was immensely rich, with a theatre and a stable of racehorses to her name.

'Is she very beautiful at close viewing?' Madame asked Velvet when she went to give her usual report on the newly arrived guests.

'She is.' Velvet nodded. 'She has the most remarkable skin – she glows, almost.'

Madame, who had been reclining on her chaise longue, suddenly opened her eyes. 'But she's ageing now, of course. Ah! The portraits she inspired in her youth. Everyone who saw her fell in love with her, and every great artist in London wanted to paint her. Did she speak to you?'

'Only to wish me good evening,' Velvet said. 'She was deep in conversation with a gentleman the whole time. She even waved away her glass of wine.'

'*Champagne*,' Madame reminded her with a smile. (Since Velvet's visit to Miss Cook, Madame had decided that they, too, should serve this more sophisticated and costly drink.) 'And everyone is quite composed?'

Velvet nodded again. 'I think so,' she said, 'although it's difficult to tell, of course, because last week Miss Formgate seemed completely at her ease . . .'

'And then went quite wild when I managed to contact her fiancé.'

'Indeed!' exclaimed Velvet, for it had turned out – unbeknown to anyone except Miss Formgate herself – that her fiancé, who had unfortunately died in a hotel fire, had been staying at the hotel with another woman. When the errant fiancé had come through from the Other Side, Miss Formgate had hurled herself towards Madame, demanding that she ask him what he'd been doing there with the woman, and seeming more upset about his infidelity than his death.

It had taken all George's strength to hold Miss Formgate back from Madame, for it looked likely that, as she could not reach her fiancé, she would throttle Madame instead. (Velvet wondered afterwards at the wisdom of his turning up at all. Wouldn't he have known that Miss Formgate was going to be fearfully angry with him? Surely it would have been better for him to have adopted a peaceful life on the Other Side and remained there?)

'I did have a few words with the poor lady whose

little girl died,' Velvet resumed. 'She's wearing her child's christening shawl.'

'That would be Mrs Fortesque, I believe?'

'Yes, she seems very low,' Velvet said. 'She told me that she'd visited another medium, a Mrs Russell.'

'That charlatan!' exclaimed Madame.

'Mrs Russell had promised to materialise the baby so that Mrs Fortesque could actually hold her. This never happened, even though Mrs Fortesque had paid her a great deal of money beforehand.'

'Scandalous!' Madame said. There was a pause. 'Did she tell you the name of the little girl?'

'Claire, I believe.'

'And her age?'

'She didn't say, but she did remark that the child had just learned to sit up unaided.'

'She was six months or so, then.' Madame sighed. 'How tragic. I'll certainly help the poor woman if I can.' There was another pause. 'Apart from Miss Langtry, is there anyone else of especial interest here tonight?'

Velvet shook her head. 'But there are two young gentlemen who've placed themselves in the back row and are being rather boisterous.'

'Really? In what way?'

'I believe they must have been imbibing liquor before they arrived. They certainly drank their champagne very quickly and asked for more.'

'Is George aware of them?'

'Oh certainly,' Velvet said. 'George has been most courteous and efficient in his handling of them. He requested that they remember they are in the house of a great lady and in the presence of distinguished people, so they must act accordingly.'

'Dear George!' exclaimed Madame. 'What it is to have a man about the house. And thank you, too, for your help, as ever.'

The first part of that evening's session began with a short recital of piano music, then Madame entered on George's arm and, without using the cabinet, she spoke to the seated audience of thirty in a conversational way, bringing in this and that spirit from the Other Side, delivering messages and making certain observations.

Several times the two young gentlemen made comments – 'Madame, do you have to take spirits to see spirits?' and 'It's getting mighty crowded with ghosts in this room!' and other remarks they obviously thought were witticisms – until George reminded them that Madame was a highly respected medium and they were lucky to be able to attend one of her evenings at all.

'Lucky?' one of them called back. ''Twas not luck which got me here, but a certain amount of guineas!' There were a few titters from others in response.

Madame kept herself aloof from these interruptions and delivered her messages without acknowledging them. She then went off to rest for fifteen minutes before the main part of the evening, which began with her going into the cabinet and Velvet turning down the lamps as usual.

'We ask for complete silence at this time,' George said, with one eye on the young men, 'for Madame is about to attempt something she has never attempted before.'

'Will we get our money back if no spirit appears?' one of the young men replied, and was promptly hushed by those sitting on each side of him.

'As always, we are never sure what spirits will attend us or what might happen, but we ask you to stay in your seats at all times, please,' George said. 'If Madame is interrupted whilst she is in trance, the consequences could be serious.'

A hush duly fell on the audience.

'If materialisation of a spirit does occur, remember that the shape will emanate from ectoplasm produced from Madame's body as the spirit appears and takes form. Please be patient whilst this happens. Anyone who attempts to light a match or otherwise illuminate the room will be evicted from the house immediately.'

The ensuing silence was profound. The curtain across the cabinet was drawn open and, by the light of the one candle in the room, Madame could be seen sitting in her chair. She was dressed in a midnight-blue silk gown and looked very elegant and very vulnerable, so much so that Velvet's heart went out to her; she felt that if either of the rowdy young men started anything she would turn on them herself. But she reminded herself that that was what George was there for, of course. Strong, dependable, gorgeous George. George who had kissed her. She couldn't wait to get to bed that night and go over and over that kiss in her mind . . .

Madame began by saying, 'I have a lady here whose name begins with an "E". She passed on towards the end of last year and left behind a grieving family.'

A woman in the audience called, 'It may be my mother. Her name was Emily.'

'Yes, she says her name was Emily!' Madame announced, and there was a stir of excitement in the audience.

Emily had a multitude of messages for her daughter, some of which were understood by her and some not. Madame explained that Emily had not been on the Other Side for long enough to come back in visible spirit form, but if the daughter was to attend Madame's séances on a regular basis then she might eventually find her way through.

'What are we going to see tonight, then?' someone in the audience called. 'We were assured there would be a materialisation.'

'That's what we've paid for!' came another voice.

'I'm afraid I'll have to ask you to leave if you cannot respect the medium,' George said sternly.

Everyone's eyes were still on Madame. There was another long silence, then she said, 'I am having difficulty this evening. Someone towards the back of the room is trying to exercise control, and I'd be glad if they would refrain from doing so.'

Another long silence, and some of the audience began to cough or fidget.

Suddenly, though, a deep voice said, 'I am here. I am come!'

In an instant, there was a hush.

'Who are you?' Madame said. 'Do you come in truth and love?'

'I do,' came the answer. 'My name is Percy. In my time on earth I was Sir Percy Malincourt.'

Madame gestured towards George, who came forward and asked the audience in a stage whisper, 'Does anyone claim Sir Percy?'

No one replied.

'Is there someone here tonight who is a member of his family?' George continued.

'No one will claim me,' Sir Percy's voice said. 'I was a black sheep. A liar and a cheat. But I regret my time on earth now, and regret my sins. I wish to ask the forgiveness of my descendants.'

George spoke quietly. 'Those of Sir Percy's family

– and I believe they are here – will know who he is but perhaps they're unwilling to own him.'

The audience shifted in their seats.

'He is with us in spirit ... and in body, too!' George said, pointing to the bottom of the cabinet where, around Madame's feet, a mass of something white was appearing.

A thrill of excitement ran around the room, and those towards the back stood up in order to see better.

George bade them be seated again. 'Please do not move or alarm Madame in any way. Materialisation is a rare and difficult procedure ...'

Velvet stared hard at Madame's feet and, in spite of having seen a similar occurrence at Miss Cook's, was incredulous as she gazed at the white mass which could be seen very dimly in the cabinet. At one glance it looked like smoke, then something akin to a flimsy white fabric. As it grew more substantial, its shape altered so that it became about the size of a kneeling man. A lady in the audience screamed and George called again for calm. Another moment and it was taller, almost the shape of someone standing. Because of the poor light and the vagueness of the form, however, it was impossible to distinguish any features, or even tell for definite if it was male or female. The grey-white shape wavered and then stilled. The audience – even the two rowdy young men – were completely silent.

'I cannot rest until my family forgives me for my sins,' came the deep voice.

Madame spoke up then. 'The family of Sir Percy are here tonight and know well who he is,' she said, 'but their shame at his conduct when on earth prevents them from speaking out. They should be assured that the sins of the fathers do not fall upon the heads of those still living, and should forgive Sir Percy in their hearts so that he can rest in peace.'

Just after she'd spoken, the form of Sir Percy vanished. To Velvet, who'd been close to the cabinet and watching intently, it seemed to waver, fall to the ground and then disappear. The audience gasped and sighed in turn, murmuring to each other that they'd never before seen anything like it.

Amidst this stir and muttering, there came something like the sound of a child's voice, far away, saying, '*Mama!*'

Mrs Fortesque, the lady in the front row wearing the child's shawl around her, suddenly jumped to her feet. 'I heard a baby! Is it Claire? Will you do more, Madame? Will you materialise my child?'

George nodded to Velvet, who immediately went to urge Mrs Fortesque to sit down again. 'It may not be possible tonight,' she whispered. 'Please be seated, Mrs Fortesque. Madame knows you're here and I am sure she'll do her best.'

'Claire!' Mrs Fortesque burst into tears. 'Claire, I must see you!' She wriggled from Velvet's grasp and ran towards Madame's cabinet, but George stopped her just before she reached the chair.

'Please! You mustn't go near the medium. It could be dangerous.'

'But my child! I heard her, I tell you. I want to see her . . .'

Between them, George and Velvet escorted Mrs Fortesque back to her seat, where she was comforted by the woman accompanying her. During this time, Madame gave a groan and her head fell forward, then after a moment or two she sat up. She pressed her hand to her forehead, then looked out to the audience as if waking from a deep sleep.

'My child . . . I heard my child . . .' Mrs Fortesque said brokenly.

'I'm so sorry,' said Madame, fully herself now. 'Your child wanted to come through, but I didn't have the strength left to communicate with her at this point in the evening.' Madame motioned to Velvet to light the lamps. 'Perhaps another time . . .'

Whilst Mrs Fortesque sat crying, the rest of the audience stayed in their seats, stunned and speechless. Neither those members of the audience who were famous nor the two boisterous young gentlemen had anything to say for themselves.

'What a success it was,' George said to Velvet later. Sissy had been walked home and both Mrs Lawson and Madame had retired for the night, leaving the two of them in the kitchen finishing off the last few inches of a bottle of champagne. 'I was captivated by Madame's performance. Wasn't she wonderful?'

'She was,' Velvet agreed.

George swilled the liquid around his glass, holding it up to the light in order to see the bubbles. 'Indeed! But then we believe – do we not? – that Madame is wonderful in whatever she does.'

'We do!' Certainly she did believe that, Velvet thought, but there were so many things she didn't understand. 'Do you think she will always be able to materialise spirits now, at every séance?'

'Perhaps not,' George said. 'It's too demanding. Too exhausting! Madame would find her energies so depleted that she wouldn't be able to do her normal work.'

Velvet nodded. 'I see.'

'She may do a smaller materialisation next time. A child. I think that would be easier.'

'You mean Mrs Fortesque's child?' Velvet asked.

George winked. 'Most likely.'

Velvet hesitated. 'What a shame no one owned up to having Sir Percy as one of their ancestors.'

'A shame,' George said, 'but perhaps safer that way.'

'What do you mean?'

'I mean it's safer to materialise someone whom no one knows.'

Velvet looked at him, puzzled. 'I don't understand what you mean. Why is that?'

'Well, because a few weeks ago one of the other big-name mediums materialised a sitter's father only to find that, although in real life the gentleman had only had one leg, she had materialised him with two!'

Velvet gasped, then laughed. 'What happened?'

'Oh, I believe the medium got away with it. She said that in the spirit world, diseases are cured and those with missing limbs become whole again.'

Velvet frowned a little. *The medium got away with it*, he'd said. She found it all very difficult to understand. She didn't like to ask such a question, but was he saying that the whole materialisation process was fraudulent?

George lifted his glass. 'To mediums everywhere!' he said, draining it.

Velvet forgot her concerns. 'And especially to Madame,' she added.

Then they just sat there for some comfortable moments, each contemplating the coals glowing within the open door of the kitchen range and busy with their own thoughts.

'This morning . . . I was asking you about your early life,' George said after a while.

Velvet held her breath, remembering the kiss and trying hard to maintain her composure. 'Yes, about when I was at the laundry.'

'I didn't really mean about then. I was interested in your life as a child, way back. Were they happy days for you?'

Velvet thought for a moment before answering. She hadn't wanted to speak about her father – not to anyone, not ever – but if she was going to have a special relationship with George then perhaps everything should be open between them. Madame obviously trusted George implicitly, so surely *she* should, too. She should not tell lies to the person she hoped (dare she think it?) might become closer to her than anyone else in the world. Resolved, she took a deep breath.

'Before my mother died my life was also hard, but I remember some happy days. Mother and I had outings to the park on Sundays, and sometimes went on an omnibus to see her sisters – just for the day, you understand, as my father wouldn't allow her to stay away longer.'

'Her sisters. You had two aunts, then. Are they in spirit now?'

'I don't know,' Velvet said. 'We lost touch. I think they may have written to me after Mother died, but my father never let me have any letters.'

'So there were three sisters altogether. Did they all have pretty names like yours?'

'My aunts were named Verity and Patience,' Velvet said, sidestepping the issue of her own name, 'and my mother's name was Hope.' She smiled. 'I believe my grandfather was a Quaker.'

'Indeed, they love names of that nature,' George said. 'I once knew a Quaker chap who had been christened Fearless! He was quite a little fellow, too.' They laughed. 'And you used to go out with your mother washing linens?'

'I did.' Velvet nodded. 'There were two big houses we used to go to once a week, and she'd take in washing for our neighbours the rest of the time. I was allowed to dunk the blue-bag in the rinsing water and turn the handle of the mangle, and later, when I was big enough, I'd help her fold the sheets.'

'You attended school?'

'Mother educated me at home. Before she married, she was a governess,' Velvet said with some pride. 'She taught me how to read and write, and all sorts of other useful things: cooking, house-hold accounts, the use of herbs, needlework and drawing.'

'And your father . . . I believe you told Madame he was a children's entertainer?'

'Yes, but before you ask, that doesn't mean he was a jolly man in a clown suit.'

'No?'

'No, he was not! He was a miserable devil who was only happy when he was goading my mother or I.' She hesitated, finding a few drops of champagne in the bottom of her glass and drinking them before continuing. 'My father was a wicked man. I can hardly bear to speak about him. When my poor mother died . . .'

'Your poor mother? Was she very ill, then?'

'She wasn't ill so much as run-down with worry, hard work and trying to keep bread on the table,' Velvet said heatedly. 'My father was a no-good gambler who drove her into her early grave.'

George put out a hand and stroked her arm. 'Hush!' he said. 'That part of your life is over now. You are with Madame – and with me – and you are safe.' As they gazed into the fire, he asked gently, 'When was it that your father died?'

Velvet swallowed. 'Some time ago,' she said in a whisper, for she did not feel ready to tell him everything. It would have relieved her mind to confess, but she desperately wanted George to think well of her and how could he possibly do so if he knew she had all but murdered her own father?

'Poor Velvet,' George said, putting his hand over hers. 'I'm so sorry you're an orphan.'

'You mustn't be,' Velvet replied. 'As you said, I'm all right now, and so are you. We've come through it, we've got Madame and we've . . .' In the middle of the sentence she suddenly realised what she'd been about to say and stopped herself just in time.

Blushing furiously, she willed George to kiss her and say that she must speak freely and speak her heart, because he felt the same. But he did not. Instead he looked at his pocket watch.

'My goodness. It's past midnight and here we are still talking. How indiscreet we are being.' He raised his eyebrows. 'How your reputation will suffer if anyone finds out!'

Never mind about that – just kiss me again, Velvet wanted to say, but she did not dare.

Madame Savoya's Second Private Sitting with 'Mrs Lilac'

'**M**rs Lilac!' Madame exclaimed, getting up to kiss the cheek of the elderly lady who had just been escorted into the room by George. 'How lovely it is to see you again.' Madame stood back and seemed to make a brief survey of the shape and height of Mrs Lilac. 'Your aura is looking very pink today – almost more pink than lilac.'

'Is that good?' Mrs Lilac asked nervously.

'Indeed it is! Whilst you're under my roof you are suffused with peace.'

'It **is** lovely to be here again,' said Mrs Lilac, looking about the room. 'Everything is so fresh and modern. The flower arrangements, the linens, the colours . . .'

Madame smiled. 'Surrounded as I am by spirits from the past, I enjoy having everything new about me. I think **they** like it when they visit, too.'

'What a pleasant thought,' Mrs Lilac said. 'Figures from the past enjoying all that's best about the present.'

'I could not have put it better myself,' said Madame.

George settled Mrs Lilac into an easy chair and shook out a rug ready to put across her knees.

'I did wonder if we were ever going to see you again,' Madame said.

'I've been rather poorly,' said Mrs Lilac. 'There was a fog which got into my lungs. I was laid low for three weeks and my physician said I shouldn't venture out.'

'Madame Savoya and I were beginning to think you had deserted us!' said George, tucking the rug securely around her.

Mrs Lilac shifted uncomfortably, plucking at a stray cotton on her glove. 'My physician did say that I shouldn't get myself overwrought by attending séances or the like. He was rather disparaging of them, as a matter of fact. He said he didn't believe in such things.'

Madame shook her head sadly. 'Some people have very closed minds.' She took Mrs Lilac's wrinkled hand in her own. 'My dear lady, you must do as your heart tells you. If you gain comfort from coming here, then how could it possibly be wrong? How could you disbelieve messages which come from your own nearest and dearest – messages containing information which only you, and she, could possibly know?'

'Yes, but –'

'I'm rather cross with this physician of yours, to tell you the truth,' Madame interrupted somewhat sternly. 'I would not dream of interfering in your bodily health or prescribing medicines for you, and I'm of the opinion that he should return the compliment by not interfering with your spiritual health.'

'Madame is renowned and uniquely qualified in that capacity,' George put in.

Mrs Lilac looked suitably chastened.

'I wouldn't tell you how to cure whooping cough or diseases of the blood!' said Madame. 'How is it that he thinks he can advise on your spiritual well-being?'

'It's just that he was Mother's doctor . . .'

'Ah. And he seeks to control you just as your mother controlled you.'

'Yes,' Mrs Lilac said with a sigh. 'Perhaps he does.'

'My dear lady,' said Madame, 'have you thought of keeping your visits here strictly to yourself? If you don't tell your doctor about them, then he cannot possibly censure them.'

'Perhaps that would be the best thing,' said Mrs Lilac. 'I rather think – being a man of science – that he wouldn't understand certain things. About Mother's jewels, for instance, and the magnetism.'

'Ah, yes. The vital magnetism,' Madame said.

'Since you – since Mother – told me about it, I haven't been wearing her jewellery very much at all. Although as it's her birthday today, I'm wearing a little gold pin which belonged to her. I didn't think she'd mind that.'

'We'll see, shall we? Would you like me to go into trance and see if your mother is beside you?'

Mrs Lilac nodded nervously. 'Though if she is in a bad humour . . .'

Madame smiled. 'I shall first of all ascertain what sort of mood she's in, and if she's feeling irritable then I shall ask her to come back another day!'

Mrs Lilac, not knowing if Madame was joking or not, gave a squeak of a laugh.

Madame closed her eyes and, after a few moments of breathing normally, began to draw in her breath slowly and wheezily, as an old lady might breathe. 'Esther!' she said suddenly, her voice deep and strong. 'Is that you?'

'Yes, Mother,' Mrs Lilac answered quickly.

'About time, girl. Here I've been, looking out for you every day, whilst you've been idling in bed listening to that fool of a doctor!'

'Doctor Inman has been our doctor for thirty years,' Mrs Lilac cried.

'And much good he did. If he'd had any degree of competence I wouldn't be here on the Other Side, would I? No, you killed me between you: the doctor, you and that so-called nursing home.'

Mrs Lilac began to look anxious. 'Now, Mother, we've been over this before, and I've apologised several times for having moved you into Runnymede.'

'Anything to get rid of me! That's what it was, wasn't it?'

'No, Mother, I didn't want to be rid of you. I actually missed you very much. I miss you still.'

'I expect you've forgotten today was my birthday.'

'Indeed not. I went to the cemetery today and put a posy of flowers on your gravestone.'

'I've seen it.' There came a sniff. 'You've stopped wearing my jewellery, then.'

'I have.' Mrs Lilac touched something on her lapel. 'Except this little gold pin. I'm wearing it today in your memory.'

'No need.'

'What do you mean?'

'You should be remembering me in your head. Wearing my jewellery doesn't prove a thing.'

'I do remember you in my head. Every day!' Mrs Lilac protested. 'I have nothing else to do in my life but remember you! Everything is just how you left it, Mother. I haven't changed a thing. The drawing room, the parlour, the bedroom. I still keep the curtains closed in your bedroom in honour of your memory.'

'Hmmm.'

'What else can I possibly do?'

'That jewellery of mine . . . there's no point in leaving it in the box at home.'

'But you told me not to wear it because the magnetism might call me early to the Other Side.'

'Nor should you. You must give it away. Let someone else have a use for it. You've got no one to leave it to, have you?'

'Only Cousin Evie on Father's side, and I haven't seen her for years. She didn't even come to your funeral.'

'Certainly you're not to give it to that foolish Evie. You must give it to the cause. The spiritualist cause.'

'Oh!' said Mrs Lilac.

'It could be sold in my name to help people who've been made destitute through no fault of their own.'

'Do you mean all the jewellery?' Mrs Lilac asked in some dismay. 'All the things that Father gave you? Your emeralds and your diamonds and the five rows of pearls? What about that tiara you wore to your coming-out ball?'

'All of it. What's the point of keeping it? When you die whoever finds your lifeless body will search the house and take whatever they can get hold of.'

Mrs Lilac was silent for a whole minute, until her mother sniffed and said, 'There's not much point in my being here if you're not going to speak to me.'

'Sorry, Mother. It's just that you've given me a lot of things to think about.'

'Go home, then, and look into your heart. Think about what I, your dear departed mother, want, and about how you can make amends for forsaking me at the end of my life.'

There was another long silence and then Madame opened her eyes and said in her own voice, 'Ah. Your mother has gone now.'

Mrs Lilac looked at her wonderingly. '**Where** has she gone? Where does she go to?'

'If we only knew,' Madame said.

'There are more things in heaven and earth . . .' George said wisely, taking up the rug and folding it.

Chapter Ten

In Which Mrs Fortesque Asks
the Seemingly Impossible

It was still quite early in the morning when Velvet, busy in the front room arranging yellow roses in a crystal vase, saw Charlie striding down the road.

Her first emotion, to her surprise, was one of pleasure. It had been a long time since she had seen a friendly face from her past life and Charlie could usually be relied upon to make her smile. She would be able to tease him, too, about walking out with Lizzie and maybe find out whether he was serious in regard to her or not.

She watched him from behind the pale silk window drapes. As Lizzie had said, he had a proper uniform now – dark-navy wool with bright silver buttons, black boots and leather gloves – and he did look rather smart. The only thing she didn't particularly like was his policeman's pointy helmet, but then she'd always thought these rather ridiculous.

It also hid all of Charlie's tawny-lion hair, which was one of his best features.

He approached the door. The *front* door, she noticed, the cheeky thing. He didn't look for the tradesmen's entrance, but came up the front steps with a purposeful stride. Quickly, before he could hammer on the knocker and alert the rest of the house to his visit, Velvet ran to the door to open it, checking on her appearance in a mirror and twirling her finger around a side curl on the way. She didn't want him as an admirer, but it didn't do to let standards slip.

'Really, Charlie!' she said, opening the door. 'Don't you ever give up?'

'Oh!' he said, acting surprised. 'It's you. I forgot you lived here.'

'You never did!'

'I thought you would have moved on by now.'

'Don't be silly, Charlie!' Velvet frowned at him, almost (but not quite) sure he was teasing her. 'I know you've come here to try and see me again. What is it you want?'

'See you again?' Charlie said. 'Oh no, I'm here to speak to a Mr George Wilson.'

Velvet blinked. 'George? Why?'

'Excuse me, but it's a matter of police business. I'd prefer to give that information to the gentleman himself.'

'Police business?' Velvet repeated, stunned.

Charlie tipped his helmet smartly. 'Yes, miss. I am, as you see, a policeman. Well, a police cadet, to be perfectly accurate. Anyway, I'm a member of the Metropolitan Police Force.'

'But you don't work around here.'

'That's where you're wrong, miss.'

'Why are you calling me "miss" all the time? It's very annoying.'

'It seems safer,' Charlie whispered. 'In case you've changed your name again.'

Velvet looked over her shoulder to make sure no one in the household was close by. 'Of course I haven't!'

'Well, anyways, as part of my on-going training I am now attached to Lisson Grove station in the Marylebone Division of the Metropolitan Police.' He gave a brief wink. 'I did get a choice of stations, actually, and chose that one because I knew it's on your patch. I can keep my eye on you this way and see you don't get into any trouble.'

'Charlie!' she protested.

'You can laugh, but there are some shady people about.' He grinned. 'I sometimes see you in the mornings, very early, when you're taking that little dog around the square.'

'I never see you.'

'I'm not surprised. You're usually half-asleep.'

Velvet smiled in spite of herself, a little relieved that things hadn't changed that much between them.

She didn't want Charlie chasing after her and declaring his love, of course, but neither did she want him calling her 'miss' and speaking in that strange and distant way. She wanted him to stay what he'd always been: an especially good friend.

'So, *Velvet*,' he said, with particular emphasis on her name, 'if you would be so kind as to let me know the whereabouts of Mr George Wilson. Does he reside in this house?'

'Yes, he does.' Velvet nodded. 'You'd better come in.'

Very intrigued, she led Charlie downstairs to the kitchen. Here they found Mrs Lawson cleaning the range with black lead polish, and George bent over the table cleaning Madame's boots on a sheet of newspaper.

'A policeman to see you,' Velvet said to George. Startled, he straightened up so quickly that he hit his head on the oil lamp that hung above the table. 'What is it? What do you want?'

'Would you mind coming down to the station with me, sir,' Charlie, who had now removed his helmet, asked politely.

'Come down to the station?' George blustered. 'Why on earth should I?' He gave no indication of having seen Charlie before, Velvet was relieved to note, so obviously didn't remember the 'carpet salesman' who'd called.

'It's just this, sir. A young man's body was found

in the street right outside our station last night. There was no identification on him, but in one of his pockets was a piece of paper with your name and this address scribbled on it.'

'Oh dear,' George said, looking shocked.

'We'd like you to come down and identify him, if you would.'

'Right . . . right,' George said, wiping his hands on a rag. 'Who the devil could that be, I wonder?' He shook his head. 'What sort of a man was he?'

'I'm afraid he was a tramp, sir. He was seen two days earlier begging outside the law courts. He made a nuisance of himself, as a matter of fact, and nearly got arrested.'

'What does . . . What did he look like?'

'Tall and thin, grimy, smelly, dressed in rags. Not an old man, by any means. But a poverty-stricken one.'

'That description could fit half the vagrants in London,' George said. 'But I'll come. Of course I'll come.'

Charlie was handling the situation very well, Velvet thought. She hadn't known that he could be so confident and capable. She looked at him, then at George, and couldn't help comparing them. Charlie was quite tall, a policeman's height, but George was even taller. He was also sleeker, smarter and much more pleasing to the eye, his dark hair slicked back with Macassar oil, his green eyes keen and watchful. Charlie had quite ordinary blue eyes and a few freckles across his cheeks. Although he had a kind and cheery face, he didn't look in any way distinguished, especially as his hair had been squashed in some places by the helmet and was sticking up in others.

The two men in my life, Velvet mused, and then thought how ridiculous that sounded. One was too keen – and the other not keen enough.

George and Charlie went off to the station together and the moment they disappeared, Mrs Lawson, who was not usually given to idle chatter, said to Velvet, 'Well, I could see what was going on in Mr George's mind!'

'What do you mean?'

'Proper nervy, he was. Thought the law had come for us, didn't he?'

'Really?'

'Well, they're out to get mediums, aren't they?' On Velvet looking at her blankly, she added, 'Those spirit hunters! The Society for Psychical Research, as they call themselves. Don't you read the papers?'

'Not often,' Velvet admitted.

'Oh, they're shocking, they are. They attend séances to try to discredit mediums. They turn lights on when they shouldn't and take photographs during materialisations. They insist on mediums being searched before and after séances, and they startle mediums out of their trances. They cause big trouble.'

'But our Madame has a wonderful reputation! She's not one of those catchpenny women you get at the end of Brighton Pier.'

'You know that and I know that, but not everyone does. The psychical research people say that there are frauds about, and they make it their life's work to hunt them down.'

Velvet considered this. 'Well, I suppose if they can weed out all the frauds it'll be good for us,' she said, and then went back to pondering the relative merits of George and Charlie.

George didn't return to Darkling Villa until midday, and from the smell of beer on his breath Velvet knew that he must have called at a tavern on his way home. He looked so woebegone that she would have liked to have pulled his head down on to her shoulder and put her arms around him, but instead she busied herself making him a strong brew of tea.

'Madame hasn't asked for me, has she?' he asked, sinking down on the easy chair by the kitchen fire. 'Only I couldn't come back without having something to fortify me.'

Velvet, handing over the tea, assured him that Madame had been ensconced in her rooms with a jewellery designer all morning as she was having some of her old-fashioned rings and brooches put into more modern settings.

'That's a bit of a shock to a chap, that is, seeing someone dead,' George said heavily.

Passed over, she thought, but didn't say it.

Mrs Lawson had gone out shopping, so Velvet felt free and easy enough to sit herself down on the mat beside George's chair. 'Did you know the man? Who was he?'

'I hardly knew him at all, poor chap, just that his name was Aaron and he came from Brighton. We stayed two nights at a mission house together when we were both very hard up a few years back. In fact, the night we met he only had a ha'penny, which – perhaps as a young lady you wouldn't know this – meant he could only spend the night in the mission house standing up.' Velvet frowned, so George explained, 'If you have only a ha'penny you're not permitted to lie down to sleep, but may only prop yourself against a wall.'

'Oh! How awful!'

'I fear there are many degradations and humiliations which you don't know about, Velvet. And I am glad that you do not!' After a moment, George continued, 'I had a few pence on me, so I paid for Aaron to lie in the next sleeping box to mine, and bought our hot tea and bread in the morning. The lad was grateful, of course.'

'And did you see him again?'

'Not really. Things started to go wrong for me after that. The weather turned, my raree-show disintegrated, my clothes were stolen and I thought I was finished – but then Madame came along and saved me.'

'But how did this chap have your name?'

'Oh, much later I managed to get a message to him saying that I'd give him a square meal if he came to the house. I think that's why he had my details in his pocket. He never came, though.'

'The poor lad.'

'That body this morning could have been mine, Velvet,' George said.

Velvet nodded, put out a hand and grasped his.

'I owe everything to Madame. Everything! There's nothing she could ask of me that I wouldn't do.'

Velvet squeezed his hand, then knelt up so that their faces were on a level. 'I feel the same.'

'Then we are of one mind . . .'

Velvet lifted her face to his and their lips met, softly, beautifully, a pledge of their feelings.

Two kisses, Velvet thought immediately afterwards. Two kisses must mean something. Surely it could only be a matter of time before George declared his love?

That evening there was to be a séance on behalf of Mrs Fortesque, the woman whose baby had died. Mrs Fortesque had requested a semi-private meeting to which she could ask relatives and friends who were of the same mind – those who espoused the spiritualist cause and were sympathetic to her plight – as she was very much hoping that her child could be materialised. Her husband, apparently, was not a believer, so would not be attending, although he had no objection to his wife doing whatever she needed to do to get through the days.

'Tonight will cost Mrs Fortesque quite a large sum of money,' George said. 'She wants everyone here to be concentrating on contacting the little girl, so she doesn't want other spirits getting in the way.'

Velvet sighed. 'How tragic it all is.' She and George were in the hall, waiting for the first arrivals. 'It must be terrible to lose someone you love so much.'

'It doesn't have to be *so* terrible,' George said. 'I mean, you don't have to lose them completely now.'

'Not if you come to someone like Madame, you mean?'

'Exactly,' said George. His green eyes smiled into hers. 'Thank you for being so sympathetic this morning – about Aaron.'

Velvet, returning the smile, leaned slightly towards him. Mrs Lawson was downstairs putting the finishing touches to the canapés, her daughter was setting out glasses on trays, Madame was upstairs resting before her performance and the silent, dimly lit hall was suffused with the heady fragrance of lilies. The setting was perfect for another kiss . . .

But no – the clinking of glasses heralded the appearance of Sissy Lawson, who had an uncanny knack of appearing at the wrong time. 'You're very quiet up here, you two,' she said. 'I hope you haven't been doing something you shouldn't.'

Before Velvet could think of a smart reply there was a knock at the front door and, whilst George disappeared into the front room to check that all the chairs were positioned correctly, Velvet put on her welcoming smile and prepared to open the door to the first members of the Fortesque party.

Within fifteen minutes about a dozen people, mostly women, had been seated and Madame was within the cabinet and ready to go into trance. Velvet, after turning the lamps down, used the subsequent moment of utter stillness to close her eyes and think about George and the two kisses. Had she been too forward in allowing them? When would he say how he felt about her? Would there be more kisses, or did he think too highly of Madame? Did he, in fact, love Madame? But then, she reasoned, she also loved Madame – in a different way, of course.

The curtain which separated Madame from her small audience was opened by George, and people began shifting in their seats, craning their necks in order to try and see into the cabinet. Madame spoke to say that the evening would be slightly different in that only one spirit's appearance was requested.

'I'm not sure that the other spirits will be pleased with what we're asking, for we are, in fact, denying them a chance to speak to their loved ones. I beg your patience, therefore, and request your complete silence and spiritual cooperation whilst I try and communicate with the Other Side.'

Several minutes followed. The observers shifted in their seats. It would have been better, Velvet thought, to have had the pianist there; at least her playing would have filled the eerie quiet.

'No,' Madame said suddenly, speaking to some-one not visible. 'I'm so sorry. I must leave my mind clear for the one whom I'm expecting.' There was another brief interval. 'Thank you for being so understanding,' she said then. 'Yes, I'm waiting upon a child who passed over. I have here some of her closest relations on earth.'

Another ten minutes passed and George went to stand at the front of the room to request that every-one keep a serene and untroubled mind to help the spirit of little Claire come through. He also asked if they would please remember that Madame had to wait until the spirits were willing and could only work with their cooperation. If, for some reason, Claire's spirit chose not to appear, then nothing could be done about it. 'The veil between earth and the spirit world is only slight, but sometimes it takes a mighty strength to draw it aside,' George said, whilst Velvet mused how knowledgeable he was, how elegant his speech.

Five more minutes went by, during which Madame saw off another stray spirit, then she suddenly held out her arms. 'Come, child!' she said softly. 'Come and let your mama see you.'

There was a strangled cry from Mrs Fortesque in the first row. After a few seconds, a child's voice, high and tremulous, said, '*Mama! Where are you?*'

'I'm here, my darling!' Mrs Fortesque called. 'Come to me.'

'*Mama! It's dark over here.*'

'But where are you?'

'*I don't know.*'

'Can you let me see you?'

There was a groan from Madame and she slumped forward slightly, then the voice said, '*I don't know how.*'

'Try, darling! Your mama loves you very much. She's waiting here for you to appear.'

After another silence and some laboured breathing from Madame, startled calls came from those in the front row: 'Something is forming on the ground! Something white . . .'

Mrs Fortesque dropped on to all fours to be closer to whatever it was that was appearing.

George quickly stepped in and barred her way. 'I

beg you, madam, go back to your chair or Madame Savoya will not be able to continue the séance.'

As Velvet helped Mrs Fortesque back into her seat, the eyes of every other person in the room were on the white shape that was forming at Madame's feet. This seemed to be of a similar composition to the spirit which had appeared there before, although this time it did not grow in length, but stayed small – baby-sized.

'Can you stand now, darling? Can you come to me?'

'The ectoplasm which is forming a likeness of your child's body is attached to Madame Savoya,' George said. 'It cannot come towards you.'

'But I must hold her!' Mrs Fortesque cried. 'Just let me touch her.'

'Madam, that is not possible.'

'I can hardly see her . . . Can she become more distinct?'

'Not at this time, I fear,' George said. 'Madame Savoya is a skilful practitioner, but this is an inexact science.'

'Oh, let her speak to me herself! Let me see more of her and hear what she says!' Mrs Fortesque pleaded. 'Oh, my darling! Are you amongst the angels?'

'*They play with me and teach me,*' came the piping voice, '*but I miss my mama!*'

'And I miss you, my dearest.' Mrs Fortesque stood

170

up again and attempted to go towards Madame's cabinet, so that Velvet had to intervene and hold her back. 'I implore you, madam,' she whispered. 'It may be injurious to Madame's life if you touch her. It may even be injurious to the spirit of your own child!'

'*I have to go now, Mama.*'

'Not yet, surely! Don't leave me!' Mrs Fortesque screamed, but the white cloud shook a little and then dropped and disappeared, as it had before.

There came the sound of Mrs Fortesque sobbing, then Madame stirred and opened her eyes and the audience, who had been holding their collective breath, let out a lengthy sigh.

Madame was still slumped over as if she had lost all her strength, and George ran to close the curtain so that she could start to recover in private.

The Fortesque party were soon dressed in their outer clothes and waiting on the steps of the open front door, but when Velvet went back into the front room, Mrs Fortesque was still speaking to Madame and George.

'Please, I beg you. Would you just consider it?' Mrs Fortesque was asking Madame as Velvet entered.

'Impossible,' Madame said. 'Or near impossible. Certainly I've never heard of it being attempted before.'

171

'But you, Madame Savoya, have a reputation as one of the most skilful mediums in London. Everyone swears by you!'

'My dear Mrs Fortesque,' Madame said, 'even if I could manage to do such a thing, it would very probably damage me. At the least, I would be so depleted, so drained, that I'd never be able to work again.'

'But you'd never *need* to work again. I'd pay you enough to last the rest of your life! My husband is very rich and he'd give everything he has to make me happy.' So saying, she broke into sobs.

Madame and George exchanged glances. 'My dear woman,' Madame said, 'I've never heard that such a thing is possible but will only say – and this must not be repeated – that I will investigate further.' On Mrs Fortesque straightening up and looking at her joyfully, Madame repeated, 'I only promise that I'll look into it, but you mustn't tell a soul. Leave it to me. George will contact you if I have any news to impart.'

Mrs Fortesque's face, though wet with tears, broke into a shaky smile. She kissed Madame, was helped into her coat and bonnet by Velvet and taken to the door. Velvet returned to the front room, ostensibly to collect the vases of flowers and take them downstairs, but secretly keen to know more of what Mrs Fortesque had been asking.

Madame beckoned to her. 'I expect you're curious as to what was being said.'

'It sounds as if Mrs Fortesque is expecting you to work miracles.'

'Indeed she is,' said Madame.

'What is it that she wants?'

Madame spread her hands wide. 'She wants her child back! She wants me to materialise her baby completely, so that she can carry her away.'

Velvet started. 'But surely that is impossible?'

There was a long silence between the three of them, then George said, 'Know only this: with Madame, nothing is impossible.'

Reflecting on everything later in her room, Velvet thought what a bizarre evening it had been. Did she really and truly believe that a dead child had, that night, come back to life – or almost to life? How had the ectoplasm been formed? Was it made of smoke or something more substantial? If it was made of some material thing, then might there be some trace left in Madame's cabinet?

Velvet went over and over these questions in her mind and, finally, finding it impossible to sleep, decided to go downstairs to see if she could discover more about this so-called ectoplasm. She put a wrap over her nightdress, lit a candle and went downstairs. The house was, of course, silent and dark, but Velvet was not nervous.

She pushed open the door to the front room, intending to go straight to Madame's cabinet and examine the floor for traces of white foam or something similar. Someone was already in the room, however. Two people, in fact, in a lovers' embrace. As Velvet gasped with shock, the person who was facing her opened his eyes and looked directly at her.

Horrified, she realised that it was George.

Madame Savoya's Second Private Sitting with 'Lady Blue'

'**D**o be seated, Lady Blue,' Madame Savoya said. 'I hope this warmer weather is agreeable to you. I'm finding it rather hot in town, myself.'

'Oh, I do so concur,' Lady Blue said. 'It's just a pity I can't get down to our villa by the sea – such a long journey on one's own.'

'A villa by the sea sounds lovely! Where is it?'

'Brighton, on the south coast. We find the sea breezes most invigorating. That is, *I* find the sea breezes most invigorating.' She shook her head. 'I find it so difficult to remember that I'm alone now.'

'You're not entirely alone,' Madame said gently. 'Your husband is near you always. You know that, don't you?'

'He's close by, whether you can see him or not,' George put in.

'Yes. Thank you,' Lady Blue said. 'Knowing that is such a comfort.' She dabbed her eyes. 'Dear Bertie . . .'

'Did your husband enjoy it beside the sea?' Madame

175

asked. On Lady Blue nodding and sniffing into a handkerchief, she went on. 'I hear that sea-bathing is quite the thing nowadays. They're even talking of having mixed bathing.'

'Really?' Lady Blue said. 'I don't know whether my husband would have approved of that. However, he did love sea-swimming, whereas I find the waves much too rough.'

George sat down, his notepad under his arm. 'I'm with milord on that,' he said. 'I find swimming in the sea very exhilarating.'

'Oh!' said Lady Blue. 'He used to use that word, too. He'd tell me that fighting the waves let him know he was still alive!' Suddenly realising what she'd said, she collapsed over her handkerchief once again.

'There, there,' said Madame, patting her client's arm. 'Let us look for the positive in all things.'

'Yes, yes, of course,' said Lady Blue. She tucked the handkerchief into her reticule and managed to smile at George. 'You really are very much like he was as a young man.'

Madame smiled indulgently. 'It's quite uncanny, isn't it? I think we've remarked before on George's similarities to his lordship.' She paused, then added, 'It's almost as if your dear husband's spirit lives on in him.'

'How wonderful that would be,' said Lady Blue.

Madame patted a fold of her silk skirt into place. 'But your villa at the seaside – how often do you go there now, Lady Blue?'

'Not very much at all. I suppose it's silly to keep it, really, when you think of the cost of employing a permanent housekeeper, but . . . well, I haven't got round to doing anything about it yet.'

Some other chit-chat followed and then, when Lady Blue was completely at her ease, Madame said that she thought the time was right to see if her husband could be contacted.

Lady Blue assented and Madame closed her eyes, saying that she didn't think he was far away; in fact, she could feel his presence quite close by.

After two minutes of silence, Madame lifted her voice and said, 'Of course you may. Welcome to my home, milord.'

'Oh!' exclaimed Lady Blue, all of a flutter. 'Are you there, Bertie?'

The same deeper, stronger voice as before replied, 'I am, my dear. I am beside you.'

'I want to ask you how you are,' Lady Blue said anxiously, 'but that hardly applies, does it?'

'It really does not. I am as I am,' said her husband. 'Are you happy?'

'Such concepts are impossible to understand in this realm. It's more important to me that you are content.'

'I can never be content without you!' Lady Blue gave a strangled sob. 'I'm lonely, Bertie.'

'Ah, my dear! If only we'd had children,' came the reply. 'Children would have filled the gap that my death has left in your life.'

'Yes, they would have been such a comfort.'

'Have you thought any more about what I said?'

'About . . . about helping the young man here make his way in the world?'

'Indeed. Acting as his patron and his benefactor.'

'I have,' Lady Blue said, giving George a sideways glance, 'although I did wonder about your nephew.'

'Who?' Lord Blue barked.

'Well, I suppose he's not really a nephew. Your cousin Myra's boy, Albert. He was named after you, you know.'

'Never set eyes on him!'

'You have, dearest. Not very often, granted. But he came to your funeral.'

There came a grunt. 'I know why that was: he hoped I'd left him something.'

'He seemed quite a good sort. Going into law, I believe.'

'Being a good sort isn't enough reason for me to make him my heir. Come to think of it, I never liked the boy!'

'Did you not? You never said, dear,' Lady Blue protested mildly.

'I want my houses and my money to go to someone who is like me in spirit. Someone who'll enjoy our villa by the sea! Someone who'll change his name to mine and carry on the title and the family line.'

'But such a person could not inherit your title!'

'He could assume it, with your permission' was the response.

'Oh!' said Lady Blue. 'I hadn't thought of that.'

She toyed nervously with her handkerchief again. 'Is that what you really want, Bertie?'

'Of course. What's the point in sitting on my money? When you die it'll go to the blasted government. Take the lot in taxes, they will.'

'But what about cousin Myra's boy?'

'I don't like cousin Myra's boy. He's a fortune hunter! I don't like the idea of him lording it in our house. I want someone sensitive and thoughtful, someone who'll look after you like a son.'

Lady Blue nodded. 'Very well, dear.'

'I want you to look into it, then come back again and tell me how you're going to do it.'

'I shall go to Burgess and Burgess –'

'Not them! They'll try and talk you out of it. No, go to one of the new firms of solicitors in Church Street and insist on having what you want. No shilly-shallying.'

'All right, dear.'

'I shall be so proud if you do this for me, Ceci. It would make me very happy.'

'That's what's important to me, Bertie. I shall take advice as soon as I can.' Lady Blue glanced at George, who had been sitting mute during most of this discussion, hunched over his notepad and occasionally shaking his head in disbelief. 'Provided, of course, that the young man here is agreeable. He may not want the responsibilities that come with big houses and large sums of money.'

The deep voice chuckled. 'Ceci, he is like me! Of course he will.'

'Very well, dear.'

There was subsequent talk about the maintenance of the two houses and then Lord Blue had to go, drifting back into that unknown land on the other side of the veil where spirits dwelt and, it seemed, occasionally sought the attention of those still on earth.

Madame came out of her trance and the three of them discussed what had occurred during the séance. George proved very reluctant to give his point of view, saying that he was utterly incredulous; he could hardly believe that Lord Blue had meant what he said.

'But spirits speak from the heart,' Madame said. 'There's no concept of artifice in the spirit world. Spirits have nothing to lose, so why should they confuse things by dissembling?'

'Bertie **was** a bit of a philanthropist,' Lady Blue said. 'Always giving to charity, trying to help those less fortunate than himself.'

'Spirits have the highest aspirations,' Madame said. 'Whatever they were like on earth, those qualities are doubled, even tripled, after death. I find this time and time again.'

'I must take further advice,' said Lady Blue.

'Of course, dear lady,' Madame said. 'But when all is said and done, remember your husband's specific words . . .' Madame looked at George, who glanced down at what he had written.

'Regarding the solicitors, he said you must insist on having what you want,' George said.

'Especially if you want him to come to you again,' put in Madame.

'What do you mean?'

'Just this,' said Madame gently. 'I find that if those left on earth fail to carry out the wishes of those on the Other Side, then the spirits are most reluctant to attend them after.'

Lady Blue's eyes filled with tears; the handkerchief was utilised once more. 'You mean that my husband might not want to communicate with me again?'

'Oh, let's not be hasty!' Madame said. 'It's just that sometimes – when the spirits realise their wishes are being ignored – they feel there's little point in returning to give advice.'

'I see.'

'But we've all been cooped up here too long,' Madame said, 'and I'm about to send George into Regent's Park to enjoy the sight of the beautiful shimmering water of the boating lake.'

'Yes . . . yes,' said a distracted Lady Blue.

'Keep your husband's words in your head,' said Madame. 'I hope – if you trust in what your heart tells you – we'll see you here again very soon.'

Chapter Eleven

In Which Velvet and George
Share Some of Their Secrets

Geeorge and Velvet entered Regent's Park through the ornate, wrought-iron gates and, as they did so, George raised his boater and offered Velvet his arm. It was the afternoon following the materialisation of the Fortesque baby, and they were taking a walk in the park amidst the happy families, courting couples and well-dressed gentlemen. Boys in sailor suits rode hobby horses, nannies pushed perambulators and little girls in white petticoats bowled hoops along the pathways. Everyone seemed pleased to be out in the sunshine. Except for Velvet, who pretended not to see George's proffered arm, but instead concentrated on putting up the pink parasol that Madame had lent her.

'Velvet, please,' George said. 'I can explain.'

'There's nothing to say,' Velvet replied. Having fled from the front room, she had spent a sleepless night, most of it at her window, gazing out at the moon and feeling desperately miserable. Sissy Lawson and George! How *could* he?

She wouldn't have come out with him at all, except that Madame had insisted that – it being such an unexpectedly lovely day – her two favourite people, as she called them, should take the air. She was only sorry she couldn't join them, but she had some important business to attend to after a client's visit that morning. Had she somehow sensed the atmosphere between George and herself, Velvet wondered, and wanted them to make up? Well, it wasn't going to happen! If George thought that just because he had sea-green eyes and gave all the old ladies the vapours, he could play her off against Sissy Lawson, then he was quite wrong.

'Velvet, she means nothing to me!' George went on. 'It's always been you. When I kissed you, it was something I'd been longing to do ever since you first arrived at Madame's with your little brown paper bag.'

There had only been two kisses between them, Velvet thought. She'd been a fool to think that they amounted to anything.

'Please speak to me, Velvet.' George sat down on a seat and pulled her down beside him. 'How will we work together if you're going to be like this?'

'I have no idea,' Velvet said coldly.

'Look, let me explain.'

'Please don't bother.' Velvet wondered what on

earth she was going to do. How would she cope if Sissy Lawson and George began walking out together? What if they became betrothed ... married? She couldn't bear it. She would have to leave Madame's!

'I can explain.' He tried to turn Velvet around to face him, but she wouldn't budge. 'Sometimes one has to do things one really doesn't want to. You understand that, don't you?'

'No,' Velvet said. One did not kiss someone in the dark when one really did not want to. 'I saw you!' she burst out. 'I couldn't believe it. I saw you with her – you were kissing. Not that that's any business of mine and of course you must kiss whoever you like, but don't think you can make up to me as well.'

'My dearest Velvet –'

'Don't call me that! Is *she* your dearest, too?' Velvet asked childishly. 'Is she your dearest Sissy?'

At this, George suddenly jerked back from her as if he'd received a shock. 'Dearest Sissy?' he repeated.

'Or is it darling Sissy? And had you been longing to kiss *her* since the moment she arrived?'

George looked at her steadily before saying with conviction, 'Sissy Lawson means absolutely nothing to me, Velvet. I don't care for the girl in the slightest.'

He actually sounded as if he meant it, Velvet thought. 'It didn't look like that last night,' she said, lips pursed.

'Believe me, it's true. I swear it on my life. I swear

it on the life of the girl I hold most dear.' Saying this, he looked her straight in the eyes. 'You are the only one for me, Velvet.'

Velvet hesitated – he sounded so sincere. 'I don't believe you,' she said nonetheless.

'She flung herself at me, Velvet. She's the most extraordinarily forward girl I've ever met. Why, she hid in the front room in the dark, and practically leaped on me when I went to put on the window locks.'

Velvet gasped, shocked at such a show of vulgarity. 'But surely you could have pulled away or made an excuse or something.'

'Well, at first I didn't react – I was just so astonished and appalled at her behaviour – but then I looked up and saw you and pushed her from me.' George shook his head, his brow furrowed. 'It pains me to say it of one of the fairer sex, but she's a vulgar girl of dubious morals. Ever since Mrs Lawson brought her to work in the house she's been the same. And it's not just me she goes after – have you seen the shameless way she talks to tradesmen?'

'Can't you complain about her behaviour to Madame?'

'How could I do such a thing?' George said. 'It would seem so weak, as if I'm unable to deal with one silly girl on my own. And besides, Mrs Lawson would get involved and then the whole thing would get out of hand.'

Velvet was silent for a long time, wondering how

much she believed. Had the Lawson girl really thrown herself at him in the dark? What might there have been between them in the past, before she came? And what of, just a moment ago, when he'd looked at Velvet and called her the girl he held most dear? Was that true? How was an inexperienced girl such as she supposed to tell?

They remained sitting together there on the bench whilst people promenaded around them, and Velvet, already more than halfway to forgiving him, could not help wondering if they made a handsome couple. Certainly George was drawing sideways glances from nearly every woman, young or old, who walked by, because he, in his Sunday best – striped blazer, boater and spats over brown-and-white shoes – was easily the handsomest man in the park.

'Please don't spoil everything we have,' George said. His hand reached for hers and squeezed it. 'I've never met anyone like you, Velvet. You and I are surely meant to be together.'

With a lump in her throat, Velvet decided that, yes, she had almost forgiven him.

'You're blushing,' he said, looking at her intently. 'Your cheeks look pink enough to kiss . . .'

'Please!' she protested, pretending to fan herself. 'Such behaviour on a Sunday afternoon.'

George, laughing, got up from the seat and, this time, when he offered his arm, she took it.

'I shall endeavour, as much as I can, to never be

alone with Miss Lawson again,' George said, squeezing her arm against his. 'From now on, we must both be truthful with each other. If she makes a nuisance of herself I'll tell you, and in return you must tell me all your secrets.'

'If you wish,' Velvet said, but immediately thought of the big secret regarding her father's death. Whatever happened, she could not tell George about that. She wanted him to love her and surely he would never love a murderess.

'I say we must be truthful and let's start now. You recall that policeman who took me to the station to identify Aaron?'

'Yes.' Velvet felt a chill run through her.

'Did you know him at all? Because I thought he looked at you in a very warm manner and spoke in a most informal way.'

Velvet hid a little smile. George sounded positively jealous.

'We do know each other,' she admitted. 'At least, we did. Charlie is a friend from my childhood, someone I used to play with in the street.'

'Forgive my asking, but is a friend all that he was to you?'

'Indeed! We went scrambling for pieces of coal together following the cart, vied with each other to see who could get the best stale cakes from the baker and fought to be first in line when the organ-grinder passed the monkey around.'

George looked at her questioningly, head on one side. 'And . . . ?'

She shook her head. 'There was not so much as a kiss between us.' But she suddenly thought of the mock wedding she and Charlie had had when they were about eight. She'd worn her mother's lace petticoat pulled up high under her arms and placed a daisy-chain circlet on her head. Charlie had tried to kiss her, she remembered, but she'd turned her head at the last minute and his lips had landed on her ear. 'It was all very innocent,' she reiterated.

'Although he wishes it was more?'

Velvet shrugged. 'Perhaps he does.' She'd had a train to her 'wedding dress', she recalled: a ragged curtain of Charlie's mother's, which had been knotted in the front and trailed in the mud behind. She could even remember that her mother had smiled to see her dressed so and said, 'One day, Kitty. One day . . .'

'So in that respect he's an unwanted suitor – and a little like Sissy Lawson?'

'Well, yes,' said Velvet.

'Then if he becomes persistent or too annoying, you must tell me and I'll challenge him. I won't have my girl upset or disturbed in any way.'

Velvet, pleased to be called his girl but rather horrified at the thought of him challenging Charlie to a fight, quickly said that she was quite sure it wouldn't come to that, and they walked on.

By the time they returned to Darkling Villa, she had forgiven him entirely – indeed, had convinced herself that there had been nothing to forgive him for. Sissy Lawson was a forward baggage who had instigated the whole business, and Velvet would certainly be watching her like a hawk from now on.

Later that afternoon, Velvet was called to Madame's private apartments and went there wondering, rather nervously, if she'd done anything wrong, for Madame was not usually so formal in her invitations. Had Madame detected the feelings between her and George, perhaps, and wanted to put a stop to things? Had Velvet neglected to pay enough attention to Madame's tiny yapping dog, or had she made a stupid mistake when that morning (for the first time) she'd answered that frightening telephone?

It was none of these.

'My dear girl,' Madame said, 'do sit down and stop looking as though I'm going to eat you.'

Velvet smiled and sat, relaxing a little.

'You've been here several months now and I just want to know if you're still quite happy with us, or if there's anything that might be improved.'

Velvet shook her head. 'Nothing. Nothing at all. I'm very happy.'

'Excellent.' Madame hesitated a moment, then continued, 'You heard some of what poor, dear Mrs Fortesque was saying the other evening.'

'I did,' Velvet said. 'I could hardly believe what she was asking, because surely, *surely*, such a thing could never happen?'

Madame looked reflective. 'Mediums are achieving near miracles nowadays.'

'But *that*.'

'With the help of the spirits, nothing is impossible.'

'That's almost what George says, although he says that with *you*, nothing is impossible!'

'Dear George.' Madame smiled. 'Where would we be without him?'

Velvet smiled as well, flattered by the 'we'.

Madame hesitated once more. 'But you may also have a part to play in the recovery of Mrs Fortesque's child.'

'I?' Velvet stared. Privately, she had been wondering if poor Mrs Fortesque was deranged in some way, perhaps sent crazy by the loss of her child. She'd thought about it and did not, could not, believe that anyone could come back from the dead – but this was precisely what Madame seemed to be saying.

'When the time comes and I call on you to do something important, will you aid me in this great undertaking?'

'Of course,' Velvet said without hesitation, for hadn't she and George taken a vow – sealed with a kiss – that they would do anything for Madame?

Madame seemed more at ease once she had

extracted this promise from Velvet. She showed her a magazine which depicted a new hairstyle she was contemplating, discussed next season's colours with her and said she was thinking of having an ice-cream maker installed in the kitchen.

'We'll serve dishes of ice cream at séances,' she said gaily, 'for we must be à la mode! Mediums are terribly fashionable now, but it's only the youngest and most beautiful who'll thrive. I've already heard a rumour that Conan Doyle is enamoured of Mrs Palladino, and if this is true we must win him back.'

'Who is she?'

'Eusapia Palladino is an Italian peasant,' Madame said somewhat witheringly. 'One who can do as many tricks as a performing horse. According to her supporters, she's able to float in the air, fill a room with flowers, produce the handprints of the dead in wet clay and issue ectoplasm from her body at will!'

'Really?' Velvet marvelled.

'Oh, every day brings forth a new skill from her!'

'But I'm sure that no one could rival you, Madame,' Velvet said, 'whether in skill, in temperament or in beauty.'

'Ah. You're too kind,' Madame said, and she kissed her fingers and wafted the airborne kiss in Velvet's direction.

Madame Savoya's Second Private Sitting with 'Mr Grey'

'My dear Mr Grey,' Madame said, extending a pale, ladylike hand. 'How have you been faring?'

'Not so bad, not so bad,' Mr Grey said, shaking Madame's hand with a little more vigour than she was expecting and holding it longer than she would have liked. 'I've been moving lodgings. Ha, ha! Apartments, I must learn to say. I'm going up in the world, you know. I'm renting something rather grand in Chelsea. I've also ordered three suits from a gentlemen's outfitters and been measured for new false teeth.'

'How nice,' Madame said, managing to withdraw her hand. 'So you are feeling better in yourself?' She surveyed the shape of him. 'I see no improvement in your aura, unfortunately.'

'That'll be because of my terrible wickedness in the past,' he said, winking at her. 'I've started having nightmares, too. The worst nightmares known to man or beast.'

'I'm sorry to hear that,' Madame said.

'Every night is the same. I fall asleep straight away, then immediately start dreaming of the time when my wife was alive. I dream that I'm standing outside our house – oh, what a poor and ramshackle place that was – and she won't let me in. It's snowing and I'm pleading and pleading for her to open the door, but she won't, and the next thing I know I've frozen into a solid lump of flesh, like that puppy I told you about –'

'Mr Grey,' Madame interrupted, 'I am a medium, not a dream interpreter. I cannot tell you what your nightmares mean.'

'Ah. No. Of course not.'

'What Madame can do is try to contact your wife to ask for her forgiveness,' George said. 'Once you know you're forgiven for your past sins, this may bring you peace.'

'So you say,' said Mr Grey. 'It's just that last time I came here it was all very general, if you don't mind me saying – bits and pieces of this, dates and times of that, names of people I'd never heard of. I didn't get a look-in with my wife.'

'I believe this was solely because she was reluctant to appear,' said Madame.

'But who were all those other blighters crowding in? It was like Cheltenham on Gold Cup Day.'

'Mr Grey,' Madame said, 'you must understand that when I first sit for someone, the line through to the one they wish to speak to on the Other Side is often shaky and the link is insecure. It's like the telephone. You are familiar with the instrument called the telephone receiver?'

'Certainly I am. I'm having one in my new apartment.'

'Well, with a telephone sometimes the line is unclear and you hear other voices butting in. People speak and you don't know who they are or what they're doing there.'

'You do! You're right.'

'Then as you grow used to the telephone, you're able to disregard interference on the line.' Madame paused. 'What I'm saying is, the more often I act as a link between you and your wife, the better the connection will become. Even today I'm sure you'll sense a great improvement.'

'Once you can speak directly to your wife and ask her forgiveness for your past sins, then most probably the nightmares will cease,' said George.

'But you may have to come here several times to convince her that you're truly sorry about the way you acted towards her,' added Madame.

'Ah. Right.' Mr Grey clicked his new teeth. 'Now, there's something else I want to say.'

Madame nodded.

'I've got this friend, see, Donald Duffy, a chap I met racing,' said Mr Grey, 'and he told me that it's impossible to speak to the dead. He said spiritualism is a load of baloney; that once someone's in the ground, they're in the ground, and you might as well try and speak to the winning post at Ascot.'

'Did he really?' Madame asked, and even a casual observer might have been able to detect a trace of irritation in her voice.

'He said there are some so-called mediums who are crooked and prey on bereaved people, and that there's a society going around trying to expose them.'

'Mr Grey,' Madame said rather sternly, 'your friend has a right to his opinion, and of course there are dishonest people in the world in all trades and all callings, but perhaps you'll be reassured to know that no less a figure than Arthur Conan Doyle graces my modest evening soirées.'

'Arthur Conan Doyle?' Mr Grey asked, much impressed. 'The author of Sherlock Holmes?'

'That's right. And don't you think a clever and learned man such as he – a doctor and famous writer – might possibly be trusted to know what he's doing? Don't you think that someone with his vast knowledge and experience might be depended upon to distinguish true from false?'

'Ah. Yes.' Mr Grey wriggled uncomfortably in his seat under Madame and George's stern gazes. 'I read one of his stories once. He's quite a clever chap.'

'Will you please relax now, Mr Grey.' Madame closed her eyes. 'With your permission I'll go into trance.'

'Permission granted,' said Mr Grey. 'Conan Doyle. Who'd have thought it?' he muttered. 'Wait till I tell ole Duffy.'

Madame tilted her face towards the heavens. 'I have a gentleman with me who's seeking his wife, who passed over several years ago. He's a very strong-minded gentleman who was, until recently, a children's entertainer and magician. Is his wife there on the Other Side? Will she claim him?'

Mr Grey looked up, too, as if he were trying to see through the ceiling to where the spirits gathered.

'Wait!' Madame said to the ceiling. 'Then, no, I'm afraid it's not you. It's a woman who has been in spirit for more than five years. Yes, you over there, dear, please come forward.'

'Is that her?' Mr Grey asked. 'Is she there?'

Madame spoke above his head. 'Please, dear lady. Don't turn your back.'

'It seems that your wife may not want to speak to you,' George said in a whisper.

'It might not be her,' Mr Grey said, his teeth clicking in his jaw. 'How do you know you've got the right one?'

'Your name, dear? What was your name on earth?' Madame's eyelids fluttered. 'She says her name was Hope. Is that right?'

Mr Grey's mouth dropped open and stayed open. 'Well, how d'you know that? I never told you that, did I?'

'I'm seeing her amidst sheets and towels and washing. Did she work in a laundry?'

'That's her all right,' Mr Grey croaked. 'She took in washing.'

'She worked very hard, she's telling me. Impossibly hard. She had very little free time. She had two sisters named Verity and Patience, but you never liked them and tried to stop her visiting them.'

'That's because we never had no money to spare for trips out,' Mr Grey said, tears of self-pity beginning to form in his eyes. 'Lived from hand to mouth, we did. Crusts was all we had most days. And pickings from the butcher's bins.'

'But . . . but Hope is saying that you, Mr Grey, earned money from your children's parties and she hardly saw it. You wasted it all gambling. She says that she and your little daughter, Velvet, often went hungry because of this.' Mr Grey heaved a sob and Madame went on, 'Hope is telling me now that she came from a good family. She was a governess once and she had a proper education.'

'That's right. An' marrying me was the end of her. Brought her right down, I did.' He sat up straighter in his chair. 'I can see the error of my ways now, though, and I want her to forgive me.'

'Oh. I'm afraid she's turning and walking away,' Madame said.

'She can't just go! Make her come back so I can say sorry.'

'It's too late – she's disappeared,' said Madame.

'The spirits aren't ours to command,' George added under his breath.

Madame slowly opened her eyes and looked at Mr Grey. 'Your wife suffered years of neglect and abuse when she was married to you. You can't expect to come along and have her forgive you all in a moment.'

'No, I suppose not.' Mr Grey sniffed thoughtfully and clicked his teeth several times. 'Wait till I tell ole Duffy what happened here, though,' he said. 'You got the names and everything. Marvellous!'

'I think you need to make recompense for all the times you abused your wife, kept her short of money and let your child go hungry.'

'How can I do that? She's dead.'

'You can give to the needy and the poor now,' Madame said. 'I'll tell your wife how sorry you are and what you've done to make up for it, then perhaps she'll forgive you.'

'What, you want me to go round giving out ten-shilling notes?'

'Not that, Mr Grey. Now, let me think.' Madame was silent for a moment. 'Perhaps you could endow a foundation like . . . The Charity for the Rehabilitation of Washerwomen. George would help you set it up, and you'll be the chief patron. When word gets out, everyone will be very impressed with your compassion and generosity.'

Mr Grey thought for a moment. 'Maybe Arthur Conan Doyle will hear about it . . .'

'Possibly,' Madame said.

'It's the only way you can prove to your wife that you're truly sorry,' said George.

'Right-o then,' said Mr Grey. 'And you'll tell her all about it next time I come here, will you?'

'I will,' said Madame.

The sitting now being at an end, Mr Grey prepared to leave. As George handed him his top hat and they shook hands, however, Mr Grey said, 'I've just thought of something – you got one of the names wrong. My daughter's called Kitty, not that other name.'

'**Kitty?**' Madame asked, looking at George.

George shook his head. 'That's nothing,' he said dismissively, 'just a little disturbance on the spirit line.' He hesitated, then asked, 'And you're not in touch with your daughter at present?'

'No. Kitty thinks I'm dead.'

'Oh?' Madame enquired.

'She thinks I drowned after falling in the canal,' he said. 'I'd had a bit too much to drink, I suppose. I was chasing her and in I went.'

'When was this?'

'Oh, a year or so back. I was that close to drowning, I was, and Kitty never tried to come back to save me! A waterman plucked me out of the canal and cleared my lungs, and then his wife slowly nursed me back to health. I was proper poorly, mind you – caught a fever from the fetid water and it took four or five months before I was back to normal.'

'And then what happened?' Madame asked.

'When I got back on my feet, I discovered I'd missed my own funeral! Some other cove – an old tramp – had fallen in the canal round about the same time and he'd been fished out, dead as a doorknocker. The neighbours all thought it was me.'

'How very odd,' said Madame.

'I never spoke up because it rather suited me to start over again. I owed money to the landlord as well as the bookies, y'see. I moved away and changed my appearance. When I eventually decided to go racing again, it was like fate agreed with what I'd done, because I won all that money.'

'So,' Madame asked delicately, 'have you never thought of trying to find your daughter?'

Mr Grey shook his head. 'Wherever she is, she's probably dancing on my grave – or what she thinks is my grave.' He blew his nose heartily. 'Never loved me, she didn't. Maybe if she'd loved me a bit I'd have been a better father to her. Sometimes I lie awake at night and think about how it might have been if –'

'You must excuse me now,' Madame said quickly, 'but please do come and see us again soon. We can then begin to talk to your dear wife about the marvellous charity that you're going to endow.'

George ushered him towards the side door. 'May we wish you a very good day, Mr Grey.'

Chapter Twelve

In Which the Spirits Attend Egyptian Hall

'I believe you already know that my grandmother was a Russian princess – one of the Romanovs,' Madame said to Velvet. 'I grew up with the understanding that I have royal blood in me.'

Velvet nodded. She remembered that from the first evening at Prince's Hall – and to think she was now living and working for this wonderful woman who was almost a princess!

'My grandmother was extremely beautiful – men fought wars for her – but she married an Englishman for love, left Russia and came to live in London. She and my mother both had the Sight, but I was scornful of it until, on my sixteenth birthday, Grandmother spoke to me in a vision.'

She hesitated and Velvet, sitting beside her on a bench in Regent's Park, breathlessly urged her to go on.

'As well as telling me that I would have an

immense and devoted following, she said I must never allow my talents to corrupt me. I should remain chaste and pure, and devote myself to a spiritual life.'

'You did tell me once that you would never marry or have children,' said Velvet, slightly embarrassed at discussing such an intimate topic with her employer.

'Ah, yes.' Madame nodded. 'That is one of the hardships: never to know the love of a good man or have a family of my own.'

'Although – do excuse me for mentioning it – your mother and grandmother obviously had families.'

'But they didn't dedicate their lives to their calling, as I have. Their spirituality, their psychic ability, was sublimated. They did not live by it.'

Velvet nodded that she understood. Uneasy about asking more questions, she reached up, pulled down a rose on a low bough and inhaled its perfume. 'Such a beautiful scent.'

'Your mother loved roses,' said Madame unexpectedly.

'Did she?' Velvet asked in surprise. 'I hardly think of her in terms of loving flowers. We certainly never had any growing in the yard at home.'

'She was just telling me how much she cares for them,' Madame said. Velvet gave a little gasp and Madame looked at her fondly, as if through a mother's eyes. 'Especially roses that are scented and a vivid red, very much like the one you have your nose in now.'

Velvet smiled, deeply touched by the thought that her mother could be watching over her.

'She is very near to you,' Madame went on softly. 'The mother and child relationship is the closest there is, and cannot be severed by death. She cares for you still.'

Velvet felt tears come into her eyes.

'She is saying . . .' Madame frowned a little. 'Oh, she's asking why you've changed your name. She says the name she gave you at birth was Kitty! Can that be true, or have we got a naughty spirit here making mischief?'

Velvet looked at Madame, awestruck. Truly, she was the most brilliant medium in the world. She gathered herself and after a moment said, 'It is true, yes. I wanted to make myself into another person, so I called myself Velvet when I began working at the laundry.'

Madame laughed. 'My spirits never let me down. I can find out all your secrets!' she said. Then she frowned and added quickly, 'No, sir, I cannot speak to you at the present time.'

'Who's that?' Velvet asked.

'How strange are the spirits on the Other Side! Your father is here – I believe he was attracted by the spirit of your mother. But your mother will not tolerate his presence and has disappeared.' She raised her voice slightly. 'I'm sorry, sir. Your attendance here is unwelcome at the moment. Please go back from whence you came.'

Velvet clenched her hands within her lace gloves. Her father had come to make trouble, for sure – to try and incriminate her in his death.

'Ah, he's gone,' Madame said after a moment. 'But your mother has been frightened by him and won't return. Another day, perhaps.' She got up from the bench and opened her parasol. 'Shall we walk to the rose arbour?'

They did so, but the heavy scent of the massed roses there was too overwhelming for the delicate nose of Madame and she decided they should return to Darkling Villa.

'I have a little favour to ask of you,' she said as they turned for home.

'Of course,' Velvet said. 'Anything.'

'You may have heard me and George speaking about an engagement at the Egyptian Hall this Friday.'

Velvet nodded.

'You've attended one of my public sessions before.'

'I have, before I came to work for you,' Velvet said. 'You gave me an invitation to Prince's Hall at Christmas.'

'Of course. Well, it'll be an evening similar to that, with questions written and put into envelopes, and the spirits answering the queries through me.' She paused. 'I don't particularly enjoy these entertainments, but we hold one or two a year, whenever we want to gain new clients. To put it in the vulgar manner it deserves,' she added, 'it's to drum up numbers.'

Velvet, very surprised, said, 'But surely you already have more clients than you can handle?'

'Not really. I have a great deal of commitments, you see; money that I have to set aside for my charities and foundations and committees, also the rental on our beautiful house is rather large.' She smiled and nodded at a passing man who raised his hat to her. 'There are so many mediums competing for business now that, rather sadly, it has become a race – a matter of always keeping ahead, of gaining clients before they can be taken by others.'

'But what a shame that a gift like yours has to be treated in such a way.'

'It is,' Madame agreed. 'But I'd like you to come along and watch us, Velvet.'

'Of course, if you wish,' Velvet said, rather pleased.

'Sometimes the audience can be a bit slow, you see,' Madame explained, 'so it would be helpful if you could lead the applause or do a little cheering if I get something especially accurate.'

Velvet smiled. 'I'd be delighted.'

On Friday, well before six o'clock, the audience for 'The Spirits Speak' began assembling at London's famous Egyptian Hall in Piccadilly.

Madame and George had left the house some time earlier in order that Madame should become familiar and easy with the atmosphere at the venue, but Velvet arrived in a hansom cab a fashionable five minutes late.

None of Madame's regular clients were expected to attend something so populist, but nevertheless Velvet was in disguise. Her dark curls were hidden under a wig of curly fair hair and a headdress of ostrich feathers, and she wore a slightly outrageous gown of Madame's – something she'd told Velvet was left over from her Russian inheritance – in flame-coloured silk, with heavy embroidery and a matching bolero.

Arriving at Egyptian Hall, a remarkable building with columns and sphinxes and lavishly painted decor, Velvet took a seat towards the back and enjoyed looking at what the ladies were wearing, taking pleasure in the knowledge that soon she would be watching George on stage at his magnificent best. Things had been very congenial between them lately; there had been another kiss, many loving looks, and George was behaving in a very cool manner towards Sissy Lawson, at least whenever Velvet was near.

When every seat in the hall had been taken and the audience hushed, George escorted Madame on to the stage. He explained that everyone was going to be given a chance to ask the spirits a question but that, sadly, Madame would not be able to address them all in the time given. People were asked, therefore, to take one of Madame's cards at the door on their way out, and if their question had not been chosen, or they wanted further explanation of an answer given, to get in touch with her privately. Everyone who wanted to do so was then given a moment to write their question on the square of paper left under their seat and put it into an envelope collected by George.

After ten or so minutes, a large basket of envelopes was presented to Madame. An envelope was selected by George and handed to her. Madame closed her eyes for a moment, holding the envelope close to her heart.

'One of the fair sex has asked this question, a stylish lady,' she said on opening her eyes. 'She has asked me to verify the wishes of someone in spirit concerning a piece of jewellery.'

There was a murmur from someone in the audience.

'Who was it who spoke?' Madame peered over the footlights, looking especially beautiful in a black evening gown embroidered all over with dangling crystals. 'I'm afraid I can't see you very well. Could the lights be dimmed a little?'

After the lamps were turned down, Madame looked across the audience. 'If I have summed up the question correctly, could the person who asked it stand up, please?'

Velvet turned to look at the lady who stood up on the other side of the hall. 'I think you're holding my question, Madame Savoya,' she said.

She was a lady in her thirties, Velvet noted, attractive, with slightly prominent front teeth.

'Can you just confirm that we do not know each other in any way, and that you have not asked a question of me before?'

'I confirm it,' the lady said clearly. 'I do not know you, nor have I previously asked a question.'

'Very well.' Madame smiled. 'You asked about a piece of jewellery?'

'Yes, it's –'

'Please don't help me,' Madame said. 'It's glittering and it's green. Is the jewel in question an emerald?'

'Yes!' she exclaimed, and Velvet and several other members of the audience gasped excitedly.

'I think it may be a brooch. No, it's a pendant on a gold chain!'

'That's quite right.'

'And it belonged to a lady who is now on the Other Side. Your aunt?'

'Yes.'

Velvet started the smattering of applause which ran across the theatre.

'She passed over in the month of . . . February.'

'She did.'

'And her name began with a . . . "G". Or perhaps an "O". An unusual name . . . Ori—?'

'Her name was Oriana,' the woman said, smiling.

Led by Velvet, everyone clapped enthusiastically. Velvet craned her neck around in order to see more of the woman who was speaking. Looking at her she frowned, puzzled. There was something vaguely familiar about her . . . something about the way she spoke.

'I shall now concentrate on the question you've asked,' Madame said. 'Your aunt died and . . .' She spoke into the ether. 'Yes, I see. Thank you. Your aunt is here, and she's telling me that she left her daughter most of her jewellery.'

'That's right, but she had always promised me the emerald pendant.'

The lady who was speaking lisped slightly as she spoke, perhaps because of her prominent teeth, and it was this slight speech defect which nudged at Velvet's memory. Where had she heard her before?

'Your aunt says that she left a letter telling her daughter this.' Madame paused and then delivered the final grand disclosure. 'It's hidden in her study, in a secret drawer!'

'Oh! That's wonderful,' said the lady as the applause rang out. 'I shall tell my cousin, and I'm sure she won't keep the emerald from me any longer.'

Velvet suddenly realised where she'd seen the lady: she'd been at the evening of mediumship she had attended with Lizzie. She hadn't asked a question about an emerald then, but about whether she would get married or not, and Madame had given her a very precise answer. How very curious, Velvet thought, still strongly clapping Madame.

'Thank you very much,' the woman said to Madame, whilst Velvet and the rest of the audience continued to applaud and murmur to each other how skilful Madame was. 'I'm most grateful.'

'I'm happy I was able to be of help,' Madame said. When the audience grew quieter, she tore open the envelope and read out the woman's question: *Did my aunt mean me to have her emerald pendant?*

This received more clapping and an amount of cheering.

The next question Madame answered was from a gentleman who didn't know whether to propose to his young lady or not, and then came one from a woman who suspected that a member of her family was stealing from her. As the evening went on, Velvet continued to lead the approbation, but could not stop thinking about the first questioner. It was certainly very puzzling and very odd.

It was some days before she plucked up the courage to ask George if it was just a coincidence that the same young woman had started the questions on two occasions.

George hesitated for some time before he answered. 'Yes,' he said, 'probably just a coincidence.'

'But wasn't it strange that she didn't admit to having asked a question before? Especially as Madame specifically asked her if she had.'

'Oh well, perhaps she thought she would only be allowed to ask one thing.'

'And how could it happen that she was the very first to be answered once more?'

George shrugged. 'Who knows, who knows,' he said dismissively. 'Madame will probably explain it to you some time.'

Velvet, sure that there must be more to it than she'd been told, couldn't bring herself to question George any further in case he became cross – and she certainly didn't dare to ask Madame anything. Besides, it had already occurred to her that she might not want to find out the truth about Madame. She decided, therefore, that she must put the matter out of her mind.

Madame Savoya's Third Private Sitting with 'Mrs Lilac'

*T*he usual greetings and salutations having been exchanged, Mrs Lilac sat down opposite Madame and permitted George to administer the rug.

'How have you been faring, my dear Mrs Lilac?' Madame asked.

'I've been very well, considering,' replied Mrs Lilac. 'And I'm feeling somewhat easier in my mind since I've been able to speak to Mother through you.' She looked around her a little fearfully, as if she thought that lady was lurking nearby, hidden somewhere. 'It suits me to come here to speak to her rather than have you . . .' she laughed nervously '. . . spirit her up at home, so to speak.'

Madame nodded. 'She was a strong woman, your mother. Nothing daunted her, did it? Not even death.'

'Not even death,' Mrs Lilac echoed. She lowered her voice. 'I do adore her jewellery, but I'm only wearing a *little cheap amethyst brooch today because wearing the larger stuff seems to really set her off.'*

'Ah, yes, the jewellery,' Madame said, and a look flashed between her and George. 'If you don't mind, I won't discuss your mother's jewellery with you. I know she's adamant that you shouldn't keep it, but I'd rather not be involved in your decision either way.'

*'That's really gracious of you,' said Mrs Lilac. 'It's been a difficult task trying to make a decision about it. So **very** valuable, you see. I think – hope – that she'll be happy with what I've decided.'*

Madame waited for Mrs Lilac to continue speaking and then, when she did not, closed her eyes briefly. 'Do you wish me to go into trance now?'

'Please do.' Mrs Lilac's expression was nervous, that of someone who was putting a brave face on things.

Madame closed her eyes and seemed to speak to several people before getting through to Mrs Lilac's mother. At one time she said, 'I'm so sorry. You're not the lady whose daughter I have here. Please allow her mother through . . .'

Mrs Lilac swallowed. 'I do hope she won't be in a bad mood.'

'If she is, you can rely on Madame to treat her with the utmost delicacy,' George whispered.

Another few moments went by and then a stern voice said, 'Fuss and bother, fuss and bother! Is that you, Esther?'

'It is, Mother,' Mrs Lilac answered up quickly.

'What do you want this time?'

'Just to converse with you, Mother,' Mrs Lilac quavered, 'and to know that you're quite well.'

'There is no well-being over here. You're either here, or you're not. **Well** doesn't come into it.'

'I hope you're content, then. And I want to tell you what I've decided to do about your jewellery.'

There came a sniff. 'I see you're not wearing anything valuable today.'

'No. I've taken to heart what you told me about its magnetism pulling me to the Other Side, and so I've stopped wearing it. It's all in your big leather jewellery case at home.'

'Good. I'm very glad to hear it.'

'And I've made up my mind to do what you've asked me to do: I will give it all away. Apart from the sapphire necklace, that is. I'm rather fond of that.'

'The sapphire necklace! Sapphires have the strongest magnetism of all. Utterly lethal, they are.'

Mrs Lilac sighed. 'Do you want me to give away everything, then? Every single piece of jewellery that you owned?'

'Well, there's not much point in half measures. As I've told you before, jewels mean nothing in the world over here. It's the light from one's soul that is important, not tricking yourself out in gee-gaws.'

'Yes, Mother.'

'So, are you donating my jewels to the spiritualist church?'

'No. I've thought long and hard about it, Mother, and I want the money raised from their sale to go to Runnymede, the nursing home where you spent your last months.'

There came a scream. 'Not that place! Not that wicked prison you consigned me to. It's a hellhole!'

'Such language, Mother!' said Mrs Lilac. 'Runnymede is a perfectly pleasant place. They were very patient with you when you used to go wandering about, and didn't even mind too much when you threw your meals across the room. They need the money to build a sun room and –'

'Oh!' The exclamation was from Madame and a pause followed. 'I'm afraid your mother's gone, Mrs Lilac,' she said then. 'She just disappeared.'

'What?'

Madame looked about her in a bemused manner. 'Was there an exchange of ideas between you? She seemed most displeased.'

'A slight disagreement, certainly,' George said.

Mrs Lilac sighed, looking defeated. 'I suppose it was my fault, telling her I was giving all the proceeds from her jewellery to Runnymede.' She looked from Madame to George imploringly. 'I know she wanted the money to go to the church, but spiritualism is such a new thing for me, and Runnymede has been going for years and is badly in need of funding, so I thought that would be the sensible thing to do.' Here she broke down and Madame handed her a lace-edged handkerchief.

After a moment she said, 'Can you get her back again, please?'

Madame said, 'I don't know. I'm very tired now – your mother has such a strong character that it exhausts me when she comes through.'

'But if Madame can get her back, what would you say?' George asked. 'How would you improve the situation?'

'Oh, I'll let her have her own way,' Mrs Lilac said, a look of patient resignation on her face. 'She was selfish all her life and seems likely to continue to be so after death. I don't know why I thought things might change.'

'So do you intend to follow your mother's wishes and give the jewellery into the care of the church?' Madame asked, choosing her words carefully.

Mrs Lilac shrugged. 'If I'm not able to wear the jewellery because of the magnetism then it doesn't really matter what happens to it, and if that's what she wants . . .'

There was a pause. 'Shall I advise you on how to proceed, in that case?' Madame enquired.

Mrs Lilac sighed and nodded, a defeated woman.

'I'll speak to your mother – I'll do my absolute best to get through to her – and tell her of your change of heart, whilst George here helps you draw up a legal Deed of Transfer. You'll then be able to pass all your mother's wealth to the church, with me as a go-between.'

'Very well,' Mrs Lilac said. 'And I suppose they may

216

as well have the sapphires, too – and even this little amethyst.' She unpinned the purple brooch, put it on the small table and gave a sigh. 'Then do you think she'll be pleased with what I've done?'

'My dear Mrs Lilac, I'm sure that she will,' Madame said, and she gave Mrs Lilac's hand a comforting squeeze.

Chapter Thirteen

In Which Two Young Ladies
Attend a Séance

Velvet caught Lizzie's eye and gave her the trace of a smile. What a night *this* was turning out to be. Not only were they the youngest – and perhaps the prettiest – girls in the room, but they had been toasted with champagne by two well-dressed young gentlemen who seemed very keen to further their acquaintance. And, Velvet thought, even though she was mad about George, it did a girl the power of good to know that when one raised one's eyes there was a gentleman standing opposite, all ready to give her a flirtatious wink.

Velvet and Lizzie were attending an evening of mediumship at the villa of Mrs Eusapia Palladino, who had rented a house in Chelsea for the season. Madame Savoya, anxious to know what her rival was up to, had asked Velvet to attend and suggested that she take a friend with her. Together they were to act the part of two young ladies attending their first séance – and as long as they acted modestly and kept their voices down, Velvet hoped they could pass as such.

It was mostly, she thought, those at the very peak of sophisticated society who attended Mrs Palladino's evenings. Hardly anyone behaved as if they were bereaved, and the evening of mediumship seemed born less of a desire to contact the Other Side and more of a wish for a congenial evening of gossip. Whilst waiting to go into the main room, Velvet and Lizzie heard several scandalous rumours about the new king and his mistresses, some fears voiced about the Whitechapel Murderer and whether he might, even now, strike again, and the latest news on the utterly amazing feats of Harry Houdini.

Lizzie had been eager to come with her and even more eager to borrow one of Velvet's outfits for the occasion. That afternoon, Madame and George both being busy at an accountant's office, the two girls had had a high time trying on gowns and hats and mantles in Velvet's room. Velvet had ended up in her clover-pink outfit; Lizzie was wearing watered silk in a pretty pale green.

The first thing Velvet had wanted to do on meeting her friend that afternoon was to dispel any awkwardness about the situation regarding Charlie. Once Lizzie had been taken on a tour of Darkling Villa and gasped admiringly at everything, Velvet began discreetly with 'I know you're probably walking out regularly with Charlie now, but –'

Lizzie had interrupted her with a sigh. 'We're not really,' she said. 'In fact, not at all. Since he moved to his new beat I've hardly seen him.'

Velvet stopped, surprised. She'd been about to say, in as open and generous a way as possible, that – as far as she was concerned – it was quite all right for Lizzie to continue seeing Charlie and she shouldn't feel in the least bit bad about it.

'I don't know why he doesn't visit now,' Lizzie continued with another sigh. 'Pa says it's because he's doing shift work, but Ma says he only ever came round to talk about you.'

'Oh!' said Velvet. She realised she should have felt irritated by this news but, strangely, only felt pleased.

'Have you not seen him either?'

Velvet shook her head. 'Hardly. Apart from when he came round to see George.'

'That's what you wanted, though, isn't it? For him to leave you alone?'

After a moment, Velvet nodded. 'It *is* what I wanted. Although I hoped we could remain friends.'

'George, though! What a catch for a girl. Has he declared himself?'

Velvet hesitated another moment. 'Not exactly, but I think he loves me.' She bit her lip. She wasn't sure of this; how was a girl supposed to know without being told? She loved him, of course. Yes, she was almost certain that she loved him.

'There! We are both unsure about these young men, aren't we?' Lizzie said. Then she added (for she had just read a desperately sad love story in a magazine), 'The path to love is a stony one, is it not?'

'It is,' Velvet agreed, and then looked at Lizzie trying on a fur hood back to front so that it covered her face, and they both dissolved into giggles.

When Eusapia Palladino entered the room where the séance was to be held, Velvet knew that Madame would be pleased to have it confirmed that her rival was no beauty, but a sturdy, rather homely-faced woman. She was dressed in one of that season's newest fashions – a gown with huge lace-bedecked puffed sleeves – which unfortunately made her look even more sturdy. She took her place at a large round table and gestured for everyone – fourteen people in total – to join her.

There were some formalities to go through first: a woman checked Mrs Palladino over for anything that might be concealed about her person and then her feet were tied to the legs of the chair she was sitting on, so that she couldn't move them or lift the table. (Madame had told Velvet that this might be expected, for Mrs Palladino had, apparently, been accused of fraud several times in the past.)

A male attendant, the equivalent of George (only nowhere near as handsome, Velvet and Lizzie agreed), locked the door, lowered the black blinds and pulled the drapes. The room was now only lit by one tall wax candle standing on a sideboard at the back.

There being no piano in the room and thus no hymn singing nor recital, Mrs Palladino went into action straight away, asking what she termed 'a vast number of spirits anxious to speak' to please get themselves in line and wait their turn; she would receive them as soon as she was able. She asked everyone to touch hands around the table and to take particular note that her own hands were also touching the person on each side of herself.

'If, at any time, anyone believes that the chain of hands around the table is broken,' Mrs Palladino said, 'would that person call out immediately.' She paused. 'I'm now going to enter a trance state.'

For some moments there was complete silence in the room and then Velvet heard a *tap-tap-tap* on the table, which brought a startled gasp from Lizzie next to her.

'Don't be alarmed,' Mrs Palladino said in her ordinary voice. 'These are just my spirits letting me know they're arriving.'

More tapping ensued. At first it was like finger-nails and then it became more of a thump, as if a fist was being banged down hard.

'Someone sounds very displeased!' Mrs Palladino said, and two or three people around the table laughed.

The table then buckled, as if it had been picked up and tilted, and Mrs Palladino asked the spirits to please be careful as she didn't want anyone harmed at her séance.

There were more silent moments, then a trumpet sounded somewhere in the room, followed by a bugle call. To Velvet's amazement she then saw these instruments floating above the centre of the table, glowing in the darkness with a strange luminescence. Several flowers flew across the heads of the guests and landed, with a scattering of petals, in the table's centre, and then came a few oranges, two of which rolled past Velvet, off the table and on to the floor, so that Velvet had to force herself not to break the circle and go after them. She tried to peer through the gloom and work out from which direction all these things were appearing, but the almost complete darkness in the room made this impossible.

There was further tapping and Mrs Palladino commanded, 'Spirits! Please let us have more proof that you are truly with us.'

Velvet felt something brush across her head, but whether it was a draught of air, a hand or a spirit, she couldn't have said.

A woman screamed in the darkness that she had

felt a hand stroking her cheek, and a male voice – the young man who had winked at her, Velvet thought – was heard to say that someone had patted him on the head.

'There's someone behind me!' another person called. 'I felt a hand on my shoulder.'

Velvet felt Lizzie wriggle in her seat. 'I'm scared,' Lizzie whispered to her.

'It's all right. This sort of thing always happens,' Velvet whispered back, trying to sound brave when she wasn't at all. The truth was that she was used to Madame's ways and of the methods she employed to get in touch with spirits, but had no experience of musical instruments playing by themselves, or of floating hands stroking her cheek.

'I'll try to materialise one of my spirits,' said Mrs Palladino. 'I'll call up a will-o'-the-wisp, which is a type of faery that often comes to speak to me.' She began whistling softly, an eerie sound in the dark room, and suddenly there appeared, dancing above the table, a little swirl of white, bobbing and turning this way and that.

'Oh, I don't like it!' Lizzie squealed.

Velvet, rather terrified herself, was trying to think of something comforting to say when a light flared in the darkness. One of the young gentlemen had lit a match!

The faery disappeared and in the half-light Velvet looked towards Mrs Palladino, seeing immediately that her gloved right hand was lying in her lap covered by a white silk scarf. Her left hand was still flat on the table, but the man and woman to each side of her both touched this same hand with their own, thus leaving Mrs Palladino's right hand completely free to throw flowers, brandish trumpets, stroke cheeks and the like. An uncomfortable thought suddenly came into Velvet's mind: if, during the first proper séance she'd attended at Darkling Villa, Madame had had a hand free, it would have been the simplest thing in the world for her to reach under the table for flowers which she'd hidden previously, and throw them into view.

'Mrs Palladino, I'm very much afraid that you've been found out!' said the other young gentleman. He reached across the table, lifted the square of white silk by one corner and flicked it about. 'Here is your "will-o'-the-wisp"! It's nothing more than your black-gloved hand holding a silk scarf.' He moved to the window to raise one of the blinds. 'The Society for Psychical Research will be very interested to hear of this séance,' he concluded.

Much to Velvet and Lizzie's wonder, the evening then descended into chaos, with Mrs Palladino answering her accusers by fainting clean away and having to be carried from the room by her young assistant and a maid, and her clients, incredulous and appalled, hailing cabs to go home.

*

'It was utterly shocking,' Velvet reported to Madame later, in her private sitting room. 'It became clear that she had had one hand free the whole time, and when they looked under the table, both her legs – previously tied up – were also free. They said that she'd been lifting the table with her knees.'

'So there were two members of the Society for Psychical Research there?' Madame asked.

'Those devils are appearing everywhere these days,' George said, frowning.

'They just looked like two ordinary young gentlemen,' Velvet said. 'It was one of them who lit the match. They said afterwards that they'd had several reports that Mrs Palladino was acting dishonestly once more, and were hoping they might expose her. They're going to report her to the authorities this morning.' Velvet shook her head wonderingly. 'I was completely taken in, especially by the bugle and trumpet.'

'Ah,' Madame said. 'That's a well-known trick – holding wind instruments painted with luminous paint with your free hand, and blowing into them to make sounds. And getting the person on each side of you to hold the same hand is a very old trick indeed.'

Velvet, rather taken aback at Madame's composure in the light of the revelations about Mrs Palladino, said, 'Excuse me for saying this, but you don't seem at all startled by anything I've told you.'

Madame shook her head. 'There's always some

fraud or other being perpetrated by so-called mediums.' Her eyes shone as she spoke, as if challenging Velvet to dare ask if *she* had ever done such a thing. On Velvet certainly not daring to do so, she added, 'Cheating is especially prevalent in London, where there are so many of us and each medium is trying to prove they're more gifted than the next.'

'I see.' Velvet found she could not meet Madame's eyes.

'It may be, of course, that Mrs Palladino is a true and talented medium who just occasionally uses her wits to aid her clairvoyance.'

'Yes . . .'

'As we know, sometimes the spirits need a helping hand.'

Velvet did not say any more, but could not help wondering what would happen if no one ever helped the spirits and they were left to their own devices.

It was two days later that Madame came upstairs to Velvet's room, quite early, before she'd even finished dressing. Madame had never been to her room before and Velvet was not quite sure how she should act; if she should speak to her at the door, or allow Madame to come in and sit on the bed.

But Madame decided this point for herself, stepping over some shoes and sitting down on the window seat. 'I dare say you're very surprised to see me this early in the morning.'

Velvet nodded, hurriedly doing up her buttons.

'I fear I've had a very disturbed night. There's something urgent I need to speak to you about.' Madame looked at her searchingly. 'My dear, I'm loath to say this, but I believe you haven't been altogether honest with me.'

Velvet, feeling the blood drain from her face, wondered what on earth Madame was going to accuse her of. 'I don't know what you mean,' she protested. 'I've always tried to tell the truth in all my dealings and have never touched anything of yours that I shouldn't have. You're always so generous anyway that I wouldn't dream of taking anything that wasn't mine.'

'No, you misunderstand me,' Madame said. 'It's not stealing which I want to speak about; stealing is comparatively straightforward and can be dealt with quite easily. What I mean is that you've been dishonest by not telling me of the terrible circumstances surrounding the death of your father.'

Velvet sat down heavily on her bed. How much did Madame know? And *how* did she know it? 'Please, it's not that I tried to deceive you . . . But how did you find out?'

'I found out because I'm a medium, and your father's spirit came to tell me of it.'

Velvet began to shake.

'He told me about the night you defied him, and the chase, and how he fell in the canal. He said he screamed for you to come and help him, but you didn't, although you knew the water was very deep and icy cold. In effect, you let him drown, wouldn't you say?'

Velvet fought the urge to cry. 'Yes, and I know I should have helped, but I despised him! They say it's wicked to hate your parents, but I hated him for how he'd treated my mother and all the awful things he'd done over the years.'

'Your father says that your ignoring his call for help was tantamount to manslaughter,' Madame said. 'This puts me in a very difficult position.'

Velvet held her breath. What could she mean?

'I rely on the spirits for my living,' Madame continued. 'And you rely on these same spirits for *your* living. This is why we must always be honest with each other. The spirits hate deception, lies and double-dealing. If we lie to the spirits, they will lie to us.'

Velvet looked at her, heart in mouth, wondering what was coming next.

'You should have told me of these circumstances before now.'

'I . . . I know, but . . .'

Velvet couldn't say any more for a sudden terrible fear that Madame was about to cast her out on to the streets, that she would lose her job, her lovely room, her clothes – and George.

'But I can hardly believe you are capable of real deceit, Velvet.'

'No, indeed I am not,' Velvet pleaded. 'I love working for you and love everything about living here. Please let me stay! I'll always tell you the absolute truth from now on.'

'And help me in all my endeavours?'

Velvet nodded vehemently. 'Of course! I'd do anything for you.'

Madame got up from the window seat and clasped Velvet's hand. 'Then I shall speak to the spirit of your father on your behalf, and ask forgiveness.'

'Oh please, if you could,' Velvet said. 'The matter has been much on my mind.'

'And so we shall be friends now,' Madame said, 'and never speak of these things again.'

Madame Savoya's Third Private Sitting with 'Lady Blue'

'*H*ow well you look, Lady Blue,' Madame Savoya said. 'There's quite a spring in your step and a twinkle in your eye.'

'Thank you very kindly,' said Lady Blue. 'I must admit that since I've been coming to you and speaking to Bertie I have felt more like my old self.' She smiled at George. 'George here has been most helpful. He's taken me to the solicitors in town several times and read through the legal niceties with me. He's even advised me on matters concerning the motor car Bertie bought just before he . . . before he –'

'Passed peacefully to the Other Side,' proffered Madame quickly.

'I feel it's the least I can do,' George said to Lady Blue. 'To tell you the truth, I'm rather embarrassed to be the recipient of such a large amount of money. I can scarce believe it even now.'

'Dear boy!' said Lady Blue, patting George's knee.

'Didn't Bertie say – in this very room – that he would rather someone like you had it than have it disappear in taxes and trifles?'

George shrugged. 'I know, but . . .'

'But nothing!' said Lady Blue gaily. 'You shall have Bertie's money and that will make him happy. When I die you shall have mine, too.'

George spread his hands out and shook his head in wonder, as much as to say that Lady Blue was incorrigible but there was nothing he could do about it.

'Did you mention a motor car?' Madame asked.

Lady Blue nodded. 'And what a nasty, noisy thing it is. I can't abide it! It needs to be cranked to get started and – well! – however am I supposed to do something like that?'

'I'm sure George will help you.'

'George can have the thing!' Lady Blue said. 'I've told him so. Take it and be done with it. It stinks of petroleum – horrific! Give me the smell of plain old horse dung any time.'

Madame and George joined in with her laughter, then Madame grew more serious and asked if Lady Blue was ready to speak to her husband.

'Oh, I am,' said Lady Blue, 'because I know he's going to be so pleased with me.'

It did not take long for Lord Blue to appear before Madame, and yes, he did seem remarkably pleased with what his wife was about to do with his money.

'It's very satisfying to find that you've taken my

advice, dear,' came the deep, strong voice of Lord Blue.

'I listened to you when you were alive, and I shall listen to you after death,' said Lady Blue. 'The solicitors were rather surprised, mind you, but they came round in the end when I told them it had been your express wish.' Lady Blue dropped her voice a little. 'I didn't tell them that you'd communicated this wish in spirit, however, for I didn't think legal men would understand such things.'

'Quite,' replied Lord Blue. 'And more fool them.'

'The paperwork has been completed and everyone has signed,' said Lady Blue. 'It just remains for the money to be drawn down from your bank.'

'Jolly good,' said Lord Blue. 'And the question of the title can come later.'

'Of course,' said Lady Blue, looking at George in a new, fond light.

'We'll see how this young man gets on first, eh, what? I shall be watching over him and making sure he invests my money in the right funds!'

Lady Blue and George smiled at each other.

'My dear Ceci,' said Lord Blue, 'you look like a young girl today. Just the way you were when we first met.'

'Oh, Bertie, do you remember that? Our first meeting?'

'At your coming-out ball, wasn't it?'

'It was at my friend Lucy Bonneville's birthday party!' She smiled. 'But you never have been able to remember important dates. I don't suppose you even remember our wedding anniversary!'

No reply came to this and Lady Blue laughed, then said to Madame, 'This may be rather a strange question, but can you tell me how Bertie is dressed as he stands before you? Only, he was buried in his regimental uniform and it was rather small for him, so I wonder if he's quite comfortable.'

Madame's eyelashes fluttered. 'Spirits aren't attired as such,' she said.

Lady Blue looked shocked. 'You mean they are . . . **naked**?'

'No, they're draped in white. A haze surrounds them.'

'Oh, of course,' Lady Blue said. 'A haze. Most appropriate.'

'The Brighton villa,' said Lord Blue suddenly. 'You're passing the deeds over to George, aren't you?'

'I am,' Lady Blue said. 'That's what you wanted, isn't it?'

'Of course. He'll no doubt get married some day and have a family who'll use it. No point in it sitting there empty.'

'No point at all,' echoed Lady Blue.

George made a slight noise of protest but both Lord and Lady Blue insisted, so he held up his hands in a gesture of surrender and whispered that it was very, very generous – too generous – but of course he would accept the villa if that was what they really wanted.

Chapter Fourteen

In Which Velvet Has to
Prove Her Loyalty

'The time has come to prove yourself to me and to show your commitment to our cause,' Madame said to Velvet. They were in Madame's private sitting room, she sitting on one side of the fireplace with Velvet facing her on the other side.

Velvet bit her lip, wondering what was going to be asked of her. Since their conversation a few days before, she had been careful – even more so than usual – to be polite and respectful to her employer at all times. In the London streets she could see countless impoverished young people in rags, begging, sleeping in doorways and prostituting themselves in order to obtain food and shelter, and she knew that the fall from rich to poor was short and permanent. If Velvet had any doubts about the veracity of Madame's calling at this point, then she did not allow herself to consider them further, or to question the rights and wrongs of the profession she was involved in. She loved Madame, who had saved her from the laundry and much else – and she loved George. She would do everything she could to stay with them.

'Yes, Madame,' Velvet replied rather nervously. 'What is it you want of me?'

'I want you to help me with a very special task: to help Mrs Fortesque recover her lost child.'

Velvet stared at Madame in wonder. *Lost* child? she thought. It was surely more than just lost. She nodded, however, for she didn't want to look as if she doubted Madame's capabilities. 'And ... and how will that come about, Madame?'

'We will recover the child. Or at least, we will recover *a* child.'

Velvet frowned, looking at the arrangement of orange lilies and golden sunflowers in the fireplace and trying to work out what Madame could possibly be speaking about. 'Do you mean the child will develop from ectoplasm?'

Madame shook her head. 'No. I know that no power on earth could make that happen.'

'Then how?'

There was a pause. Madame said, 'May I speak to you in complete confidence, Velvet?'

'Of course, Madame. Nothing that you say to me will ever go any further.'

The pause this time was much longer and Madame

looked at Velvet steadily, as if weighing her up. 'The life of a medium is a difficult one,' she said at last. 'One is constantly trying to come up with new ways of communicating with those on the Other Side, of proving one is as capable and competent as the newest medium in town, of trying to go that little bit further than the one before.'

Velvet nodded. She had certainly picked up that much from her visits to Miss Cook and Mrs Palladino.

'It's fearfully expensive to live the life one's expected to lead, because a medium's house, her clothes, jewellery and accoutrements are seen as measures of her success. The richer the living, the more talented the medium. No one wants to visit a medium whose skills have only bought her a room in a run-down lodging house.'

'I can see that, Madame.'

'So one has to try and keep ahead of the field, as it were.'

Velvet nodded.

'My dear, I am going to ask you to do something which may shock you.' There was a long, long pause, and then Madame said, 'I want you to steal a baby. A child for Mrs Fortesque.'

Velvet almost smiled, thinking she must be joking, but Madame continued intently, 'Never fear. It'll be an unwanted baby . . . a baby that no one will miss.'

'A – a real baby?' Velvet stuttered.

'Precisely,' said Madame.

'But . . . but how will we get it? And anyway, it won't be Mrs Fortesque's baby! We'll be deceiving her, won't we?'

Madame sighed. 'Velvet, you and I haven't had the experience of having a child of our own, but – as you know from your mother's spirit, which watches you still – the maternal bond is like no other. Poor, grieving Mrs Fortesque wants her child back most dreadfully, and it's doing her an act of supreme kindness to reunite her with that child.'

'But it won't be her child!' Velvet blurted out before she could adjust her manner of speaking. 'And surely she'll know it's not hers.'

'She won't. I'll tell her that the child has been changed somewhat by its time on the Other Side. The poor woman is so desperate to have Claire back in her arms that she'll believe anything.'

Velvet put her hands to her head, trying to understand. 'The spirits, though – what will they have to say about that?' she asked. 'And what about the messages you received from the spirit of the real Claire?' There was something else which had been troubling Velvet and now came to the fore. 'Excuse me for saying so, Madame, but Mrs Fortesque's child died when she was no more than a babe in arms, so how could she have spoken as she did that evening?'

'Those were messages from the child's mind,' Madame answered straight away. 'The words she would have said had she been able to talk.'

'Then they weren't true?'

'Of course they were true, my dear. They were what her spirit said to me.'

'And . . . and what about the evening when the child actually began to take form? I saw her!'

Madame shrugged. 'Just between us, I'll tell you that it has proved impossible for materialisation to go any further. Which is why I'm asking you to do this now.'

'But . . . but it doesn't seem . . .' Velvet could not finish the sentence, because whatever word she used – truthful, right, ethical? – it would have sounded like an insult to Madame.

'Mrs Fortesque is so distraught that, without her child, she'll surely take her own life,' Madame said. She paused and then added softly, 'But you have doubts about what I'm doing?'

Velvet swallowed and hesitated. Of course she had doubts! But how could she voice them?

'We all have our little indiscretions, do we not? Our little transgressions from what we know to be right.' Madame stared upwards, beyond the ceiling. 'You have the death of your father on your conscience, for instance.'

Velvet dipped her head. Madame's meaning was clear: her will must be done, or it would be the worse for Velvet. Some would have called it black-mail. 'No, I have no doubts, Madame,' she lied.

There was a pause, and when Madame spoke again, her slightly intimidating tone had disappeared, making Velvet wonder if she had imagined it. 'Besides, my spirits have informed me that the soul of little Claire will go into the new child, the child that you'll choose, so it won't be stealing, but merely putting things right.'

'I see,' Velvet said, and suddenly wondered what Charlie might have had to say about this 'putting things right'. Mediums had never been rated very highly in his list of trustworthy persons.

'My dear,' said Madame, 'as you know, sometimes the spirits need a helping hand. All will be well, I assure you.'

'Yes, Madame.'

'Just think, we'll be making everyone happy, and Mrs Fortesque will pay me such a very large sum of money that our stay in this house – yours, mine and George's house – will be guaranteed for at least another five years. I hope that by then we'll be working together on stage. Two attractive lady mediums will certainly draw in the gentlemen!'

Velvet barely heard this last prediction, so focused was she on asking her next question. 'But if I might ask something, Madame?'

'Of course.'

'What will Mrs Fortesque tell her friends and

relatives about the reappearance of the baby? Won't it seem strange to others, to unbelievers, that a child can come back from the dead?'

'That's easily resolved,' Madame said. 'Mrs Fortesque has already told me that, should this near miracle occur, she'll tell everyone that the new child has been adopted by her from an orphanage. Nothing could be more natural than that she should seek to replace the child who died.'

Velvet shivered, trying not to think about the fact that she had been ordered to steal a baby. 'When must I take the infant, Madame?'

'Tomorrow.' *Tomorrow.*

'And where will I find it?' she said to Madame.

'I'll give you the address and final instructions in the morning.'

Whilst Velvet sat, stunned, trying to come to terms with what she had to do and wondering what would happen if she got caught, Madame took off the amethyst brooch she had been wearing and pinned it on to Velvet's lilac satin waistcoat.

'A present,' she said. 'To show how much I appreciate your help, and to mark the beginning of our closer collaboration.'

Velvet looked at the brooch and gasped. 'Oh, but I couldn't!'

'You must!' Madame's eyes hardened and sparkled like the gem she held. 'The colour perfectly complements your waistcoat.' She gestured towards the door to signal that their interview was at an end. 'It belonged to a great-aunt of mine, a Russian tsarina.'

Velvet rose and curtseyed low. 'Then I thank you very much indeed, Madame.'

Leaving Madame's presence, she looked down at the brooch. It was very pretty and was possibly worth a good deal of money – but oh, just think of what she was going to have to do to earn it. Velvet ran to her room, lay down on her bed and wept.

Madame Savoya's Third Private
Sitting with 'Mr Grey'

*A*fter 'Good morning's, handshakes and enquiries as to one's health had been given and received all round, Madame bade Mr Grey sit down.

'Have you thought any more about the advice I gave you?' she asked.

'The idea about starting a charity for washer-women,' George added.

'Yes, I have,' said Mr Grey. 'I've thought long and hard about it, and I'm going to do it.' He poked George lightly in the ribs. 'I've had another win, too – that helped decide me. Talk about money to money, eh?'

'Allow me to congratulate you,' said George.

'You see, the spirits are rewarding your philanthropy,' said Madame.

Mr Grey looked puzzled for a moment, then obviously decided that 'philanthropy' must be a good thing, for he nodded.

'Good always comes from doing good,' said George.

'Well, I suppose it's about time I started doing some,' said Mr Grey, 'seeing as I've spent most of my life being bad. I was an utter cad to my wife – I've told you about that, haven't I?'

'Yes, you –'

'An utter scoundrel and rotter!' Mr Grey elaborated. 'One year the wife –'

'Hope,' Madame corrected.

'Yes. Hope. Well, one Christmas she saved up some of her laundry money to buy Kitty a real china doll. Jointed, it was, with a porcelain face. She sat it in the top of a stocking and pinned it up over the fireplace.'

Madame glanced at George, who gave the faintest roll of his own eyes heavenwards.

'But when I came in a bit the worse for wear on Christmas Eve I took that little dolly from its Christmas stocking and went straight to the pawnshop with it. Non-stop to Uncle's, I went! Ain't that the wickedest thing you've ever heard?'

Madame and George were both silent.

'We didn't have no Christmas to speak of that year. Y'see, I'd already taken the leg o' pork back to the butcher's, so we had nothing but tatties.' Tears started in his eyes. 'Oh, when I think of the terrible cruel things I've done. One year our Kitty had a pet rabbit and I put it in the pot with a couple o' turnips!'

There was an appalled silence until Madame said, 'Come, come, Mr Grey! Let's forget the past and concentrate on the future, shall we? You've resolved to turn over a new leaf, you're going to start a wonderful charity and subsequently your wife will forgive you. Your life is improving all the time.'

'You're one of the very few lucky people who can – with our help – rewrite the past and start again,' said George, handing him a handkerchief and bidding him wipe his eyes.

'That little rabbit, though,' said Mr Grey, unwilling to give up the subject. 'White and fluffy it was, with brown whiskers as long as a cat's –'

'Mr Grey, I'm now going into trance,' Madame interrupted. After a moment she said quite briskly into the ether, 'I'm seeking Hope, the wife of the gentleman before me. Hope passed through this vale of tears some years ago and is now on the Other Side. Hope, can you come before us again? Are you willing to speak to the man who was once your husband?'

'Have you got her? Will she talk?' Mr Grey asked eagerly, and George put a finger to his lips to quieten him.

'Spirits, can you help?' Madame intoned.

Mr Grey beckoned to George and whispered in his ear, 'Have you had Conan Doyle around lately?'

George frowned and again put his finger on his lips. ''Spect he's busy, what with those detective stories.'

Madame's eyes remained closed. 'Ah . . . here she is at last. You won't hear her voice, though. She'll only speak through me.'

'I'm not surprised at that,' said Mr Grey. 'She hates me and who could blame her?'

'Please, Mr Grey,' protested George.

'I've been a wicked old devil all my life!'

'Your husband is truly sorry for the way he treated you and your daughter,' Madame said into the air. 'He wishes to make recompense for this and is prepared to give some of his newly acquired fortune towards setting up a foundation, a charity to aid washerwomen and laundresses who have fallen on hard times.' Madame listened for a while, then nodded. 'Hope says that to make sure that you actually do what you say, she wants you to carry out all the negotiations through George and myself. She says that too often in the past you made promises which you never kept.'

'Fair enough, fair enough,' Mr Grey said, peering all around Madame as if hoping to catch a glimpse of his wife.

'She wants you to sign the paperwork before you leave us.'

Mr Grey nodded absently. 'And then will she forgive me for being such a shocking bad husband?'

Madame closed her eyes in order to commune with the spirit, then replied, 'She will.'

'That's good,' said Mr Grey. 'You know,' he continued, 'I was thinking that I ought to find my young girl Kitty, and tell her that I've been converted. She might want to come and live with me and be my housekeeper, look after her old dad in his dotage.'

'No!' Madame's eyes sprang open. 'Your wife doesn't want you to do this. She says that Kitty has suffered enough and must not be contacted under any circumstances.'

'Fair enough,' Mr Grey said. 'If that's what she says, that's what I'll do. I want to make up for being such a dreadful beast all my life.' He peered around Madame again. 'Here, can you ask the wife if she's seen anything of my old pa up there?'

Madame closed her eyes again, then opened them and said, 'I'm afraid your wife has gone. Now, about your foundation . . .'

Chapter Fifteen

In Which Velvet Visits
Mrs Dyer's Baby Farm

Sometimes, Velvet thought to herself determinedly on the train to Reading the following morning, the spirits need a helping hand. *The spirits need a helping hand,* she repeated to herself several times, but it didn't make what she was about to do sound any better. She was going to steal a baby! What she was doing was fraudulent, illegal and wicked, but she was doing it for Madame, who surely had the best of reasons – amongst them the saving of Mrs Fortesque's sanity, maybe even her life – for her plan. Did that make it all right?

Velvet had been given the money for a second-class ticket from Paddington to Reading and as she had not had the experience of riding on a train before, this part of the journey, at least, was exciting and enjoyable. As London gave way to the suburbs, then to fields with horses and cows and sheep, she managed to clear her head of worrisome thoughts and found herself exclaiming with pleasure at every new scene. Picturesque cottages, pretty churches, ponds with white ducks, allotments with rows of vegetables and blooming gardens passed in a blur of colour. Daydreaming, she envisioned being married to George and living with him in one of the little thatched cottages. However, though she could just about imagine herself in the parlour sewing a patch-work quilt, the figure of George stubbornly refused to appear beside her. George seemed too tall, too dapper, too urbane a fellow to be chopping wood or toasting hunks of bread in front of the fire.

Early that morning, Madame had called her upstairs and shown her some particular advertise-ments in *The Telegraph*. They came under the heading of GOOD HOMES and there were seven of them, all saying more or less the same.

> A lonely widow offers a good home
> to a baby under six months.
> If sickly, will receive a mother's love.
> No questions asked about provenance.
> £12 annually, or for £20 would adopt entirely.

Velvet knew about baby farms, of course. Knew that many a young girl, desperate to keep her employment and her reputation, would sometimes give birth in secret and take her baby straight to a woman who would mind it until she was able to take care of it herself. If, as often seemed to happen, the baby died before she could reclaim it, then the girl would mourn the loss in private and try to get on with her life. Mrs Amelia Dyer of Reading had such a baby farm, and it was hers which had been selected by Madame.

Velvet was wearing her oldest clothes (those she'd been wearing the day she'd arrived at Madame's, which she'd hoped never to wear again), her hair was deliberately unkempt and she had no gloves. She was posing as a girl in the family way and, wearing a roll of muslin as padding, might have been trying to conceal a pregnancy of seven months' duration, or merely have been plump. To save her from any unpleasant comments or unwelcome speculation whilst on her journey, however, Madame had supplied her with a cheap wedding ring and Velvet, her hands crossed over the lid of her wicker basket, kept this in sight.

George had studied a map of Reading and had told Velvet where to go on leaving the station. He had also kissed her and said it was a wonderful thing that she was doing for Madame – for all of them – and she should feel very pleased and proud that she was helping in such a significant way. The closer she came to her destination, however, the more she realised she did not feel either of these things; she just felt ill. Her hands trembled, beads of sweat stood out on her forehead and there was a dull ache in her stomach. What was she doing here? How had she got herself into this situation? When she had said that she would do anything to stay with Madame, she hadn't envisaged *this*.

Mrs Dyer's terraced cottage was at the end of a row of equally shabby dwellings. In the front yard was a broken-down perambulator, a chair with two legs, a quantity of old wood, several stained mattresses of various sizes and two large, filthy dogs fighting over a bone. It did not seem the sort of place where one would choose to leave one's child, but Velvet realised that unmarried mothers had little choice, so great was the stigma against them that it was well-nigh impossible for them to obtain work or shelter. To have their illegitimate children cared for was difficult, too, for most children's homes were attached to the church and would only take orphaned or desperately poor children who'd been born in wedlock.

Velvet tapped on the front door, listening for any noises. Madame had assured her that Mrs Dyer would have at least half a dozen babies, but that they would be drugged with opiates to make them docile, so it was unlikely she would hear any crying in the house. Drugged babies were also too sleepy to drink milk, and this saved money. Of course, sooner or later, Madame explained, lack of nutrition would lead to a baby's death, but the baby farmer would pocket the monthly fee for as long as the mother continued to send it. If the mother wrote to ask about her child, a false report would be given, and only if she turned up at the door to enquire would the sad news be given out that the child had just died. Recalling all these details, Velvet shuddered as she tapped at the door again.

This time a rough female voice shouted, 'Round the back!'

Velvet took a deep breath and, walking round, tried to affect the gait of a pregnant woman, putting her hand on her back as if it pained her. 'Mrs Dyer?' she called.

Attached to the back of the cottage was a little glass outhouse looking as if it had been constructed of ancient doors and windows. Just outside sat a stout middle-aged woman smoking a clay pipe. She wore a dirty apron over a black cotton dress and her hair was patchy and balding.

'Who wants 'er?'

Velvet fought to control a sudden urge to be sick, reminding herself that she was supposed to be anxious and desperate. 'I saw . . . saw your advertisement in the paper.'

Mrs Dyer looked her up and down. 'Expecting, are you?'

Velvet nodded.

'Know who the father is?'

Velvet nodded again.

'Has he got money?'

'He has not,' Velvet sighed. 'And his parents have sent him to France in order to keep us apart.' She had cooked up this sad tale on the train. 'They say we are never to see each other again.'

Mrs Dyer blew out a cloud of smoke through lips which were cracked and stained with nicotine. 'Usual tale,' she said. 'Want me to adopt it, do you?'

Velvet had already decided she could never in a hundred years leave a baby – even an imaginary baby – with such a woman. 'No, just to have it minded.'

'A year's fee in advance is my terms. That's twelve pounds. You'll need to provide clothes and bedding for the year, and there's no refund if the child dies.'

Velvet looked round. There was no evidence of any children: no cots, toys, or clothes drying, no napkins, bottles or any other nursery paraphernalia. 'Have you many babies here?'

'One or two,' Mrs Dyer said. She coughed and spat on to the ground. 'A mother's love, I gives 'em.'

Velvet shivered.

'Got somewhere to lie-in, have you?'

'Not yet. I . . . I have about a month to go, I believe. I'm trying to persuade my sister to take me in.'

Mrs Dyer puffed on her pipe. 'You better book a place here for the child, then, because you'll not find many what'll take bastard children.'

Velvet nodded, thinking how fraught, how achingly

desperate a young girl would have to be to leave her baby here, with such a woman.

'I'll need a deposit, non-refundable, in case of anything going wrong.' Velvet winced and Mrs Dyer added, 'Risky business, childbirth. Plenty don't make it through.'

Velvet handed over the ten-shilling note which Madame had given to her for a deposit, adding, 'Here's something else that my sister said you'd like.' She delved into the basket and brought out a bottle of gin. 'She said you may look especially kindly upon my child if you have a little treat.'

Mrs Dyer's eyes lit up and her gnarled, yellow-stained hand reached for the gin. 'Good on you, girl,' she said. 'Yer sister is the kind of woman who understands an old lady's needs.' She pushed the bottle into the pocket of her apron. 'See you in a few weeks, then,' she said, then crossed herself piously. 'God willin'.'

Velvet hesitated, then asked, 'Could I see the babies' accommodation?'

'No, they're all asleep.' Mrs Dyer gestured up to a little window. 'Wouldn't want 'em woked up, would we?'

'Then I wish you good morning,' Velvet said.

She set off, but before she had reached the front of the house she heard – just as Madame had predicted – the sound of the bottle of gin being unscrewed, of someone taking a gulp of liquid and giving a grunt of satisfaction. Now all she had to do was wait.

Velvet passed what seemed like an interminable time walking around the back lanes of Reading, not enjoying being poor. She was too used to being Madame's companion, to travelling in her pretty carriage, to wearing satin shoes and taffeta under-skirts that swished as she walked, to take kindly to walking the streets wearing cheap shoes and raggedy gowns again.

She sat in a park and thought about George. When, oh *when* would he declare himself? What was holding him back? She sighed, closed her eyes and imagined him kissing her passionately, then getting down on one knee and telling her he loved her. Was that ever going to happen?

Thoughts of George led inexorably to thoughts of Charlie. It was surely more than a month since she'd seen him, so perhaps he'd finally realised that there was no future in their relationship. Either that or Lizzie had won him over. This notion, for some reason, made her feel breathless and anxious, so that she had to start walking and quickly think about something else.

Judging that near two hours had gone, she walked back to Mrs Dyer's, passing the dogs in the garden, still fighting, to tiptoe to the rear of the cottage. If Madame was right (and she was usually right about such things), Mrs Dyer would be in a drunken sleep.

If she was not, then Velvet had a question ready as an excuse for returning, and would have to think again about what to do next.

That Mrs Dyer was sound asleep, however, was immediately evident. Her pipe had dropped on to the ground, where it still smouldered, the gin bottle was empty and the lady herself was snoring loudly. Velvet slipped past her and went inside, where, once through the glass outhouse and into the kitchen, the stench hit her like a wall, so much so that she gagged and had to return to the outhouse to take in some fresher air.

Three deep breaths, then, trying to steady herself for what she might see, Velvet went back into the house, straight through the kitchen (which was full of newspapers, stinking clothes, old plates covered in flies, torn towels and rags, cups and bottles half-full of sour milk) and up the stairs. At the top were two rooms, one with its door open and one shut, and it was into the latter that Velvet went.

She opened the door slowly, her eyes closed, then peeped out through screwed-up lids, unwilling to take in the scene all at once. There was a tatty screen standing in front of the window to stop the light coming in, but her first view was of boxes lined up across the floor – rough wooden crates, such as vegetables came in at the market. Turning to take a breath outside the room, for the stench inside was even more appalling, she went right in and saw that each of the crates contained a comatose infant. None of them wore napkins and each was lying in its own mess on straw or newspaper, apart from one, the smallest, who was swaddled around so tightly that it looked like a little Russian doll. The infants looked to be of slightly different sizes and ages, for only some had hair, and – probably according to the length of time they had been with Mrs Dyer – some were in a worse condition than others, with gummed-up eyelids, cradle cap or bloodless lips.

Velvet, surveying this scene, pushed her nails into her palms and felt her body folding in on itself with horror and grief. Stealing a baby had seemed such a terribly wicked thing to do, but now she had seen these poor innocents, she wanted to take them all out of the hell they were living in. Which one to choose? Which to condemn to death? Oh, their poor, desperate mothers . . .

Hurriedly, Velvet looked the babies over. Madame's only stipulation was that the child should be a girl, and there were four of these. The smallest, the wrapped baby, looked to be the pinkest and healthiest, so it was probably a new arrival, but Velvet could not spare the time to undo its wrappings and discover what sex it was in case Mrs Dyer woke up. She therefore picked up the girl nearest to her and quickly cleaned her as well as she could on a piece of newspaper. The child was as thin as a skinned rabbit, with legs held in a frog-like position and stick-thin, dangling arms.

Quickly opening her basket, Velvet lifted out a blanket, unfolded it and placed the little girl within it, then loosely rolled it around her and put the bundle on the cushion in the basket. The child did not move or murmur during these attentions, and Velvet, suddenly frightened that she might be dead, made herself open the blanket in order to watch the baby's little chest rise and fall several times before she went on.

Going downstairs and finding Mrs Dyer in the same position as before, Velvet was filled with a fearful anger. She realised she need not have concerned herself about the ethics of stealing a baby, for Mrs Dyer would be only too pleased it was off her hands – it would save her the trouble of slowly starving it to death. Seeing the evil woman slumped there before her, lumpen, drunk and gross, Velvet felt she could have kicked the chair from under her, but knew that to do so wouldn't have helped the poor infants upstairs. All at once it struck her that there were many degrees of evil in the world. She'd thought her father wicked, but his doings were nothing compared to the heinous crimes of this woman.

Upon arriving at Paddington station, Velvet decided to walk to Madame's house, not wanting to take the basket on to a crowded omnibus in case it got bumped and caused the baby within to start crying. For this reason also she had travelled from Reading back to Paddington standing alone in the guard's van, peering in at the baby every few moments and hoping and praying that, once Mrs Fortesque had taken possession of her, she might recover her health and strength. How dreadful it would be if she had chosen a child to replace Mrs Fortesque's dead Claire, only to have that child die, too.

Reaching Lisson Grove, her mind refusing to dwell on anything but the horrors at Mrs Dyer's house, Velvet came to the street corner and stopped abruptly. She knew her way home quite well, so could not have said exactly what prompted her to turn, quite deliberately, in the wrong direction. And then she came in sight of the blue lamp which indicated a police station, and she knew why she had come that way.

Clasping the basket tightly in her arms, she began running towards the gleaming blue lamp. She wanted – oh, most desperately wanted – to see Charlie.

Chapter Sixteen

In Which Velvet Speaks to Charlie about Baby Farms

Sitting in the vestibule of Lisson Grove police station with the basket beside her, Velvet had to wait ten minutes or so for Charlie to appear. She checked on the baby repeatedly, but she did not make a sound in all that time. There was a duty policeman behind the desk but, busy with paperwork, he didn't even glance their way.

A headache pounded Velvet's skull and she felt giddy, her mind whirling, so that she hardly knew what she was doing or what she was going to say. When Charlie appeared around the corner, his tawny hair showing bright as a lamp in the dark corridor, she was so terribly relieved to see him that she felt she wanted to cry.

He surveyed her anxiously. 'Ki— Velvet, whatever's wrong?'

'Charlie,' she said, 'please will you sit down a

moment?' She patted the bench on the other side from the basket and tried to calm herself.

He sat. 'It's lovely to see you whatever you've come for – but you're not ill, are you? You look very flushed.'

'No, Charlie.' Velvet shook her head. 'I'm fine.'

'Something upsetting has happened to you, though.' He studied her carefully. 'I can see it in your face.'

'Yes, it has. There's something really important I want to report, Charlie.' She lowered her voice. 'But I don't want anyone to find out that it's me who told.'

Charlie nodded. 'It's that Madame Whatsit of yours, I bet. You've found her out and she's as crooked as a five-bob note, eh? Or is it that folderol fancy man of hers who's playing you up?'

'No, it's neither of them,' Velvet said, 'and really, I don't want to fall out with you about them, Charlie. I just want to tell you something and please, oh, *please*, you must tell someone and they must do something!' And so saying, Velvet burst into the tears that had been threatening ever since she'd set foot inside Mrs Dyer's house.

Charlie put an arm around her. Even though Velvet made an effort to shrug it off, he persisted and she was immensely comforted by crying on to a navy serge shoulder. But she only allowed herself to be fragile for a few moments before turning to face him.

'We're wasting time, Charlie,' she said urgently.

'It was the most terrible thing I've ever seen. You must tell your superiors and get a deputation and go and take them all away!'

'What on earth do you mean, Kitty?' Charlie asked, and it was a measure of Velvet's anxiety that she didn't put him right about her name. 'What are you talking about?'

'Babies. A woman who runs a baby farm. She lives in Reading – Parkby Close, right at the end of the road. She's got about seven babies there and they all . . . all . . . look close to death.' Tears trickled down Velvet's face and though she had a handkerchief in her basket she didn't dare to reach in for it in case she disturbed the baby and Charlie realised what she'd done. 'Please, please don't ask me how I know, Charlie. Just go there as soon as you can.' She pushed him away from her. 'You must go now!'

'What's her name?'

'She calls herself Mrs Dyer, but I don't know if that's her real name.'

'Ah, yes,' said Charlie, nodding sagely. 'Amelia Dyer. Sometimes she goes by that name, sometimes by the name of Smithers, sometimes Lee. When she was Mrs Lee she had a house on this patch.'

'Really?'

'Oh yes. She's been in prison several times. She gets caught, serves her time, comes out and starts another baby farm under a different name.'

'Then she must be stopped again! Please say

you'll go down there now and arrest her and take the babies away. *Please!*'

Charlie stood up. 'We're a different division, you know,' he said. 'We're the Met, and that'll be down to Reading Borough Police.'

'But . . .'

'It's all right.' Charlie patted her shoulder. 'I'll go and tell the chief right now. He'll get on to it, alert the other force.'

'Straight away?'

Charlie nodded. 'He's got children of his own. Besides, he knows that wicked witch from old.'

Velvet heaved a great sigh of relief. 'Oh, thank you, Charlie!' She rubbed her wet cheeks with the back of her hand and picked up the basket. 'I must get home.'

He caught hold of her hand – her right hand, thankfully, so he didn't notice the false wedding band. '*Home.* Is that big place really home to you?'

'Charlie! Don't start all that again.'

He looked at her and gave a rueful half-smile. 'Very well. But come back to the station in a day or so and I'll tell you what happened to the wicked witch.'

'I will,' said Velvet. 'But go and tell your chief now. Please, just go!'

Charlie patted her shoulder awkwardly, and went.

The baby, Claire, as she was called henceforth, was received gladly by Madame, who had already bought blankets and a set of baby clothes. Madame had also taken advice from a physician regarding the best and most nutritious way of feeding an ailing infant, and little Claire was bathed, swaddled, put to sleep in a drawer in Velvet's room and fed a small amount of goat's milk every two or three hours throughout the night. This regime was continued all through the next day and night until, on being taken to a doctor to be checked over, she was pronounced healthy and likely to survive.

On the morning of the séance, although she was still unnaturally quiet after days of being fed sedatives, her cheeks were certainly pinker and she even opened her eyes briefly. 'The child is desperately undersized because of lack of food,' Madame said to Velvet as they looked at her in the drawer, 'but the doctor said she'll soon catch up.'

'I'm afraid I didn't think about size or age – I just took the nearest girl and got out,' Velvet said. She shuddered. 'Is there anything more wicked than a baby farmer?'

'I'm sure they're not all like that,' Madame said. 'Some do care for the children they look after.'

'But not she. Not Mrs Dyer.'

Madame shook her head. 'No. She appears to be one of the very worst. She feeds babies sleeping powders so that they're too tired to feed, and they gradually die of starvation.'

'But the mothers of these babies, don't they ever report her?'

'The mothers are too ashamed and guilty about using her in the first place,' Madame explained. 'They're young, unmarried girls who have little experience of life and nowhere else to turn.'

Velvet looked enquiringly at Madame, still not quite sure how the subterfuge was going to work. 'Won't Mrs Fortesque think it strange that her baby is younger and smaller than when she died?'

'Don't worry, we'll resolve that,' Madame said. 'I'll tell her that Claire has been in a sort of limbo, a halfway house between this world and the next, and that's why, missing her mother, she hasn't progressed.' Madame straightened up from bending over the baby and pressed Velvet's hand. 'You've been an excellent and efficient help to me, Velvet. This enterprise could not have been carried out without you.'

'Not at all, Madame,' Velvet murmured. Who could blame Madame, she thought, for wanting to be the best at her profession, for seeking to do something that no other medium had done? And though she was deceiving Mrs Fortesque, it was surely a deceit of the kindest sort – and one which had also saved a baby's life. Several babies, if the police force had acted swiftly.

'Now, I have to tell you something which will come as a surprise,' Madame said. Whilst Velvet reflected that many things at Darkling Villa came as a surprise, she went on, 'I intend that we, our household, should relocate to Brighton for the winter season.' As Velvet looked at her in astonishment, she added, 'Because – what do you think? – I will shortly become the owner of a beautiful house there, a villa facing the sea.'

'How lovely!' said Velvet. She had never seen the sea, but she knew that the seaside, and sea-swimming, were becoming extremely fashionable amongst the upper classes.

'Would you enjoy living there, do you think?' Madame asked. 'Brighton has some very rich residents, I believe, and our new king spends a great deal of time at the wonderful palace there.' She smiled. 'I could have a whole new clientele in Brighton! It would be wonderful if I could make my name as well known in Sussex as it is in London.'

'Indeed, Madame,' Velvet said, feeling quite excited. She would miss Lizzie, of course, but then she hardly ever saw her now. And Charlie, yes, he was a good friend and she would probably miss knowing he was nearby, but her move away would be one more door closing on that miserable early part of her life.

'Perhaps, when we get settled there, it will be time for you to begin learning my ways so that eventually we can work together.'

Velvet smiled her thanks. She remembered that Madame had spoken of this before, and was pleased – at least, she thought she was pleased – that

Madame wanted to have her as an assistant on stage, but was not at all sure that she could develop the necessary skills in order to become a medium. She had never heard voices or seen spirits, never received messages from beyond the grave and no one in her family had ever been psychic. Her mother had not been a Russian aristocrat, either. If Madame thought Velvet could be a medium, then could anyone be a medium? Another thought followed, for which she immediately rebuked herself: could anyone *pretend* to be a medium?

'But now, this morning, we have the most important séance that I have ever undertaken,' Madame continued.

'What do you want me to do, Madame?' Velvet asked. She fought back a yawn – she had been looking after little Claire for the last two nights, so had hardly slept.

'Mrs Fortesque is arriving at eleven o'clock. Just before that, I want you to bring Claire downstairs and place her – George will show you where – inside my cabinet, concealed by a cushion. Is the child liable to cry, do you think?'

'I think not, Madame. She's still very sleepy.'

'Good. She'll only be in the cabinet for a matter of minutes, then Mrs Fortesque can take her home and the whole affair may be concluded. Everyone will be happy.'

*

The séance to materialise Mrs Fortesque's baby was to be held in near secrecy, with just Mrs Fortesque, her sister and an elderly aunt – all three of them devout spiritualists – in attendance. Madame had given Mrs Lawson and Sissy a week's leave so they would know nothing of these events.

'You, myself and George will be the only people involved,' Madame said. 'It's a solemn undertaking which will bind us together for ever.'

Just before eleven o'clock, Velvet swaddled Claire tightly in her new white blanket and went downstairs. She found George in the front room, kneeling down to adjust something in Madame's cabinet. He jumped to his feet as she appeared.

'How's our little charge?' he asked, looking down at the baby.

'Doing quite well, as far as I know about babies,' Velvet replied. 'But I'll just be glad when this is over. I can't sleep for fretting about her – and all the others in that awful place . . .'

'But just think what you've done! You've rescued this child, saved Mrs Fortesque from a broken heart and gained enormous regard in Madame's eyes.'

Velvet was still looking anxious, so George took Claire from her and settled the baby into the hollow of a large cushion on the cabinet floor. 'Now,' he said kindly to Velvet, 'you can stop your fretting.'

Velvet sighed. The truth was, she was not sure

exactly what was worrying her; she simply felt over-whelmed, anxious and beset with doubts of all kinds. Because some of the worries she had were about Madame and her methods of working, however, she did not dare articulate them to George.

'You have done the most wonderful thing,' George said. 'It will mean that we can all continue to live together. You, me and Madame.'

'Yes,' Velvet said uncertainly.

'And then, later, we must see . . .'

Tantalisingly, he said no more, but seemed just about to kiss her when there came a knock at the front door, which signalled that the Fortesque party had arrived. Velvet, pressing her hands to her flushed cheeks to try to cool them, went to answer it. If she had felt confused and bewildered before speaking to George, she felt more so now. *And then, later, we must see* . . . What had he meant by this?

Velvet showed Mrs Fortesque's sister and aunt into the darkened front room, whilst George took the woman herself upstairs to conclude some busi-ness with Madame. (How much, Velvet could not help but wonder, would it cost to materialise a baby?)

When the two ladies appeared downstairs, both were pale and anxious. Madame greeted the aunt and sister in little more than a whisper, explaining that she was conserving her strength for what was to come. She could make no promises, she said, but would do her utmost to manifest little Claire from spirit to flesh.

She took her usual position in the cabinet and George pulled the curtain across to hide her from view. 'So that Madame can begin to communicate with her spirits and ask for their guidance,' he explained.

The spirits sometimes need a helping hand, Velvet thought, and wondered just how much of a helping hand Madame had to give them. Sometimes there seemed – dare she think it? – to be no spirits, but only a very clever woman.

Velvet dimmed the lamps, Madame went into trance and George opened the heavy cabinet curtain. After a few moments Madame, her silky turquoise gown glimmering in the darkness, began to breathe in a rough, rasping way.

'I seek the spirit of Claire!' she called. 'A little child who passed before her time to the Other Side, and now resides in the Vale of Darkness.'

Velvet, her mind befuddled through lack of sleep, felt her usual shiver at these words. The work of a medium might not always be a strictly honest one, but the basic principle remained: that the dead, through the channel of a medium, were able to speak to the living. It was a truly portentous and chilling thought. If it were true . . .

'Come closer to our world, Claire,' Madame called into the air. 'Come towards those who love you best. We're not ready to lose you, Claire!'

There was complete silence. Velvet's heart was in her mouth. She just wanted it to happen quickly; for Mrs Fortesque to take up the child and go.

'Your mother wants and needs you in this world, Claire!'

Another long silence, then they heard, '*Mama! Mama, where are you?*'

'I am here, my precious,' Mrs Fortesque replied, her voice thick with emotion. 'Come towards me!'

'*I want to see you, Mama!*'

Madame began to call upon all manner of ethereal assistants. There was much talk of angels coming back to earth and spirits seeking the light, of Mrs Fortesque being given another chance to keep her precious darling close by her. Then, dimly, something – the ectoplasm, Velvet thought – could be seen floating up from the floor, gathering and billowing around the big cushion. In the almost total darkness it looked strange and eerie, a thin film of shimmering gauze. But why was it appearing at all, Velvet wondered, when the baby was already there? Was it mere window dressing to give more of a theatrical look to the whole thing? If it was false, then what had happened when Sir Percy had materialised? Had *that* been false, too?

'Is she there? Can I touch her?' Mrs Fortesque asked urgently, trying to see through the darkness. 'Oh, please let me hold her again!'

'*Mama! I want to come back to you!*'

Madame flung her arms wide. 'Your child is there,' she cried, pointing to the cushion in her cabinet. 'Take her, and let the spirits do what they will with me!'

Mrs Fortesque immediately darted forward and snatched the baby from the cushion, leaving Madame to scream dramatically as the three ladies fumbled their way through the darkness, into the hall and out of the front door.

Chapter Seventeen

In Which Velvet Tests
Her Suspicions

Velvet did not have to return to the police station to find out what had happened to the rest of Mrs Dyer's victims because, two days later, going to the shops for fresh rolls for Madame's breakfast, she noticed the headline in *The Mercury* was: *POLICE RAID BABY FARM*. She bought the newspaper, took it home and under the banner headline read the following:

Yesterday, the Metropolitan Police, being in receipt of information about a so-called 'baby farm' in Reading, raided a squalid house and found there the lamentable sight of six distressed infants of various ages from a few weeks to eight months. The children were all found to be suffering from malnutrition, sores and scabies. There was also evidence of rat bites on two of them. It is said that some of the policemen who raided the house were reduced to tears on seeing the condition of these innocents.

273

The woman responsible for this sorry state of affairs turned out to be the notorious Mrs Amelia Dyer. Dyer has been arrested at least twice previously for neglecting infants assigned to her care, sometimes to the point of death, and has twice been in prison. On leaving jail, however, it appears that she sets herself up under a different name to begin her cruel employment elsewhere.

Dyer's method was as follows. She advertised to adopt or nurse a baby in return for a one-off payment or a monthly fee, plus adequate bedding and clothing for the child. Once the unfortunate mother had handed these over, the clothing was taken straight to the pawnbroker and the child was put in rags and made to sleep on straw or newspaper. It was given opiates or sleeping powders to quieten it (Dyer's neighbours said they had no knowledge of the fact that she had so many children in her care) and was fed a mixture of cornflour and sour milk, which slowly led to the child's death by starvation. Any unsuspecting doctor asked to certify the death would merely put that age-old reason: 'failure to thrive'.

There have long been calls for baby farms to be regulated and inspected because at the moment anyone at all, with or without experience of children, is able to start their own nursery without any checking of credentials by the authorities. It is indeed symptomatic of our times that young working-class women are desperate enough to put aside their scruples and standards and to use these services. This newspaper believes it is vital that stricter adoption laws are imposed, that all adoptions should be vetted by the authorities and that personal advertisements placed in newspapers by those offering to adopt or nurse should be monitored.

The River Thames is but a short walk from Dyer's house, and there are now plans to search the river for the bodies of infants. Anyone who has left a child with Mrs Amelia Dyer is urged to put aside any consideration of propriety and go immediately to their local police station.

Velvet put down the newspaper, her hands shaking. Thank goodness. *Thank goodness!* Maybe Mrs Dyer would be put away for life this time – and surely the remaining babies would be taken to a place of safety. No one need know that Velvet had had anything to do with it.

Deep in thought, she prepared Madame's breakfast and took it to her rooms and then, George having left a message that he had gone to try out a motor car, found herself alone in the kitchen. To be alone, she realised, was exactly what she wanted; time to sit down by herself and deliberate about things. She needed to think about George and she needed to think about Charlie. She needed to think about her work and where it was leading her and, most of all, she needed to think about Madame.

Sometimes the spirits need a helping hand . . . But when did that hand stop helping and take over?

That Madame was truly psychic and spoke to spirits seemed beyond doubt. Otherwise, how would she have known that her real name was Kitty, or all those other details regarding the death of her father? Yet – and here the doubts began creeping in – there were so many other things which had proved to be counterfeit: the evenings of mediumship with the questions in the envelopes, the billowing 'ectoplasm' which looked very much like a chiffon sack filled with air, and the flowers and other objects that had appeared at the first Dark Circle she had attended at Darkling Villa. Now that she had seen Madame in action on many occasions, she knew that much of what she said at séances was carefully built on what she herself and George had found out from clients beforehand.

Stealing a baby, however, was a step too far. When Velvet had taken the job with Madame, she had never thought that kidnapping would be one of her duties. What would be demanded of her next?

And what about George? Velvet sighed to herself. Madame had saved his life, so of course he was loyal to her and perhaps willing to forgive her transgressions. If Velvet found it impossible to carry on working for her, however – and felt compelled to tell someone of the things she'd discovered – what would happen about George? Would he support her, or decide to stay with Madame? *What would George do?*

Velvet sat quietly for ten minutes or so until she'd thought of a plan. She didn't want to do it, not at all, but felt she could no longer work for Madame without discovering the truth about her. The next evening of mediumship at Darkling Villa would be held at the end of the week, so what if Lizzie, who had never been seen at close proximity by either Madame or George, came along as a potential client? Velvet would tell Madame that Lizzie was a young heiress whose grandfather had left her a fortune, and then wait and see whether Madame made use of this false information. If she did not refer to it during the course of the evening, then life could go on happily as before. If Madame pretended she was in touch with the spirit of this completely fictitious grandfather, however, then Velvet would confide in George, tell him that Lizzie's story was completely untrue and ask him to go with her to the police.

The police. Thinking of this latter scenario made her feel uneasy in the extreme.

The week passed very slowly. Madame was as charming as ever, giving Velvet an ocelot fur tippet and muff ready for the encroaching winter and engendering a terrible guilt in her. Madame was so kind and generous; how could she be so wicked as to even consider betraying her? But then she thought of Mrs Fortesque and of all the people who had been persuaded to part with their money on the basis of false communication with their dead relatives. Madame had many rich private clients, too, whom Velvet never saw. What had Madame purloined from *them*, she wondered?

One evening during the week, Velvet went to Lizzie's house and, after telling of her visit to Mrs Dyer's (Lizzie sat gasping with horror throughout), went on to confess that she had suspicions about Madame.

'I wondered if you would come to Darkling Villa and play the part of an heiress,' she said. When Lizzie began laughing, she added, 'It would be similar to the part you played at Mrs Palladino's – but not in my clothes, of course, because Madame would recognise them.'

Lizzie nodded eagerly, saying it would break the awful tedium of working at the laundry. 'Besides, Pa always said that those mediums were frauds. And I remember Charlie saying so, too.'

'Charlie,' said Velvet thoughtfully. 'Have you seen anything of him?'

Lizzie shook her head.

'I went to his police station on my way here to ask more about the arrest of Mrs Dyer, but they said he was away on a course.' She smiled rather wistfully. 'I'd have liked to have seen him. He plans to be a detective, you know.'

Lizzie giggled. 'Like Sherlock Holmes?'

Velvet nodded. 'He'll probably be very good at solving crimes – when Charlie gets hold of something he doesn't let it go.'

Lizzie gave a sad little laugh. 'He doesn't want to let *you* go, you mean. He was always talking about you.'

'We've only ever been friends . . .'

'Friends, was it?' Lizzie teased. 'He told me that you two once had a mock wedding. He wore his pa's top hat and you were dressed in your ma's petticoat.'

'We were only eight years old!'

'Even so . . .'

'Oh, I think he's realised now that I only like him as a friend,' Velvet said and, as she spoke, felt an unaccountable sadness creep over her. Suppose Charlie *had* found someone else? Suppose she never saw him again?

On the afternoon of the séance, things were very much as usual. Madame, who had spent the morning at the hairdresser's having a Marcel Wave, was upstairs resting. Velvet was putting last-minute touches to the flowers, Mrs Lawson was making savouries and Sissy Lawson was flirting with George (who was studiously ignoring this, Velvet was pleased to see). Watching him go up and down to the cellar selecting the champagne and checking the glasses for smears, Velvet wondered how on earth she would tell him about Madame. Or had he already worked things out for himself?

About forty people were attending that evening,

so the séance was not going to be held round the table, but with everyone seated in rows and with Madame in her cabinet. There might, George said after consultation with Madame, be a manifestation of spirit into flesh, but it was impossible to say for sure as this depended on so many variables. He said this so earnestly, so seriously, that although Velvet longed to make a comment about the only spirits she'd seen looking suspiciously like bunched chiffon, she thought better of it.

When the audience arrived, Velvet found there were about ten clients who had never been to Madame's before, so she took some time to speak to each of these to make sure they were relaxed and comfortable. Lizzie was amongst them, wearing her mother's best jacket over a plaid skirt belonging to her sister with a hat borrowed from someone at the steam laundry. She didn't exactly look fashionable, Velvet thought, but then not every heiress was interested in the latest styles. Dressed as she was, Lizzie could easily pass for a rather quaintly old-fashioned girl from a good family. Knowing that her accent, however, might give her away, she and Velvet had decided that she should plead a cold and speak to Madame, if she had to, in a hoarse whisper.

About ten minutes before the evening's proceedings began, Velvet went up to talk to Madame as normal. Sick with dread, she thought to herself that if Madame were truly psychic then she would detect that something was very wrong and surely know if Velvet was lying. But no, stretched out on her chaise longue as usual, wearing a gown made entirely of artificial flowers, her hair slicked to her head in wavy lines, Madame asked if everything was in order and if there were any new clients.

'Several,' Velvet reported. 'Mostly older ladies. Two sisters have come together to try and contact their brother – he passed away last year and his name was Cyril. There's a gentleman who hopes to get in touch with his wife, but is worried that because she passed over some ten years ago this might be difficult.'

'Did you get her name?' Madame asked.

Velvet shook her head. 'Not her right name. He referred to her as Pippin, though, because he said she had a pretty round face, like an apple.'

'That is most helpful,' Madame said. 'Anyone else?'

'There's also a girl who has only recently been bereaved of her grandfather, who she lived with from a young age,' Velvet said, giving Madame the story, word for word, that she and Lizzie had concocted. 'He left her all his money, but she told me that she misses him so dreadfully she'd give anything just to have him back.'

'How interesting,' said Madame.

'Her family, apparently, are terribly jealous of the

fact that she was the beneficiary of his will and they're going to contest it in court.'

'That's very mean of them,' Madame commented. She was wearing a new piece of jewellery, Velvet noticed: a flower brooch heavily encrusted with diamonds. 'I shall try and help this little lady if I can. Do you recall her name?'

'Sara. Sara Pilkington-Smith.'

'Well,' said Madame. 'I'll most certainly do my best for Miss Sara Pilkington-Smith.'

The séance began as usual, with spirits arriving and departing and being claimed or not, including a 'lovely older lady who passed over some ten years ago, known to her husband as Pippin'. As the evening progressed, Velvet began to wish most desperately that she hadn't stooped to carrying out this plan. Either that, or that Madame would not select Lizzie, or would say to Velvet afterwards that it had been a pity that the young lady's grandfather hadn't come through. How pleased Velvet would be to hear this!

Halfway through the evening there was a pause for another glass of champagne, and George was besieged by middle-aged ladies wanting to confide in him. He looked across at Velvet once and gave her a faint wink, which – as ever – sent butterflies fluttering around inside her, and she wondered again what would happen if he chose Madame over her.

'I have several more spirits waiting to be heard,' Madame said as she began the second half of the evening. 'One in particular is rather reluctant to linger here too long. He's telling me that he was always very punctual in life and remains so now.' Madame looked across the audience. 'He's an elderly gentleman, possibly in his seventies or even eighties. He has a full white beard and lovely white hair. He's related to someone here. A young woman.'

As nearly every gentleman over the age of sixty-five had a grey or white beard, this appearance was a reasonable guess. Madame was fishing, seeing if 'Sara' would catch the line she was throwing out. Hearing her, Velvet went cold. She knew, with a terrible certainty, that every word Madame said from then on was going to be a lie.

Lizzie raised her hand. 'I believe I know the gentleman you're speaking of,' she said hoarsely. 'He was always very punctual, and he had a beard.' She put her hand to her throat. 'Will you please excuse my voice – I've taken a chill.'

'Of course,' Madame said. She closed her eyes. 'He says he's the grandfather of someone here tonight. Is that you? Does your name begin with . . . "S"? It's Sara, isn't it?'

'Sara' nodded, smiling, and the audience applauded enthusiastically.

'And your second name, and his, is something double-barrelled. The first name begins with "P", I believe, and then there is a commonplace name which begins with "S". Smith?'

'All that is perfectly correct,' Lizzie croaked, affecting great surprise.

Velvet's heart began to thud. It was turning out just as she'd feared: Madame was a trickster, an imposter, a fraud . . . one of those mediums being sought out by the psychical research people.

'May I converse with this gentleman on your behalf?' Madame asked, and Lizzie gave permission. Madame put her head on one side, in her 'listening to spirits' mode, and said, 'It seems that your grandfather only passed to the Other Side a month or so back.'

Lizzie nodded.

'And you're a named beneficiary in his will.'

'That's right,' said Lizzie.

'You're the only beneficiary, in fact. He's telling me that he has left you his entire fortune.'

There was a stirring in the audience as everyone heard the word 'fortune' and turned to see who Madame was talking to.

'I see some dark clouds over this money, however, because – please correct me if I'm wrong – it seems that there are others in your family who think they're entitled to it. They intend to take the matter to court.'

'That's right,' Lizzie said in hoarse amazement.

Madame gave a little laugh. 'But your grandfather says you must fight them all the way! He says he

284

doesn't want you to give in. If he'd wanted his money to go to anyone else, he says, he would have left it to them. His last will and testament is very clear and there's no room for any deviation from it. You'll win any case brought against you.'

'Thank you so much,' said Lizzie.

'Has that helped?'

'It has! I can't thank you enough.'

'If you come and see me again on your own I may be able to summon the spirit of your grandfather to speak to you personally,' Madame said. 'I had hoped to materialise someone tonight, but I'm afraid I'm now completely exhausted and don't have the strength. If you come to me privately, however, I'll see what I can do.'

'I will,' Lizzie said. 'And I'll tell everyone what you've done for me.'

'Just one moment!' Madame said. 'Your grandfather tells me that you are in pain with your throat.'

Lizzie nodded.

'He instructs you to gargle with an infusion of six sage leaves steeped in a cup of boiled water. He says that will cure it.'

Lizzie smiled. 'I shall try that. Please thank Grandfather for me.'

'I will,' said Madame graciously. 'And if you come for a private session you may be able to thank him yourself.'

There was one more rambling spirit message for

someone who was rather mystified at being its recipient, some general chit-chat about spirits watching over people, and then the evening was over. Velvet showed Lizzie to the front door and there was just time for them to briefly – meaningfully – clasp hands before they parted.

Velvet helped with the clearing away and washing of glasses, then Mrs Lawson went to bed and George left to walk Sissy home (Velvet, for once, hardly cared about this). After taking the flowers downstairs to the scullery, she set a candle in a holder, carried it to her room and sat down on the bed, her head swimming. She'd set the trap and Madame had fallen straight into it, but what was she going to do next? Fear flooded through her. Why, oh why, had she ever done such a thing? It meant that she would have to leave the house and never return.

Never return. At this thought – the thought of leaving the comfort, warmth and luxury of the house and of saying goodbye to everything she loved most dearly – Velvet's heart felt as if it were on the verge of breaking. But how could she stay now that she knew what she did? She couldn't live with herself if she kept her position whilst knowing the truth.

She looked around her room, seeing it in a teary haze. She could take the clothes she was wearing, of course, but most of her other things would have to be left behind. And once she left Darkling Villa, she'd be without a job, a home – or money, she realised now, for she'd scarcely saved a thing since she'd been working for Madame, so intent had she been on buying ribbons, parasols and scented lipsalves to help her look the part. She'd probably be forced to return to the laundry – if they would have her – and work there until her health gave way. Unless, perhaps, George believed her, supported her . . . and married her.

But when ought she go to the police? She had to wait for George to return, she decided, and catch him as he was going to his room, then tell him everything. He would either bitterly hate her for the trick she'd played and say that she'd betrayed them all, or praise her for her astuteness. He would either go with her to the police that very night, or she would leave the house without him and never see him again.

She went over to her door, opened it a little, then sank to the floor and rested her cheek against the door jamb to wait for his return.

It all depended on George.

Chapter Eighteen

In Which an Incredible Truth
Is Revealed

The next thing Velvet was aware of was the sound of the wooden wheels of a milkman's barrow on the cobbles outside the house. It was still dark, her neck ached and she could feel a long dent in her cheek where the door jamb had marked it. She didn't quite know how she could have managed it, but she had fallen asleep.

Shivering, she got to her feet. About an inch of candle stub remained burning; it was probably somewhere between four o'clock and five o'clock. She looked longingly at her bed with its pristine linen sheet folded back over an embroidered pillowcase. For a moment she thought about forgetting everything she had discovered and of just undressing, getting into bed and going to sleep; of letting things go on as before.

But how could she do that? Now that she knew the truth, how could she let those sad, bereaved souls who came to Madame's special evenings continue to have their misery exploited? No, she would have to go on with what she had started.

Where was George? Her candle had been burning and her door was slightly open all night, so George couldn't have failed to see her if he'd walked along the passageway to his own room. He would have known that she'd been waiting to talk to him.

Unless, of course, he hadn't seen her because he hadn't come home. Unless – the thought cut through her like a knife – he had taken Sissy home and then stayed the night with her.

There was only one way to find out.

She stood up, brushed herself down and tiptoed along the dark landing, past Mrs Lawson's bedroom and towards George's room at the end. She tapped on the door. There was no answer and she tapped again, then carefully opened the door and looked inside. The moon shining into the room showed that his bed was empty and had not been slept in.

The shock of discovering this was much greater than discovering that Madame was a fraud for (now that she really thought about it) hadn't she suspected her for some time? She had trusted George, but it seemed that he'd flattered her, led her on and made her believe that they had a future together, whilst all the time having a relationship with Sissy Lawson.

She would have to go to the police without him. Shakily, she went back to her room to gather up a few things. Feeling that she deserved one or two of the garments that Madame had given her, she pulled on an extra skirt and waistcoat, together with her mother's old lace petticoat, underneath the clothes she was still wearing from the night before, then put a spare pair of shoes, two pairs of stockings and a hairbrush in a bag and closed the door on her room for the last time.

By seven o'clock or thereabouts, she thought, Mrs Lawson would be wondering where she was and come looking for her. When she couldn't find her she would go to Madame or George and tell them that she was missing. What would they think? Would they realise that she'd gone to the police, or would they just think she'd run away?

Slowly, carefully, she made her way down the three flights of stairs, being extra careful on Madame's floor not to make a sound in case she woke the dog. Reaching the hall, she began to cry quietly, for she couldn't help remembering how, when she'd first arrived at the house, she'd been quite overwhelmed by the elegance and the ambience and the wonderful welcome she'd received from George and Madame. How happy she'd been then, how incredulous of the luck which had come her way after getting the silver horseshoe in her Christmas pudding. And now she was going to throw it all away!

Fumbling in her pocket for a handkerchief to wipe her eyes, she almost missed seeing the small white envelope lying on the mat. Picking it up, she saw VELVET written on it in Charlie's sturdy hand and was about to open it when there was a whistle from the direction of the kitchen stairs.

George's voice hissed, 'Velvet! What are you doing at this time of the morning?'

One hand already outstretched towards the front door, Velvet stopped dead and turned to look at him incredulously. '*George!*'

He looked tired and a little bit flustered. 'Where are you going so early?'

'To . . . to . . .' But Velvet couldn't bring herself to say it. She tried to keep the note of reproach out of her voice. 'Where have you been, George? I looked for you in your room.'

He shrugged and gave an embarrassed grin. 'I took Sissy home and when I came back I had one last glass of champagne – just to clear the bottle, you know. It was obviously one too many for me, because I fell asleep at the kitchen table. I only woke just now when I heard the stairs creaking.'

Velvet felt relief rush over her. 'I wondered where you were. I could only think that –'

'Out like a light, I was!' He rubbed down his arms. 'Damned hard, that table.'

'Oh, George!' Velvet discreetly stuffed the envelope into her jacket pocket and looked up at him tearfully. 'I'm in a terrible dilemma and don't know what you'll have to say about it.'

'Really? What's going on, then?'

She sighed. This, surely, was the hardest thing she'd ever had to say in her life. 'You know that we agreed that Madame was the most incredible person in the world and that we would go to the ends of the earth for her?'

'Yes. We did.'

'Well, what would you say if I told you that she'd been misleading people all along . . . that she was just a hoaxer? A fraud.'

George's face hardened. 'What are you talking about?'

She sighed again. 'There are so many ways in which she's been deceiving people,' she said. 'But I know one way most particularly because one of the girls who came to the séance last night was . . .' She paused. 'I'm not proud of this, George, but she was a friend of mine whom I'd asked to come and act a part. You remember the girl who stood up and said that her grandfather had left her a fortune?'

George gave a brief, stern nod.

'Well, that wasn't true – any of it. I asked her to play that part to see what Madame would do with the false information.'

'*What?*'

'Because I suspected Madame was a fraud, you see.' And then everything came tumbling out. 'There have been so many other things, George. The baby, the questions in the envelopes at the mediumship evenings – I know there's something odd going on there. The way Madame picks up on little things we tell her, and her materialisations look more like billowing chiffon than anything else! I know you think the world of her but it can't be right to deceive grieving people just to get at their money.' Velvet sighed and blew her nose. 'In the end there were just too many things, too many lies, to overlook.'

'And where are you going now, then?'

'I'm going to the police station,' Velvet said.

'Why? I don't understand.'

'I have to report Madame to the police. Will you come with me?'

'*What?*' George asked again, looking at her with horror.

'Please, George. You will back me up, won't you? I'm sorry and I know it's both our livelihoods at stake, but the things Madame is doing are really and truly wrong. And sooner or later those psychical research people will come and find out everything anyway.'

George did not give any answer for some time. A score of emotions ran across his face but Velvet could not work out what he was thinking or what he might do.

Anxiously, she slipped her hand into his. 'I feel terrible, awful, I really do, but I just knew I had to do something. Please say you'll come with me!'

George hesitated again, sighed and eventually nodded. 'I suppose it's only what I've been thinking myself.'

'I did wonder if you had.'

'We'd better get it over with.' He buttoned up the jacket he was wearing, unbolted the front door and opened it. 'Which police station were you going to?'

'The big one in Harrow Road,' Velvet said. 'I've heard that it's one of the few that are open all night.' She would rather, of course, have gone to Charlie's station, but didn't want to risk it being closed when she got there.

Together they went down the front steps into a dark, damp and misty London morning.

'We'll go by the Marylebone Road,' George said, turning left. Then he stopped. 'No, I know. We'll take the shortcut along the canal.'

Velvet saw no one as they crossed the road towards Regent's Canal, just heard the hollow clatter of a horse's hooves on the cobbles and a milk cart somewhere in the distance. Suddenly remembering the envelope with her name on it, she reached into her pocket as they went down the steps which led to the water. There were a few longboats moored here, but none showed a light. Here and there, however, a lamp glowed from the wall, and Velvet waited until they were under one of these, then pulled at the envelope flap.

'Just a moment,' she said.

'What have you got there?'

'Something from my friend Charlie.' Velvet was torn between getting to the police station and reading the note. Deciding that it must be something very urgent for Charlie to deliver it overnight, however, she pulled a square of paper from the envelope and held it under the light.

It was a piece of newspaper printed with a photograph of a sullen-looking couple. Underneath it said:

Mr and Mrs George Wilson, a married couple who were formerly performers at the Britannia Theatre in Hoxton, appeared at the Old Bailey yesterday on a charge of Gross Deception. They were apprehended at Epsom Races, where they were working a confidence trick which required Mrs Wilson to pose as a socialite who had had all her money stolen. Found guilty, they were both sentenced to six months' hard labour. Full story on page 3.

Velvet read the paragraph swiftly and, hardly understanding its significance, read it again, then studied the photograph.

The married couple pictured were George and Madame.

Chapter Nineteen

In Which Velvet Experiences Her
Final Moments

Velvet's legs wobbled and felt as though they might give way beneath her. Of course! It hadn't been Sissy and George she'd walked in on after the séance – it had been *Madame* and George. She knew that she should drop the piece of newspaper over the side of the canal and let it float away, or screw it up quickly and say to George that it wasn't anything important. She was so horror-struck, however, that she just stood there holding it, staring at the photograph of George and Madame outside the Old Bailey; George unkempt and looking a little younger, and Madame, her hair all anyhow, in drab, workaday clothing.

George inclined his head to look at the picture over Velvet's shoulder, then caught her wrist between his thumb and first finger. The night seemed to grow very still; the only sounds were of the water lapping against the sides of the canal and, somewhere far off, the call of an owl as it flew home to roost.

'Ah, yes, the Help the Lady Scam,' he said.

'You were . . . thieves?'

'When we stopped being actors. We weren't bad at relieving folk of their money, either. One day we cleared over a hundred pounds.'

Velvet looked up at him and blinked.

'But there was no really big money in it – it never brought the rewards that being a medium does. Mind you, *that* game's becoming a bit too popular now. People are getting careless and bringing the profession into disrepute.'

Velvet's breath felt very tight in her throat. 'You and Madame . . .'

'Been together four years now – since, like I told you, she picked me up from the gutter. Got married in ninety-seven, we did.' When Velvet didn't respond to this, he continued, 'That's why I wasn't in my room when you called – because I spend my nights with my wife. When I heard you moving around upstairs I used the private staircase to get out and went back in the house by the kitchen door.' He grinned. 'Fooled you all right, didn't it?'

Velvet began to shake all over. 'So everything you've done, everything I've seen, has been fake?'

'Indeed it has,' George said.

'The ectoplasm?'

'You were nearly right about that: it was muslin,

inflated by a foot-operated set of bellows under the carpet pumping up air. Rather clever, we thought – some mediums just dress up their assistants in white veiling and have them appear through a trap door.'

'But how do you know about my real name and everything? How could you possibly know what happened when my father died?'

George smiled a cold smile. 'I'll leave you to try and work that out for yourself,' he said. 'You'll have about . . . well, about two minutes, I should think.'

'Two minutes? What d'you mean?' Velvet tried to wriggle out of his grasp, but his hand was firm around her wrist. 'I'm still going to the police! I'm going to tell them everything I know.'

His fingers bit into her flesh, tight as a handcuff. 'Oh no, you're not. As if I'd let you destroy the neat little business that we've built up with our well-off clients and our cache of jewellery – not to mention a nice new motor car and a villa in Brighton. Oh dear me, no!'

'But how did you manage to –'

'The hows and whys don't concern you now,' he said. 'If you'd been a good girl we'd have filled you in on the whole deal – you and my wife could have worked a scam as a team. But no, you had to come over all high and mighty, and because of that – well, as I said, it'll take about two minutes.'

Velvet looked up at him and frowned.

'For you to drown, I mean.'

Before she could draw breath, George gave Velvet a hefty shove in the chest which sent her staggering across the cinder pathway, skirts flying. She fell backwards into the canal with an almighty splash.

Velvet's first thought was that – how strange, how ironic – she was going to die the same death as her father, and this was surely a just punishment. Her second thought was an angry one: no, she was *not* going to die. She was going to survive and make sure that Madame and George paid for their crimes. And then she had no more clear thoughts, for her only instinct was to survive and she started fighting, kicking and struggling. She knew that the canal could kill in other ways apart from drowning, for it was disgustingly alive with disease-bearing rats as well as the contents of countless chamber pots, and she must get herself out of the putrid mess as soon as possible.

Down, down, she went, into the murk, feeling her flailing hands touching repulsively slimy, indefinite *things* in the water all around her. Her booted feet touched the bottom and she began to rise up, fighting not only against the water but in order to try and get free of the heavy clothing she was wearing. The extra layers of skirt and petticoat clung to her legs, however, twisted around her knees and weighed her down so that she had hardly gained the surface and taken a gulp of air before she felt herself sinking again, pulled down by yards of sodden material.

Frantically scrabbling as she came up once more, she kicked out to try and reach the side of the canal and cling on to something – anything – but the walls were so slimy with filth and waterweed that it was impossible to get a grip. Struggling ineffectually, she opened her mouth to scream for help but merely swallowed a chokingly large gulp of canal water. Before she went under again she saw George standing above her on the canal-side. He had a long stave of wood in his hand which, she presumed, he was wielding to hit her on the head and finish her off.

Down she went again, taking in more filthy water which filled her nose and mouth and caused an excruciating burning sensation all the way down to her lungs. With another involuntary gulp this pain became so unbearable that she all but lost the power to struggle. She would just give up the fight, she thought, and let the all-consuming agony take over her body. She would float downstream and die, and finally be at peace. As she sank lower in the water she thought about her mother, how perhaps they could be together again, and whether she was even now waiting for her on the Other Side.

Seconds passed, and more seconds, then there was a vast splash and disturbance of the water. It seemed to her that George had jumped into the canal and was trying to hold her under, tugging at her jacket to keep her below the surface and gripping her arms hard. Having someone to fight spurred Velvet into action again. She forced her hands into fists and beat them against her aggressor's head with as much strength as she could muster. He grabbed her around the neck, however, and, although she broke the surface once more and was able to choke in a gulp of air, held her tightly under the arms, forcing her on to her back and under the water.

Her final thought was of Charlie and the strangely heartbreaking knowledge that she would never see him again. After that, everything closed in and became black.

Chapter Twenty

There followed some oddly disjointed moments when Velvet seemed to wake from a dream and found herself being jolted rhythmically up and down, as if on a horse, but it was a strange sort of ride because she appeared to be lying across the animal's back. She was aware of a tremendous rushing noise in her ears and of her clothes sticking to her, dripping and stinking, then she spewed up a great gush of warm, filthy water, and someone exclaimed in shock.

The next thing she could remember – whether an hour or days later, she couldn't tell – was finding herself lying on her side, feeling weak and ill, with a scratchy grey blanket wrapped around her. She was in a small room or cell, there was an enamel bowl just by her head and she was completely naked under the blanket, with not even her mother's old lace petticoat on. What had happened?

Muddled, she tried to reason things out. She had not drowned – that much was clear – but she was not at all certain what *had* happened or where she was. She reached for the enamel bowl, was sick again, then closed her eyes, stopped thinking of anything and allowed herself to drift off to sleep.

The next time Velvet woke, she had to work out where she was all over again, but she must have been feeling a little more normal because she immediately remembered that under the blanket she was naked. Where were her clothes and who had taken them off? What was real and true, and which were her dreams?

She was sick once more and felt a little better. Someone came into the room and she tried terribly hard to open her eyes, knowing that if she had to fight this person off she couldn't have lifted as much as a finger to help herself. This someone took her hand and stroked it gently. Her eyes struggled not only to stay open, but to focus.

'Velvet.'

Hearing the dear and familiar voice of Charlie, Velvet felt peace lapping over her, as welcome as sunlight. She did not feel strong enough to speak to him, however, so she just let her eyelids flutter down and concentrated all her efforts on not drifting off to sleep. What day, what month, what time it was she couldn't have said. She only knew that she felt safe.

'Do you know where you are?' Charlie asked. She couldn't reply, so he went on, 'You're in the sickroom at my police station. That . . . that blighter tried to drown you – he pushed you into the canal. Do you remember?'

Velvet nodded; a tiny movement.

'It was my fault,' said Charlie. 'I shouldn't have put that newspaper cutting through your door. But I suppose he would have tried to drown you before you got to the police station anyway.'

Velvet opened her eyes.

'I realised too late that the cutting might have put you in danger, so I came round early this morning to try and speak to you.' He took her hand and squeezed it. 'Of course, it was too late by then – you'd already found it and gone off. I ran up and down looking for you and a milkman told me that he'd seen the two of you walking along by the canal. I followed and heard a commotion in the water. When he saw me, the blighter bolted as fast as the king's horse.'

'Who got me out of the water?' Velvet whispered.

'Why, I did!' Charlie said. 'I jumped in for you. Reckon I redeemed myself a bit by doing that, eh?' A smile spread across his freckled face. 'Mind you, I didn't think you wanted to come out – you fought me tooth and nail.'

'I thought it was him, still trying to drown me . . .'

'And then when I gave you a fireman's carry to

the station you were sick all down my back by way of a thank you!'

Velvet, embarrassed, said that she was very sorry indeed for it. She closed her eyes momentarily. 'What about him and Madame?' she asked. 'Where are they?'

'They've scarpered,' said Charlie. 'They left the furniture and the fine clothes in the house. The housekeeper told me they'd gone off in a motor car and didn't leave a forwarding address.'

'Brighton,' said Velvet. 'That's where you'll find them.'

'Is that right?'

She nodded and sighed. 'They were both comp-letely ... utterly ... false.' After a moment she added, 'They were, weren't they?'

'Yes. I did try to tell you,' Charlie said. He lifted her hand and kissed the tips of her fingers. 'By the way, what did George tell you about his friend Aaron, the boy who died?'

'He just said that he helped him and that he invited Aaron to Madame's for a meal. That's why George's name and address were in his pocket.'

'More lies,' Charlie said. 'They were friends at one time, true, but then George seduced Aaron's sister. Got her in the family way, he did.'

'No!'

'Aaron was probably looking for George to knock him about a bit, but the poor chap died first.'

Velvet shook her head. 'But there are other things I don't understand. I mean, how did they find out my real name? And they knew about my father. I've never told anyone what happened to him.'

Charlie looked at her as if weighing up whether or not she was ready to receive more information. He decided that she was.

'Velvet, the plain fact is that your father is still alive.'

Stunned, Velvet didn't know if she was pleased or aghast at this news.

'Alive as I am! I was on loan to Chelsea police station a week or so ago when he was brought in drunk and disorderly after a race meeting. He was using another name, but I recognised him straight away. He told the desk sergeant that he and Conan Doyle were having private sessions with your Madame – full of it, he was – so I guess she must have been relieving him of his winnings and finding out your family secrets at the same time.'

Velvet shook her head in bewilderment. 'My *father*! Oh, will I have to go and see him?'

'Not if you don't want to. You might want to make your peace with him, though. In time.'

'But I won't have to live with him?'

'Of course not. It's up to you to decide.'

She felt tearful. 'But where am I going to live? What will I do?'

'You can move in with my ma,' Charlie said, as if he'd made all the arrangements already. 'I'm on nights now and I mostly stay in the police boarding house, so she's got a spare room. And as you like dressing so fancy posh, I thought you might want to work in one of those shops. I've started making enquiries in one of the stores on my beat, as a matter of fact.'

'Oh!' said Velvet, very much amazed.

'Mind you, as soon as we can, we'll get married.'

Velvet felt tears start in her eyes. 'But I've been so stupid, Charlie. Can you ever forgive me for being so awful to you?'

'Hush. You weren't to know you loved me, were you?'

She shook her head.

'Not then.'

'But I should have done.' The certainty ran through Velvet's body. 'I should have done. And I do!'

'Yes,' he said soothingly. 'Of course you do.'

Velvet thought hard. 'Charlie,' she asked, 'did you propose to me just now?'

'I certainly did.'

She did not like to think, even for a moment, of what a sight she must look. 'Then I would like to be asked again when I'm clean and presentable, please.' She squeezed his hand. 'But my answer is yes now, and will be yes then.' She suddenly remembered something and blushed. 'Oh, but where are my clothes?'

'The sergeant's drying them in front of the fire.'

'Who undressed me?'

'The sergeant's missus – she lives upstairs. Sent me out of the room first, mind, even though I told her that you were my intended and there was no need.'

'You never did. Oh, Charlie!'

He smiled at her tenderly. 'Velvet . . .'

And then there were no more words.

My Inspiration for Velvet

Like most people at some time in their lives, I've visited fortune tellers and been to theatre events where a medium purports to receive messages from the 'Other Side'. Attending these, I'd very much hoped that I would be selected by the medium and receive a meaningful message; something inspiring and uplifting. Unfortunately this has never been the case for me. What usually happened was that, after giving one or two messages that seemed to mean something to certain members of the audience (had they been planted there? my suspicious mind wondered), the medium resorted to asking basic questions, such as if any in the audience knew someone in spirit called, say, Fred, or John, or Anne. Of course, most people *did* know someone deceased who had one of these not very unusual names, and it wasn't difficult to fabricate stories around them: the medium reported that Uncle Fred had had a great sense of humour, or Cousin John had enjoyed gardening, or Anne had been a dab hand at cooking. Never did I hear any message which amazed me, or any communication which could only have come from 'beyond the grave'.

I went to two more theatre events when I was writing *Velvet*, rather hoping that the spirits might know that I was planning to write a book about them and turn up to give a good performance. As before, however, I didn't hear anything which convinced me that someone on the Other Side could make contact. At the first event the medium asked (rather desperately, for no one had 'owned' any of the spirits who had come through) if there was someone in the audience with a black handbag, and more than three quarters of the audience raised their hands, and then looked around at each other and laughed nervously. At the second event the medium and his assistant were waiting in the foyer of the theatre to greet, talk with and put the audience at their ease, rather like Velvet does with Madame Savoya's clients.

I began to wonder if it had always been thus. Had anyone ever really and truly received a message from the Other Side, or was mediumship more about intuition and clever talk? Either way, I thought the subject would make an interesting book, especially if I set it in the heyday of spiritualism, the Victorian and Edwardian periods.

I'd like to mention the naming of my main character. The first thing I do when I plan a book is to decide the main character's name. As part of my research I looked at a list of girls' names popular in Victorian times, but some of them I'd used in books before (Hannah, Lucy, Grace, Lily and Rose) and some I just didn't like very much (sorry – Maud, Agnes, Bertha and Mildred). When I saw the name Velvet I knew I'd found exactly what I wanted. Then when I started writing the book I discovered very quickly that Velvet hadn't always been called that – in fact, she'd started life as Kitty, and the reason for this change of name became part of the story.

As I wrote, the plot crowded about me, waiting to be used. I already knew the main story was going to be about a fraudulent Victorian medium, but I also wanted to incorporate a love story, and to use something I'd come across when I was researching *Fallen Grace* (set about forty years earlier), and that was baby farms. There are, in fact, several books waiting to be written about baby farms, but I'm not the person to do them; I found it impossible to read about the subject without getting upset and angry about what had been allowed to happen. Perhaps the worst thing about them is that baby farms were still in existence only a hundred years ago.

All this research was important for the book, but perhaps the single most important discovery I made was that every Victorian or Edwardian medium was accused of fraud, and that only one of these was not convicted of any wrongdoing. I am not saying that speaking to spirits is impossible, just that I haven't seen any evidence of it. I will certainly report back if I do.

Mary Hooper

Contact Mary on www.facebook.com/maryhooperfanpage

Some Historical Notes from the Author

Baby Farms

Sadly, there were many of these in Victorian and Edwardian Britain. In 1864 a law was passed stating that illegitimate children were the sole responsibility of their mothers until the age of sixteen. However, if their mothers were unable to care for them it was difficult to find anyone who would. At this time, unwed mothers and their children were seen as an affront to morality and the majority of orphanages denied illegitimate children shelter, fearing they would contaminate the minds and morals of legitimate children. Single mothers were therefore desperate enough to use people like Mrs Dyer to baby-mind or even adopt their infants, otherwise there was little hope of their obtaining accommodation or work. Laws were in place against the mistreatment of animals, but not children, and reform moved slowly for fear of violating the Victorian ideal of the sanctity of the family. Fallen women were condemned, their children stigmatised, and there was no welfare state to look after them.

Amelia Dyer was a real person, one of a breed of baby farmers. By moving around and changing her name and her methods, for some time she escaped the notice of police and the newly formed NSPCC (National Society for the Prevention of Cruelty to Children). Babies disappeared from baby farms, but their mothers were tricked into thinking that they had died of natural causes and were reluctant to take matters any further for fear of disgrace. Dyer was first arrested in 1879 after a doctor became suspicious about the number of child deaths he had been called upon to certify, but instead of being convicted of murder, she was sentenced to six months' hard labour for neglect. She returned to baby farming and murder, and began to dispose of the bodies of the infants she minded in the nearby River Thames.

In 1896, a package containing the body of a baby girl was retrieved from the river at Reading, and Dyer's house was placed under surveillance. When it was raided, police discovered that in the previous few months alone, at least twenty children had been placed in her care, and subsequently seven bodies were found in the Thames. In May that year she appeared at the Old Bailey, where it took the jury a mere four and a half minutes to find her guilty. She was hanged in June 1896. The Dyer case caused a national scandal, following which, stricter adoption laws were passed giving local authorities the power to police baby farms and stamp out abuse. However, the advertising of homes for infants and their trafficking and abuse did not stop immediately.

Mediums

Apart from Madame, all the names used in this novel are those of real mediums, although, as with Amelia Dyer, they weren't all still working during 1900–1901, the date covered by this book. Mediumship started in the United States in 1848 with the Fox sisters (who later admitted they were frauds) and quickly spread to the UK, where it became extremely fashionable. There are many photographs showing mediums exuding ectoplasm (a mysterious substance said to be produced by mediums whilst in a trance state, and at different times described as resembling gauze, smoke, mist or slime) from their bodies, but whether you are convinced by these is another matter – as is whether you believe that someone on the Other Side is able to send messages to the living.

The case for mediums has not been helped by the great number of frauds that were perpetrated in Victorian and Edwardian times against vulnerable and recently bereaved people. Two of the cases I have written about, 'Lady Blue' and 'Mrs Lilac', were based on cases from the Old Bailey records (now available online). The reason Madame gives for demanding Mrs Lilac's jewels (that the magnetism within them might draw her too early to the Other Side) was taken from these records. Spiritualism and mediumship underwent a great revival after World War I, when hundreds of people sought to get in touch with loved ones who had died in the war.

The Tricks of the Trade
The Spirits Speak

This trick is still worked now, and depends upon the medium having an accomplice planted in the audience. When the envelopes containing the audience's questions have all been collected, the medium is handed the first envelope and, without opening it, answers the question inside. The person who asked the question (the accomplice) appears very impressed, following which the medium opens the envelope in order to read the question out. What they actually do, however, is open a genuine envelope from someone in the audience, memorise the question and throw it away. They then pick up the next sealed envelope and pretend to use the spirits to answer the question inside, when what they are really doing is answering the question from the one opened earlier. They repeat this process over and over again, letting the 'spirits' answer and staying one envelope ahead the whole time.

Hands on the Table

After asking everyone to link hands on a round table, it is quite a simple matter for a medium to momentarily detach their hand from those on each side of them (perhaps by putting their hand over their mouth to cough, or saying they need to get a handkerchief). A moment after (remembering, of course, that the room is in almost total darkness), the medium reconnects hands, ensuring that the person on their right touches the fingers of one hand and the person on the left takes the same wrist, thus leaving one of their hands free. This spare hand could then be employed in all sorts of mischief: stroking those within reach, shaking bells, using a fishing line to dangle instruments over the table, throwing flowers previously concealed under the table, etc.

(With thanks to Troy Taylor for permission to include these tricks from his books.)

The Spiritualist Church Today

Spiritualists believe that when we physically die, some aspects of the mind survive and continue to exist on a spirit plane, and that mediums are able to pass messages on from those on that plane to those on earth. Meditation plays a part in spiritualist practice, as does healing. Spiritualists draw inspiration from other religions, namely Christianity, but also from faiths with a deep mystical tradition, such as Hinduism and Buddhism. Today many spiritualist churches are thriving throughout the world, mostly in English-speaking countries.

Employment for Women at the Turn of the Century

Queen Victoria apparently said that God intended women to be a helpmeet for men, and these words were used by many powerful men to subordinate women. At the turn of the century women had very few rights, not even the right to vote. If married, they were expected to dedicate themselves to their husband and children. If single and poor, they were forced to take an unskilled and lowly paid job, perhaps as a domestic servant, agricultural worker or factory hand. Only wealthy and enlightened families educated their daughters for careers – the fact that in 1900 there were just two female architects and 112 female doctors in the whole of the British Isles illustrates this.

As the twentieth century progressed, however, women began to be employed in more varied ways. The rise of shopping as a suitable activity for unaccompanied ladies presented many more opportunities for a young girl to make her way up the career ladder in a store or shop, and offices started to employ more typists and female clerks. It wasn't until World War I began in 1914, however, that women came into their own when they took on the jobs of all the men who had gone away to fight. Women over 30 were entitled to the vote when the war ended in 1918.

Arthur Conan Doyle

Conan Doyle was a doctor, cricketer and, most famously, the author of the Sherlock Holmes books. In 1893, in order to concentrate on 'more important' writing, he decided to kill off the popular Holmes by having him drop to his death from the Reichenbach Falls. The public was outraged at this, however, so much so that in 1901 he brought Holmes back to life. A famous spiritualist, he regularly attended séances at Eusapia Palladino's house in London, and was even convinced by the 1917 photographs of the Cottingley Fairies (later proved to be fakes). Conan Doyle wrote a treatise about Great Britain's conduct in the Boer War and was awarded a knighthood for it in 1902.

Please note that I have taken the occasional liberty with historical facts for the sake of the story (for instance, ten-shilling notes were not actually issued by the Bank of England until 1914).

Bibliography

Forrester, Wendy, *Great Grandma's Weekly – A Celebration of 'The Girl's Own Paper' 1880–1901*
Lutterworth Press, 1980

Gernsheim, Alison, *Victorian and Edwardian Fashion – A Photographic Survey*
Dover Publications Inc, 1963

Lycett, Andrew, *Conan Doyle – The Man Who Created Sherlock Holmes*
Phoenix, 2008

McCrum, Mark and Sturgis, Matthew, *1900 House*
Channel 4 Books (Macmillan), 1999

Pearsall, Ronald, *Table-rappers – The Victorians and the Occult*
The History Press Ltd, 2004

Sambrook, Pamela, *Laundry Bygones*
Shire Publications Ltd, 1983

Taylor, Troy, *Ghosts by Gaslight*
Whitechapel Productions Press, 2007

'By any standards, an exceptional novel'
The Times

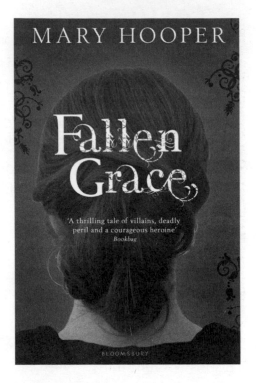

Grace Parkes has just had to do a terrible thing. Having given birth
to an illegitimate child, she has travelled to the famed Brookwood
Cemetery to place her small infant's body in a rich lady's coffin as this
is the only way that Grace can think of to give something to her baby
who died at birth.

At the funeral, she attracts the attention of the dead lady's brother and
also of a family of undertakers who hire her as a professional mourner.
These characters will have a profound effect upon Grace's life. But she
doesn't know that yet.

Follow Grace as she races to unravel the fraud about to be perpetrated
against her and her sister.

www.maryhooper.co.uk

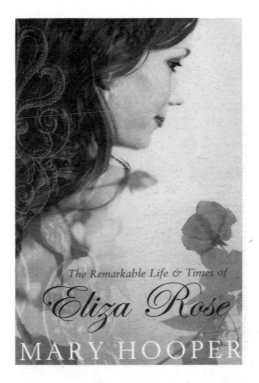

The Remarkable Life & Times of
Eliza Rose

MARY HOOPER

When Eliza Rose is ousted from her family by her new stepmother, she finally makes her way to London – only to be thrown straight into prison for stealing a mouthful of bread.

Eliza's life takes some remarkable twists as she learns to survive sordid prison life, is rescued by a woman she has never met before, and befriends Nell Gwyn, who introduces her to the intrigue, politics and glamour of the court of King Charles II.

Then Eliza discovers her true background . . .

www.maryhooper.co.uk

'I loved this ghostly romp through Victorian high society'
The Bookseller

Violet Willoughby doesn't believe in ghosts, especially since her
mother has worked as a fraudulent medium for a decade. Violet has
taken part in enough of her mother's tricks to feel more than a little
jaded about anything supernatural.

The ghosts, however, believe in Violet, and she's been seeing
them everywhere.

One ghost in particular needs Violet to use her emerging gift to solve
her murder . . . and prevent the ghost's twin sister from suffering
the same fate.

www.facebook.com/myloveliesbleeding